THE DEVIL'S LUCK

T. R. CROKE

BLUE DOOR PUBLISHING IRELAND

Copyright © 2017 by T. R. Croke

All rights reserved. No part of this publication may be reproduced, distributed, or transmitted in any form or by any means, without prior written permission.

Blue Door Publishing Ireland

Fisherstown, Ballybrittas,

Laois, Ireland.

www.trcroke.com

Publisher's Note: This is a work of fiction. Names, characters, places, and incidents are a product of the author's imagination. Locales and public names are sometimes used for atmospheric purposes. Any resemblance to actual people, living or dead, or to businesses, companies, events, institutions, or locales is completely coincidental.

Book Layout © 2017 BookDesignTemplates.com

Cover Design by Nick Castle Design

The Devil's Luck/ T. R. Croke. – 4th ed.

ISBN 978-0-9955976-1-7

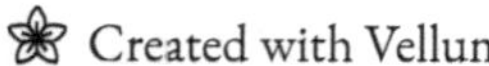 Created with Vellum

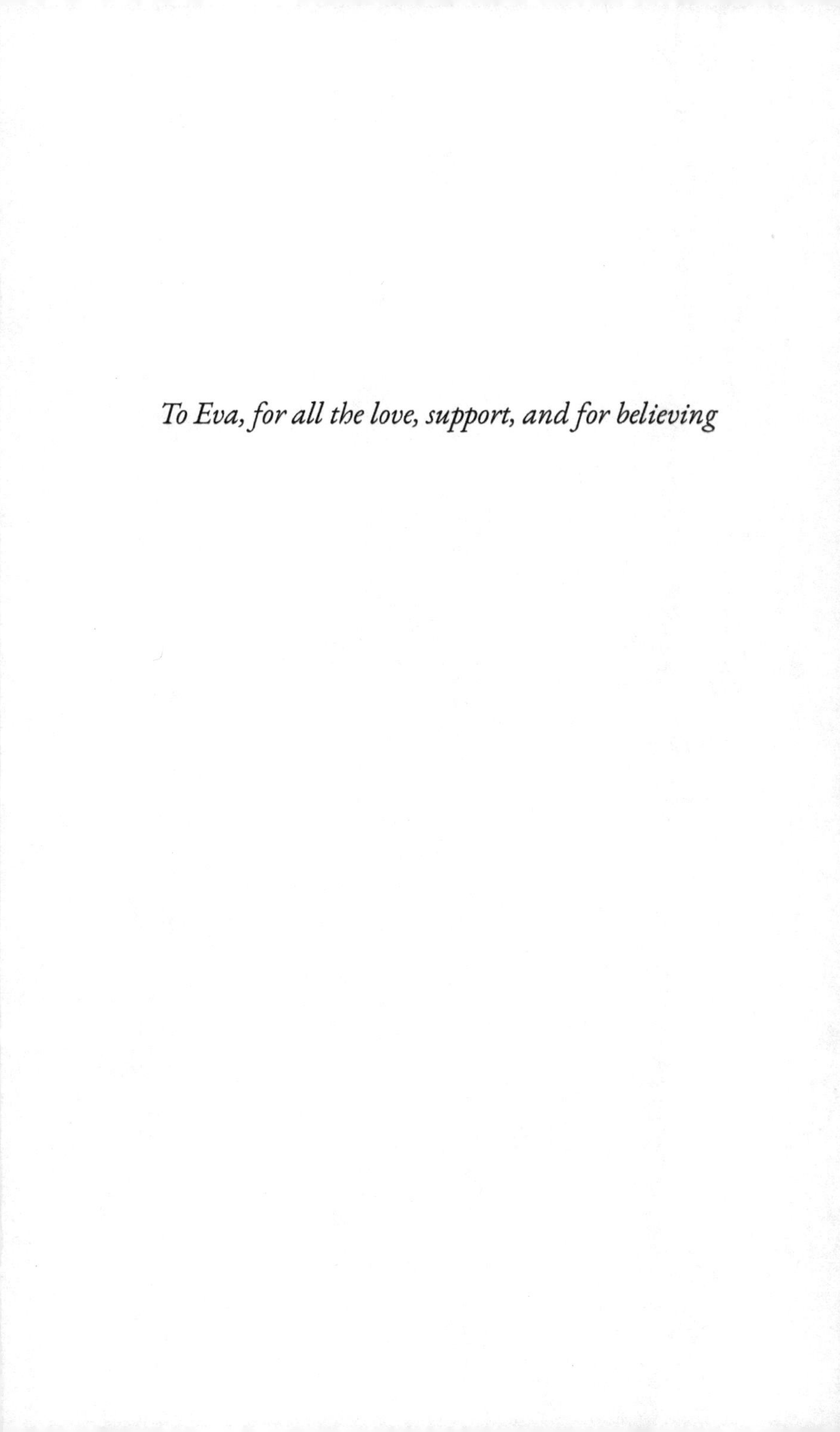

To Eva, for all the love, support, and for believing

DON'T MISS THE FREE STUFF!

I like building a relationship with my readers. It's an important aspect of my life as an author. If you would like to join my readers list, check out https://www.trcroke.com and leave your email address.

From time to time I let readers know about free or special offers, new releases, and other news. In case you missed it, the Detective Kate Bowen Mystery Thriller Series prequel, The Trinity Enigma is permanently free and downloadable on most digital platforms.

PART 1

Ireland

1

'BASE TO TANGO BRAVO 2.'

'Tango Bravo 2.'

'Sit rep?'

'No movement.'

'Base to Tango Bravo 3.'

'Tango Bravo 3.'

'Sit rep?'

'Ditto.'

So it went with the two other reports. Nothing stirred in the dark drumlin landscape. Border country. An invisible three-hundred-and-sixty-kilometre line separated the two separate jurisdictions on the island. It meandered through fields, rivers, mountains, and valleys from the east coast to the northwest. Throughout thirty years of domestic terrorist war, the Irish border proved a nightmare policing challenge on either side. Terrorists exploited it relentlessly throughout the Troubles. Despite years of peace, remnant rebels kept where the team was inserted, its eastern edge, hot.

Pre-op reconnaissance gave them a cursory aerial skim over

the terrain that yielded some insight but little relief. The night crew watched, worried, and waited from foxholes they had fashioned as observation posts. One person, one night sight, one weapon, per post.

Two kilometres from the target in a cramped command post van the clock clicked 23:30. Parked behind an abandoned cottage, the driver, Detective Pete McNally, lay across the front seats in a sleeping bag making the most of the quiet time. Time for a toilet break, team leader, Kate Bowen thought and quietly unlocked the van's back door. Using the derelict cottage as cover, she took care of the tricky business.

Overhead, an ink-black sky threatened constantly. March was clinging to winter like a limpid ensuring that after sunset temperatures fell below freezing. The forecast snow flurries were staying off, the last thing the team needed was snow. Feeling tight and tired, Kate stretched and shuffled about to keep warm. No action tonight. Despite the aches and tedium, she felt fulfilled. Perverse, given her company for the best part of two weeks in the cramped van was a dozing, farting colleague.

Twelve years earlier, she abandoned a history and politics masters at Trinity College Dublin to join the Garda Síochána. Her intuitive surveillance skills propelled her into a position as the first woman to direct specialist field operations. In her thirties, she was also the youngest.

Kate's Surveillance & Intelligence Unit developed the intel that initiated the drawn-out operation. An informant tipoff that two new bloods from a dissident IRA faction had stashed a van in a shed had led them to an out farm five hundred meters shy of the Armagh county boundary. The Police Service of Northern Ireland confirmed the black Ford Transit was stolen two weeks earlier on its patch. Kate deployed her team to find out why two locals picked it up at the Dew Drop Inn car park in Dundalk and drove it to its current location.

Inhaling a final breath of cool night air, she quietly climbed back into the van's dank stuffiness and doodled random thoughts on a notepad to pass the time. How many might come? Who? What's their plan? What's their target?

'Tango Bravo 4 to Base.'

'Go ahead.'

'Cattle in the next field very noisy tonight.'

'Ever the smart-alec,' the dozing McNally remarked.

Most nights had been noisy, wind whipped around the sparse landscape with a bone-numbing effect.

'Tango Bravo Three to Base.'

'Go ahead.'

'Those cattle could be cows recently separated from their calves.'

'Roger 'Farmer Bill', Base out.'

As the operation dragged on, the proximity to Dundalk weighed heavier. It was a reservoir of rebel support. In the distant past, tabloids dubbed it El Paso for its overload of shooters, bombers, and hangers-on from the Provisional Irish Republican Army terror group. It was also home town to Detective Superintendent Kate Bowen.

Tango Bravo 4, Detective Inspector Dan 'Digger' Rooney reported nothing new in the next 15-minute situation report. His voice betrayed boredom. Always happiest in the thick of the action, the length of this operation was even testing his resilience. Digger barely made the old five-foot-eight height requirement when he became police. He masked teak toughness behind a gregarious nature. Without an ounce of spare flesh on his narrow frame; he slipped into his surveillance role like a second skin.

Tango Bravo 1, Detective Angie Harrington, reported on

the occasional passing car. She was closest to the road, in the smallest and most precarious OP. Each night she had somehow managed to squeeze her tiny frame into it and remain concealed.

At 02:47, two radio clicks spliced Kate's reverie. The phone vibrated a text alert. Up front Pete grunted and twisted, trying to get comfortable as a message from Digger lit up the screen.

At 9, 12 & 3 o'clock from position – ten bodies entering the field – checking ditches with metal detectors.

His vigilance kicked off the game, giving them precious seconds to react. Digger would hunker down; on his own until backup cleared his area at the first opportunity.

Tango Bravo 4: Confirm. Ten-man security team? Kate messaged.

Confirm.

To McNally, she whispered sharply, 'Contact.'

He bolted upright, kicked off the sleeping bag, and fixed his headset on his ears as he stumbled awkwardly toward her. She ducked out of his way.

'Jesus, Pete.'

His job was to monitor radio traffic for emergencies. Once the unit locked onto an IRA target this close, they ditched radio comms, changing over to group-wide, encrypted text. The IRA unit would have a radio scanner. Using radios this close lost you advantage. Digger's double click was the 'game on' advance signal.

Kate propped her elbows on the van's workbench and waited. Digger did his creative work with gadgets and wires here. The phone's vibration alert hummed an incoming message.

Tango Bravo 3: *five more here, same M.O.*

Roger.

The crew had their orders and Kate trusted them. The phone screen lit up again.

Tango Bravo 1: *three on a quad bike entering the laneway.*

Roger, standby.

Almost a twenty-man group. She hit the speed dial for Twomey, the Emergency Response Unit commander. He was three kilometres away with his number one squad, the longest-serving, and the most experienced.

'Twomey, up to twenty have just landed here.'

'Christ on a bike! Twenty! How many are armed?'

'Don't know for sure, a few are, but we're more interested in whoever goes into that shed.'

'What have the ones securing the perimeter got?'

'Handguns, as far as we can gauge.'

'What do you want from us?'

'Advance to the one-kilometre staging point for now.'

'Roger.'

'I'll let you know when to get closer. We'll focus on taking down whoever's in the shed, okay?'

'Understood.'

'If you need reinforcements, I'll bring four of mine for support. Your call.'

'Roger. We're geared up and ready to rock.'

The ERU comprised the very best. They were the SWAT; handpicked after a crucifying physical and psychological selection process. ERU members were also the best trained and equipped. Taking down tonight's opposition was well within their capabilities.

No radio communication jangled everyone's nerves. The phone was a permanent fixture in Kate's hand. It buzzed.

Tango Bravo 2: *six now entering shed.*

Roger, hold your position. Everyone, standby.

Adrenaline kicked in hard. After two gruelling weeks of staking out the isolated shed, things were rushing towards a climax. Kate called SIU's Chief and her boss, Redmond McEnroe to brief him. They had managed enough operations together to know how each analysed high-risk situations. The final call was down to the on-scene commander unless the Chief had other ideas. This one seemed a foregone conclusion. Hit the shed hard and fast. Arrest the skilled operators. The capture of six-plus hardened terrorists would more than justify their budget overrun. Kate just had to line up the ducks.

'We have twenty on scene.'

'More than we anticipated,' Mac replied.

'More than we've seen in a long time.'

'Okay for bodies?'

'I'm good. We'll deal with whatever.'

'Are they fitting out the van?'

'Making noise at least. Shall I get Twomey to focus his assault on the shed? I can take four of my own to scare off the hangers-on in the yard.'

No immediate response. Did the silence come with a sting?

'What do you think, boss?'

'Don't hit it. If that van exits the shed, follow it for now. Do not intercept.'

2

KATE RUBBED HER TEMPLES, incredulous.

In the faint hope that his sleep-addled brain had not computed the situation correctly, she asked her boss to repeat his orders.

'Activate the mobile team and tail it, if it leaves. I'll alert Symons.'

There were political challenges to the night's events. Who to tell, how much intel to share. It was clear Mac wanted to tick tack with his counterpart on the other side of the border. Peter Symons was MI5's Ireland coordinator. He spent most of his time in London, visiting his Belfast office as little as possible. Kate kept him at arm's length. Content to leave the politics to someone else she focused on her operational priorities.

'Keep me posted on developments,' Mac ordered.

'Will do.'

Her boss' sleep was done. He would tune into the pursuit. Knowing as much did nothing to temper Kate's exasperation.

Once the suspect van was stashed, she knew what to expect. The surveillance unit she commanded had observed this modus operandi in the past. An IRA security team would transport a bomb maker to the shed to prepare the device. A separate Active Service Unit would deliver it to the target, likely north of the border. Tailing the van with the resources she had was possible but in this terrain, at this hour, it seemed hugely risky.

She scrambled her tail team, one car, and two motorbikes and deployed them on three roads closest to the shed. Their orders were to standby for the direction of travel. She called Twomey and told him to pull back for now. All his guys were first-rate drivers, but their training and instinct were toward intervention. Nothing about this was going to be easy.

Tango Bravo 2, Duggan, was closest to the shed and he reported sounds of hammering, drilling, and steel cutting coming from it. The sounds were incongruous. The hammering included nails being driven into wood. Kate would have expected work exclusively on metal; it didn't add up. An hour on, Duggan reported again.

Tango Bravo 2: *Shed door opening. All internal lights out. Two with balaclavas in van.*

The van exited the shed, drove down the laneway, headlights off, and paused momentarily at the end.

Tango Bravo 1: *scout cars arriving.*

Angie's sighting confirmed what they expected. A dark blue Nissan Primera drove past the laneway exit. The van pulled out and seconds later Angie reported a third vehicle, a Toyota had joined the convoy keeping far enough behind not to attract attention.

Kate had no tracking beacon to hone in on. It had not been an option. Digger spent two nights patiently scoping out entry points to the shed. He found a trip wire but could not identify what it was connected to; would it trigger a bomb or an alarm? Kate did not risk finding out. They would have to keep eyes on the van at this ungodly hour.

As the operation went mobile, Pete gunned their command post van into life and drove cautiously onto the narrow country roads. He kept close enough to maintain comms but not so close that a scout car might double back and catch them out. The team did their best boxing in the convoy by travelling ahead and behind it. Parallel runs along rural roads were incredibly challenging.

Kate considered the slew of intel. The wide perimeter established around the shed by the group indicated tactical savvy. Tonight's venture had input from experienced terrorists. This concerned her long-term but in the here and now she needed to work out their immediate intentions.

Up ahead, their target stuck to the speed limit and skirted the border. When the road veered northwards she held her breath. To the east, a weak watery light crept into the sky. Mac's decision concerned her. Was he being reckless in letting the target go mobile or was there something, some piece of sensitive intel he was holding back? It did not add up. You don't plant a bomb at this hour of the morning. Would they park the van up for later transmission to the target? SIU couldn't afford to lose them.

Back at the shed, Digger confirmed that the scene was clear of hostiles and the team emerged from their OPs. Kate ordered Twomey's squad to secure it. He lent her two of his cars. Digger took one, and Duggan and Angie commandeered the other. She would need fresh vehicles if the pursuit wore on and Duggan was her best driver. For his silky driving skills, colleagues nicknamed him Zoom.

A hundred meters shy of the border the three-vehicle convoy turned right towards the Cooley peninsula. Pete grunted with little enthusiasm.

'Still in the Republic, at least.'

Kate knew this country well. Her grandparents had lived

there and it was her second childhood home. They called it bandit country. The notion had fascinated her until she realized what it meant. Smuggling gangs and their IRA guardians moved over and back across the border through a maze of roads that were once classified as 'unapproved'. It was perfect territory for terrorists; a nightmare for those tracking them.

She rang Digger.

'Where are you?'

'Not far behind. Where do you want us?'

'We'll let the tail team do a scout run into Cooley. Take Zoom and cover the exit roads south.'

Diving directly into the isolated peninsula after the van would be disastrous. The team would be burned in an instant and the gang might abandon their operation. After ten interminable minutes of holding them back, she let the bikes off first. Like dogs too long straining at the leash, they were quickly out of sight. The rest she sent to points on the peninsula from where she felt the target might exit.

Fifteen minutes of crisscrossing highways, byways, and checking laneways turned up nothing. She had Mac's number on screen about to report a busted flush when Digger called. Her heart skipped a beat.

'Contact.'

'Location?'

'Carlingford.'

'Have you eyes on the target?'

'Roger.'

'Can we assist?'

'Negative. There's not a soul around. I'm leaving transport, going for cover. Text only from now.'

We have contact, Kate messaged her team.

Digger's first text told her: Scout cars gone north. She

instructed everyone to let them go and hang back from Digger's location. Carlingford was the destination.

'What the hell's there?' she wondered aloud.

Digger's next text told her the front seat passenger had gone into a small shop near the harbour. The shop opened early for trawler crews setting out to sea. Within five minutes the passenger returned to the van and it drove along the pier. Digger followed its progress.

He brought a Nikon Digiscope on most jobs. It filtered out atmospheric haze and ensured a clear image, even under extreme magnification. Its simple adapter allowed connection to his work digital camera. The van stopped close to where a red trawler was berthed. As the driver threw a plastic shopping bag down to one of its crew, Digger began clicking.

Tango Bravo 4: 'Shopping bag with three loaves of Pat the Baker's bread placed on boat.'

Kate acknowledged.

Three loaves of bread? Either that boat's got a big crew or there's a long trip coming up.

3

DIGGER RELATED the sequence of events on the quay during the extended debrief back at their Dublin base. The team filled the squad room listening intently, coffee mugs in hand as they watched the screen showing his photographs.

'I tracked the van as it moved slowly along the pier. There were two other boat crews there, both loadin' fishin' gear.'

'Any recognition from those crews?' Mac asked.

'Not as much as a nod. I kept scannin' the harbour; I was gettin' saturated off the grass.'

'Boo-hoo,' Kate chimed in, to a chorus of chuckles.

'I'd just settled the scope when somethin' caught my eye. Near the pier at King John's castle.'

He outlined how he had scoped the length of the ruin at ground level and saw nothing. Steadying the scope on a tiny bean bag support he continued scanning upward and midway up the rear wall glimpsed the head and shoulders of a man.

'Ivy covered every inch there and our man had binoculars trained out to sea followin' a small boat that hugged the shoreline. It motored along nice and steady as if it was headed toward the harbour. As it got closer I could make out that she was a small inflatable, a RHIB.'

Digger sipped his coffee and continued.

'I stayed focused on our friend in the castle.'

'Show us your photos,' Mac said.

They were the clincher. Mac exhaled forcefully, more a wheeple than a whistle.

'O'Hare!'

All the squad recognized Sean O'Hare. Mac had come across him in Dundalk and knew his pedigree. During the eighties and nineties, he was the Provos explosives and weapons expert. He was a full-time bomb-maker for the Provisional IRA by age seventeen. The squad scrutinized Digger's close-ups.

'Anything strike you about him?' Mac asked no one in particular.

O'Hare was six feet in height and looked strong and fit.

'Not in bad shape for a guy in his late forties,' Zoom ventured.

'Shark eyes,' Kate countered. 'There's no life in them.'

By the time Mac encountered O'Hare, he was also chief interrogator for Provo punishment squads. Hands were O'Hare's speciality. He ripped the fingernails first and followed up by hacking digits off. That an informer was unlikely to have much left to confess after losing fingers did not seem to deter him.

Digger resumed his report.

'Before movin', O'Hare waited until the van's cargo was extracted and placed on the MV Delia. They used a quayside hoist to swing the crate into the hold, the one fishermen use to land their catch.'

Mac shifted his large frame on the edge of the desk. He could not sit comfortably for long. While his six-foot-plus physique could have handled most sports, as a younger man

McEnroe had chosen rowing. A first-place finish at London's Henley Regatta was a career highlight but a pinched sciatic nerve was payback for the semi-professional training regimes of his earlier life.

'Which of them worked the hoist?'

'The van driver. Handled it with ease, he did. O'Hare moved fast when the crate was loaded. He used the castle for cover 'til he hit the shoreline, then he hopped onto the RIB and lay down, keepin' out of sight.'

Digger put more photos on the screen. With O'Hare on board, the RIB headed south as the trawler lazily pulled away from the pier and headed down the lough for the open sea. His photography was faultless given the challenges he faced. He explained that whoever was steering the RIB constantly scanned the horizon. It travelled parallel with the trawler gradually closing the gap between them. His final frame showed O'Hare jumping from the RIB onto the trawler in one fluid leap.

'I've no idea how far from land they were but O'Hare made it look easy. He disappeared into the wheelhouse straight away.'

'Looks like he held back going on board in case we hit the trawler before it left the harbour,' Kate said.

SIU was tasked with keeping watch on the defunct Provo weapons unit. Now its former main man had slipped out of the country for reasons unknown. And they had lost him. Mac thanked everyone for going the extra mile and dismissed the team. As they straggled out of the squad room, he asked Kate to hang back.

'Any thoughts on the crate?

'The cargo that was put on the MV Delia came from the shed. A crate that filled the trawler's hold.'

'Any footage from the shed?'

'Digger couldn't risk getting a camera in. It was rigged with an alarm.'

'Anything further on that?'

'We disabled it this morning, it was an anti-intrusion set-up. Entry into the shed would have triggered a message to a phone, a burner naturally.'

'Anything else?'

Mac pushed hard, his deep blue eyes holding her gaze.

'Every entry point between the concrete walls and the galvanized sheeting on that shed was sealed with expanding foam. Digger did well to pick up any audio. It's being transcribed right now.'

'When will forensics inspect the shed?' he snapped.

Fatigue was taking a toll on Kate and she wanted to leave before an acerbic comeback provoked an argument.

'I've signed a search warrant; a team is going in tonight. You said to keep it covert. We'll seal the doors and do the best we can.'

4

THE SMELL of freshly brewed coffee hit when Kate got to her apartment. Charlie was standing in her kitchen holding a pint glass filled with crushed ice and orange juice.

'Topping up on vitamin C?' she inquired.

He grinned.

She dumped her keys on the breakfast counter and slipped off her navy fleece. She had planned on hitting the shower and couldn't wait for warm water to blast away the detritus of twelve rough days away from home. Instead, she walked into the kitchen, took the glass from Charlie, and polished it off.

'Hey, I was enjoying that,' he protested.

'Try this.' She cupped his face and ran her hands through his dark wavy hair. When she kissed him he tasted deliciously cool.

He pinched his nose. 'Whoa! What have you been up to?'

Kate ignored the jibe. 'You let yourself in?'

'You gave me a key, last time, remember?'

'Only kidding! It's great to see you. How come you're home early?'

'Bloody cyclones but forget about that. It's been six weeks, two days, and four hours since…'

'I need a shower.'

'Call me when you need your back scrubbed.'

'Ever the romantic! Pour me another OJ, please,' she shouted from her wet room.

It was her apartment's wow factor. It persuaded her to buy the place in a dormant market before property prices raced out of her range. These days owning an apartment at Booterstown on Dublin's south side was the preserve of the wealthy. Car parking was in a secure underground lockup and apartment life involved no gardening. A view over Dublin Bay lit up her lounge window.

As she turned off the shower, Charlie was waiting with a luxurious bathrobe.

'Compliments of the Littoral Cruise Company!' he smirked.

He worked as a gourmet chef on the fleet's largest ship and got shore leave every three months. They had been together just over a year and were not rushing anything.

Kate savoured the warmth of the plush robe, a size too big. 'I could get used to this.'

'Stick with me, Babe.'

He took her hand and led her to the bedroom where he kicked aside his open suitcase.

'Did you stay here last night?'

'Yeah, is that a problem?'

'No, of course not; I thought you'd call first.'

'I rang a few times and left a message.'

Kate kept a separate phone for private use. She silenced it on operations.

'Come here,' he said untying the robe and slipping his arms around her waist.

'I'm soaking,' she protested as he kissed her.

Wet streaks stained the front of his tee shirt and he raised his arms over his head so she could slip it off. The touch of his skin was deliciously warm. He kissed her breasts and she quivered as his tongue caressed her nipples. She unbuckled his jeans with renewed urgency. Charlie shook them off and slipped the robe from her shoulders before laying it on the bed. They kissed passionately as she stretched out.

Together again, warm and wet, she submitted totally to his legerdemain. An attentive lover, his lips explored her milk-white skin. Ju-Jitsu kept Kate toned and her lithe body always aroused him. When they made love it was wild and urgent, a visceral release for Kate from two weeks of tension. They dozed together, her head on his chest until Charlie whispered that he had to go. He was catching up with some hometown mates.

'I'll whip up you up something before I go,' he shouted, as Kate showered.

Even with the meagre provisions in her cupboards, he came up with something special. As Kate towelled off delicious aromas wafted in from the kitchen. She looked at herself in the mirror, her dark green eyes red-rimmed. She ruffled her shoulder-length brunette hair into its usual tossed look or bed-head as her sister called it. Charlie presented a plate of French toast and Kate demolished it.

'Will you have that coffee?'

'Go on,' she replied. 'I'm awake now anyway.'

After breakfast, events at the border swirled a chaos of possibilities in her mind. She contacted the morning crew and confirmed that an air search down the east coast had gotten underway. The naval service had promised a vessel for later in the day. Digger would go on board and report directly to her. She lay down on her couch and drifted into a fitful sleep.

An instant later, it seemed, a pair of shark-like eyes loomed into her subconscious and startled her awake. She tipped over the cup resting on the seat. Dregs of coffee raced down the brown leather towards the beige wool carpet. Kate caught the spill with the end of her new bathrobe. She looked towards the clock in the kitchen. She had been asleep for barely an hour. She threw the robe into her laundry basket and pulled on sweats.

'Focus, focus,' she repeated mantra-like, as she checked the contents of her gym bag.

5

RENSHI WAS her title at the dojo but the term was rarely used. It indicated she held trainer status. She was Ju-Jitsu black belt 4th Dan and warmed up kicking and punching the heavy bags before heading upstairs to the mats. She was surprised to find Murt Butler there. When she was promoted to Superintendent, he replaced her as Detective Inspector in charge of Intelligence Analysis. He was putting a school group through a warm-up. His barrel-shaped figure testified that he had given up competition years earlier.

'Want to lend a hand?' he asked.

'Sure.'

Over the next hour, they worked the teenagers through demonstrations of groundwork, throws, strikes, and locks. For a grand finale, Kate threw Butler over her shoulder and trapped him in a headlock. When he dispersed the group Butler turned to her.

'I forget how good you are.'

She laughed.

He rubbed his shoulder. 'I've got to run. Mac wants me back

in, even though it's my only day off this week. Any idea what that's all about?'

'You'll find out soon enough.'

'Drop by this evening, if you're around.'

Stark winter sunlight streamed through the window of her old office at Garda headquarters when she linked up with Butler in the late afternoon.

'Mind if I close the blinds?'

He waved an arm expansively.

'Be my guest.'

Her former desk was a clutter of files and reports. She tried not to stare as melted butter from the slice of toast he munched dripped onto Butler's square chin. Absentmindedly, he wiped it with the back of his hand. Mac had given him details of the border operation and now he was scrambling to come up with leads in the search for the MV Delia.

'Any intel coming through on the old Provo weapons unit, at all?' she asked.

Butler picked up his cup and slurped his tea before answering.

'Fuck no. It's all towel-heads these days. Coming here for R and R, the fuckers.'

Cultural sensitivity was not part of Butler's make-up. The fact that jihadists from conflicts in the Middle East transited Ireland for rest and recuperation was well-documented. What was more worrying was the phenomenon of young Irish Muslims going to fight in the Syrian conflict.

Butler threw a pink form across the desk.

'This is the kind of crap I deal with these days.'

She read the agent handler report quickly. It had not been analysed or processed yet. The handler set out what he had gleaned during a routine meeting with his Pakistani agent. It talked about contact between an IRA splinter group and al-Qaeda, even a trade-off of weapons for IRA tactical know-how.

Had they infiltrated the Islamic groups living here? Kate doubted they had done it sufficiently to tap into that kind of information. She held up the report.

'Let me follow this up.'

'If there's anything in it, I'll need to know,' he said.

'Promise I'll keep you in the loop.'

<hr>

The total focus on operational priorities at her SIU base was like a breath of fresh air when Kate transferred from the stifling headquarters atmosphere. From the outset, Mac insisted on housing the surveillance unit away from known Garda buildings. The entrance sign read 'Government Stores.' By the time he grabbed the former Office of Public Works store, the brown brick building had almost gone to rack and ruin. Ivy still straggled up its outer wall. He had begged and borrowed from every possible budget to upgrade it. It consisted of three offices, a squad room, a canteen with limited cooking facilities, and a small conference room. Its biggest asset was its underground garage and parking, a conversion project Kate had overseen.

When she brought the report to Mac in his spartan office he shifted uncomfortably as he read through it. He was waiting on a replacement chair with enhanced lumbar support. He shoved the pink form back across his desk.

'Why do you want to go chasing this fairy tale?'

'I want to check it out.'

'We task others with intel report follow-ups. Remember?'

'I know but there's something about it.'

'There's a boat somewhere in the Irish Sea with a skilled

bomb maker on board. You'd do better to get moving and locate it.'

'Do you think I'm not aware of that?'

He drummed his fingers on the desk and waited.

'Digger's coordinating that search.'

'Where would you begin your inquiries?' he asked.

'Dundalk.'

'Why?'

'It's the south Armagh Provos natural hinterland.'

'So what?'

'If anything is stirring, someone up there might have noticed. I'll talk to Jack Quinlan.'

'Quinlan,' Mac repeated.

'He knows the place best.'

'What's your thinking? There might be a connection with Carlingford?'

'Maybe.'

'Okay. One day, no more; see Quinlan first. I'll get you clearance to talk to the agent handler.'

Digger reported no developments overnight in the search for the MV Delia and Kate met Quinlan the next day in a pub outside Dundalk. It got them away from prying eyes. The most driven anti-terrorist detectives she encountered worked in her hometown. Although she never told him as much, Detective Sergeant Quinlan was one of the best.

Trying to maintain a serious face, she asked, 'Is there anything happening up here these days, or are you thinking of handing in your papers?'

The insinuation rattled his cage.

'I'm going nowhere.'

'Pension's not getting any bigger.'

'When the time is right I'll pull the pin.

'Do you think there's still a kick left in the place?'

He checked over his shoulder.

'Who knows? There might be.'

It was coming on twelve thirty and they were the first lunchtime customers.

'What are you fishing for? Don't fuck me around; you're on to something.'

'Subtle as ever, Jack. Okay, here's a question, do you think anyone from the Provo weapons unit is active at the moment?'

Quinlan shrugged and smiled wryly.

'I knew after seeing that bastard it wouldn't be long before we had company up here again.'

'Who the hell are you talking about?'

'Don't be coy with me, Kate, I deserve better than that.'

Their paths crossed when he was a fledgling detective. Back then, she was in secondary school; there wasn't much Quinlan didn't know about her.

'Sean O'Hare turned up in one of our ops.'

Quinlan nodded slowly.

'Makes sense now. I hadn't seen him for years and last week I saw him twice coming out of Slievemish.'

'Do you know who he was visiting?'

'I've no idea. You know what it's like in there, a real warren.'

The Slievemish estate had seen more than its fair share of trouble. Economically malnourished and socially deprived, the local authority estate had been a breeding ground for the Provos. It seemed that an IRA dissident group might be cultivating the same terrain. Kate knew the estate; some of her schoolmates lived there, often surviving in impossible conditions.

'Send me a report on the sightings, will you?'

'I'll e-mail you this evening.'

'You do e-mail now!'

'If you're implying we're country hicks, don't. You were born and reared up here.'

'Touchy! What can you tell me about him?'

'Death and destruction follow the fucker. Whenever he appeared around here in the past, we tipped off our colleagues in the North, pronto.'

'Why?'

'Nine times out of ten seeing him around meant an attack on police was imminent.'

Her phone rang. The agent handler she needed to speak to requesting a late afternoon meeting.

'I've got to get back.'

'Eat first, for God's sake,' Quinlan said.

Giving in to his nagging tone, she agreed. They queued at the carvery, paid for their steak and chips, and resumed their seats.

'When I see your mother, I'll tell her I was talking to you,'

'I'd prefer you didn't.'

'She still works with the Rape Crisis Centre, I see.'

'Why would you say that?'

'Her picture is in the local paper this week. Training up new volunteers.'

'Okay, I hadn't seen that.'

She was sensitive when it came to comments about her mother from the local Gardaí. They had history. During Margaret Bowen's first year running the local rape crisis centre, a young victim took her own life when the case against her attacker fell apart. The book of evidence was not served within time limits and a judge threw the case out. The political pressure that Margaret brought to bear saw the irresponsible Superintendent demoted and transferred. Local police had neither forgotten nor forgiven.

The mention of her mother played on her conscience as she drove back to Dublin. She powered up her private phone and rang her. The greeting was familiar.

'Katie delighted to hear from you!'

'Yes Mum, I know it's been a while.'

'No, Missy, I *am* glad you called.'

They had been a close-knit unit of three growing up. Her father had left before she and Norrie started school. When they were old enough their mother told them that their dad left when he decided he was not up to the father role anymore. They discovered later that he had taken up with a new partner on his return to Wales.

'Won't you come up and see us soon?'

'I will Mum. Maybe I could bring Charlie along?'

'Still together.'

Kate winced but said nothing. Months earlier introductions had not gone as hoped. She had dropped in with Charlie in tow on their way back to Dublin from a weekend away. Her mother's reception was, at best, lukewarm. For her daughter's sake, Margaret Bowen was wary of Charlie's self-absorbed air.

'We could have a meal with Norrie and the kids,' she suggested.

'Nice idea,' Kate replied and signed off.

6

WHEN SHE GOT BACK to SIU base, she rang Digger to find out how the sea search was progressing. He was on an offshore patrol vessel the Naval Service had put at their disposal.

'Anything showing up?'

'Not a sausage, the fog's still down. It's slower than a wet week in Ballyhaunis out here, borin' as hell.'

She chuckled. 'How long can we use the OPV?'

'Captain says 'til midnight but I've managed to get Zoom onto a Customs cutter. They'll do an inshore search.'

'Symons has planes going up and down the Irish Sea since we told him about the boat.'

'Nimrods?'

'Digger, I don't have a clue. He's told us nothing. Updates every three hours, okay?'

'Roger! Can't wait to get back to dry land.'

'See you tomorrow.'

Dusk was creeping in when Kate met agent handler, Detective Gerry Grealy in a quiet car park tucked away in a secluded corner of Phoenix Park close to SIU base. Deer grazed nearby and an occasional jogger passed but otherwise, they had the place to themselves. They discussed the report that sparked her interest.

It had been a routine meeting; Grealy's agent had appeared relaxed and spoke about several new faces at the mosque on the South Circular Road in Dublin. Four of the newbies were attending an English language college. A fifth guy had disappeared quickly when prayers ended.

'The agent mentioned seeing his boss's car parked three streets away. You know, the Money Man.'

'Nasri?' Kate asked.

'The one and only.'

'Does the agent think that Nasri met this mystery man?'

'He's pretty sure he did but not certain. I'll explain later.'

Jafar 'Hajj' Nasri, the Money Man was a shadowy character who had lived in Dublin for over twenty years. He cut a corpulent figure. When dressed for prayers at the mosque, he looked as if he had stepped out of an Indiana Jones film, every inch an Arab street trader. He owned a successful company that had grown slowly and then taken off in the mid-nineties. His business imported nuts and spices from the Middle East and he had retained his wealth through the global financial crisis. His annual tax returns were meticulously prepared and submitted on time. Audits over the years failed to detect anything amiss.

SIU profiled Nasri and assessed he was financing the jihad but they could not say to what extent. They knew he was a Hawaladar, hence the Money Man tag. The hawala system operated throughout the Arab world and in Asia offering an informal way for people to transfer money between countries.

SIU investigations into militant Islamic activity among the

Irish Muslim community identified a new trend as the first war in Iraq dragged out. Jihadis who came to Ireland for rest and recuperation met Nasri.

'The way my agent described it,' Nasri ordered him to pick up his Muslim brother outside The Point and drop him back to Tallaght, where he had picked him up earlier,' Grealy said.

'Go back a bit,' Kate replied. 'Nasri supplied the transport for the earlier pick up, yeah?'

'Yes. His instructions were to go to west Tallaght, pick the guy up at seven o'clock and drop him in the city centre.'

'Did the agent recognize him from the mosque?'

'Barely. The guy was wearing a borrowed suit.'

'Did he talk much on the journey?'

'Beyond the standard greetings, Aslaamo Alaikum, nothing.'

'So he dropped his passenger in the city centre spot and then what?'

'He linked up with Nasri at the New Brunswick Hotel on the south side. Nasri gave him a phone and told him to wait in the car.'

'How long did that take?'

'He received a call about an hour and a half later.'

'And that's when he went to the Point Depot and picked up his passenger again?'

'Exactly, he dropped him back to Tallaght. When he returned to Nasri at the Brunswick he found him off his skull with drink. The agent drove him home.'

'Is that out of character?'

'We know he doesn't abstain from alcohol as the Quran requires, but we've never seen him drunk in public.'

'Does your agent know Nasri for a long time?'

'About a year and a half; Nasri has him doing runs for his business since shortly after he arrived in Ireland.'

'So what did Nasri say that night?'

'The agent says Nasri was in a stupor, muttering that soon his brothers would be trading more than nuts and spices.'

'Might your man be gilding the lily; trying to boost his image with you?'

'I agree it's cryptic.'

Grealy's large hands thumbed his notebook.

'Nasri's exact words were, Insha'Allah that which our oppressed brothers in arms in Ireland used to frighten the mighty oppressor under the table will soon be shared.'

'What does that mean?'

'You don't remember?'

Kate shifted in the passenger seat of Greally's car and looked at him.

'You know, as an agent handler you're not supposed to evaluate the information you receive. How do you make the jump to a trade-off of knowledge for weapons?'

'You know, I shouldn't even be talking to you.'

Kate was encroaching on Special Branch turf by meeting directly with Grealy.

'Keep your hair on, Gerry. I'm just trying to tease out what's behind this report.'

'You remember what made the British Prime minister and his cabinet hide under their meeting table in the dim and distant?'

'Provo homemade mortars, I know about the Downing Street attack in '91; my Granny told me about it.'

'Very witty.'

'It's a bit of a stretch, all the same.'

'Maybe, but something ramped up Nasri's mood that night.'

Kate couldn't shake her sense that something was off. Agent handling was a dodgy business, informants constantly bartered, always trying to cut a better deal. Maybe Grealy's guy was holding back. Kate did not have time for mind games; she had to find out the truth.

O'Hare was at ease on boats. He understood their rhythms and knew how they worked. He moved fluidly on the ferry vehicle deck. It was bustling with drivers checking their loads. He carried out a cursory check around the truck before opening the driver's door with a single key and climbing into the cab.

Ten minutes later, the deckhands were too busy getting the ship's bow doors ready for opening to notice another driver climb into the cab that O'Hare had entered minutes earlier. By that stage, he lay corpse-like in a compartment underneath the bunk where the driver slept on overnight stops. Before the driver gunned the engine and started to roll, O'Hare heard a thunderous clang; the ferry's ramp landing on the quay. The whiff of recently cut timber, enlarging the compartment, assailed his senses, making him gag. He forced his breathing into a slow, regular rhythm. It would be two hours before he could emerge, two hours before he could kick-start his carefully crafted plan. Provided they made it through customs.

7

THE MV DELIA was still at large as Kate read the agent's background report over breakfast the next morning.

'Anything interesting?' Charlie asked, as he looked over her shoulder and kissed her neck.

She closed the file and zipped it away in her bag. 'Just work.'

'All hush-hush, eh! Want to do something tonight?'

'I'll try my best to wriggle free.'

'It's nice having time together.'

She leaned over and kissed him. 'It's delicious. There's something I've been meaning to ask you.'

He laughed. 'Sounds ominous.'

'You said a cyclone was the reason you had to come home early.'

'Did I?'

'Yeah. I thought the Pacific cyclone season didn't begin until May.'

'I don't remember saying anything about cyclones, Babe. I got home early because the company wanted to get the boat into port for maintenance. They let me head home two weeks early.'

Kate regarded him quizzically. The weather had featured as a reason for his early return but rather than dispute his story she nodded and dropped the subject. Charlie was heading away the next day with friends. This evening would be their last together for a while and she didn't want to spoil it.

Symons was in touch to say the British searches had turned up nothing due to foggy conditions. Kate refocused SIU searches inshore when the Naval Service withdrew its vessel. Digger had been hoping for some time off after his maritime adventure when she called and told him she needed his skills.

'Herself is goin' nuts. The kids are drivin' her mad, she needs a break.'

'Tell Jane, I'll try to make it up to her,' she replied.

It was clear from Kate's review of Danesh Kundi's role as a Special Branch agent that his motivation was his desire to remain in Ireland. Grealy smoothed out bumps he hit with immigration officers. His visa had been extended three times beyond its expiration date. Now the agent had become arrogant and was failing to keep appointments. That gave them leverage.

She called Grealy and tasked him with getting the Immigration Service to stamp a warning on the agent's passport due to the no-shows. Three stamps and he would be on a repatriation flight to Pakistan. That would give him something to ponder. Within an hour, Grealy confirmed that an appointment had been set up and fast-tracked just before the close of business.

In Dublin in the early evening, Kate deployed her team to cover both sides of the river as the agent nervously exited the Immigration offices at Burgh Quay. He dropped into a nearby corner shop and chatted with the owner for ten minutes while checking out passing pedestrians. Without warning, he bolted across Butt Bridge. Grealy was waiting and pulled alongside. The agent looked around, considering his options.

'Don't be stupid, Danesh, get in.'

Grealy drove towards Dublin port, past the financial centre buildings gleaming as the last rays of weak spring sunlight hit them. Digger had picked the lock on the gate of a disused factory yard further up the quay. Grealy and his reluctant passenger drove in and parked up behind the derelict building.

Digger had wired Grealy's car for sound and vision.

'You haven't been a good honest boy, now have you?' Grealy began immediately he cut the engine.

'What you mean? I help you plenty.'

'Stop playing games, Danny boy.'

'Why do you want to see me again? It is only one week.'

'You haven't told me everything.'

'I tell you all I know.'

'Not quite everything, Danny, was it?'

Kate watched the exchange on a monitor, courtesy of the pinhole camera in the sun visor. The agent was wringing his hands as he spoke.

'Why you are doing this to me? You are not trusting me.'

'You didn't tell me the full story. I'm not interested in why; just tell me what you held back.'

'You like the rest. Brown face, no believe.'

Grealy grabbed the agent's hair from behind and knocked his head against the windscreen.

'Tell me what you fuckin' held back?'

'Stay calm,' Kate warned in Grealy's earpiece.

'Do you want to go it alone with Immigration? Do you want to see how that goes?' Grealy asked.

Danesh wiped a trickle of blood from his nose. 'I do not know what is special, what is not. This is why I did not say everything,'

'Talk,' Grealy shouted.

'Nasri, he tells me it take him a long time to arrange a meeting.'

'Lower your voice,' Kate said. 'Empathize.'

'A lot is going on,' Grealy said. 'I understand. What meeting are you talking about?'

'Nasri meet Irishman first. He told him someone will come.'

'What Irishman? Has the meeting Nasri was talking about happened?'

The meeting was two weeks ago. I do not know Irishman.'

'Who met who? Was Nasri at it?'

'No, the man I pick up in Tallaght.'

'Try and find out where they met,' Kate told Grealy.

'Do you remember where the meeting was?'

'I do not know.'

Over the next fifteen minutes, Kate watched and listened as Grealy went through every detail of the agent's conversation with the drunken Nasri. The only new element was that Nasri had met the unidentified Irishman months before the latest meeting with the suspected jihadi. Nasri was the link. Every other detail tallied with his previous telling of the tale. Grealy tried again to get a location for the mystery man's meeting but Danesh only knew it was near Abbey Street. Grealy dismissed the agent and four of Kate's team followed him to The Point tram terminus. He caught a Luas heading in the Tallaght direction, went home, and stayed indoors for the rest of the night.

Kate brainstormed possible locations with Digger. They ruled out a hook-up on the street. Hardened terrorists would not risk being rousted by a passing patrol car. Kate worked on the assumption that the visitor did not know the city. The agent dropped him near the Abbey Theatre. The only thing that fitted was a pub and they ran it down to six possibilities. She figured most would have some CCTV systems and hoped their hard drives would be advanced enough to hold footage for a few days.

Digger checked the first three and drew a blank. All had cameras in place. In one pub the cameras swivelled from side to side but were either dummies or only gave real-time coverage. Kate got lucky at The Fountain House, a pub that had successfully pitched itself at tourists. Apart from drinks of every description, it offered choices of bacon and cabbage or Guinness stew together with traditional music and Irish dancing as entertainment. She flashed her ID at the manager in the noisy bar and he beckoned her towards a backstairs to his first-floor office. He showed her their state-of-the-art system, an investment to keep drug dealers away that paid off. There was no problem getting a month's worth of images. Anything that helped keep local crime in check was fine with him. Kate thanked him without further comment.

Digger's final visit was to a tiny pub, The Hedge. It had one camera focused mainly on the till. It also gave a fuzzy view of the end of the bar. They had two weeks of recordings and he gratefully accepted a copy.

In the evening, Kate put four teams of two viewing the footage. They spliced it into hour-length digital segments and marked three images worthy of further investigation from The Fountain House footage. Digger's pub images were unclear which slowed the work down but it had to be checked out.

They almost missed it. Digger was fast-forwarding the bits containing no action with Kate looking over his shoulder. It had been a quiet evening. From six o'clock for almost an hour the barman was propped behind the counter chatting to his sole customer. Their only interruption was when a customer, small in stature, ordered a drink and walked out of shot. Five minutes on, the recording got interesting. Another customer arrived and bought a pint.

'Stop,' Kate shouted.

'Eh hup,' Digger said, as he pressed pause and rewound to where the customer came into shot.

'No, go back further,' she said, 'back to where the small guy comes in.'

Digger obliged.

'So the little dude comes in. Foreign, would you agree?'

'Definitely!'

Digger rolled the footage forward slowly.

'Feck, remind me not to use his tailor.'

Kate took up the commentary. 'He orders a Coke and goes to the back of the pub. Five minutes later, this guy, comes in and buys a pint.'

She pointed to the stilled image.

'What do you think?'

They pored over it; the resemblance was strong. They needed certainty. It was after nine o'clock when they went back to the tiny pub and spoke to the bar manager, Pat Gallagher. He recalled the particular night because most nights there wasn't much to remember.

'Wasn't that the evenin' the Man-U match was on the telly?' Digger said.

Kate did not get what men saw in football.

'Now I have it,' the barman said. 'It was midweek, things were slow. A guy with a Northern accent came in and ordered a pint of lager. He took it off to the snug.'

'What about the fella who was in before him?' Digger asked.

'The Paki?'

Digger nodded.

Gallagher laughed. 'He wore the worst bleedin' suit I ever

saw, hangin' on him it was. Come to think of it, he went to the snug as well.'

'Anything strike you about him?'

'He was jumpy. Like he had never seen the inside of a pub before. The pair left together. Five minutes after the northern lad came in, they were gone. He left half his pint behind.'

'Fair play, Pat,' Digger said. 'You've been a big help.'

The barman picked up a pint glass. 'No bother.'

He began pulling a Guinness for a customer who was settling in at the other end of the bar. They chit-chatted as the dark stout settled and Digger watched enviously when Pat lifted the pint to top it off with a smooth creamy head. He couldn't spare the time for even a sip of one.

Kate called Jack Quinlan and e-mailed him a still from the CCTV. Apart from Digger, he had seen O'Hare most recently. He confirmed the ID. Digger looked up as she hung up Quinlan's call.

'So two weeks before he disappears into the Irish Sea, O'Hare has a meeting with a dodgy Islamic. Dubious, wouldn't you say?'

'If it turns out to be a first verified contact between an IRA killer and a jihadi,' she replied. 'That would be momentous.'

She rang Mac to break the news.

'Where to from here?' he asked.

'We have to find the MV Delia. Until we do, we're shooting in the dark.'

Kate updated him on the current status of the search. She explained that the fog was lifting but their focus had switched to checking ports along the east coast.

'What about our friends in the North,' Kate asked. 'Will you tell them?'

'Let's give Zoom and the rest of the crew another 24 hours to locate the boat. We'll re-evaluate tomorrow.'

O'Hare was glad to have the jittery driver out of the picture. He slipped from the cab when they pulled into the service stop while the driver was preoccupied with a trailer tyre. He powered up the prepaid phone, punched in the number, and got straight to business when it connected.

'I'm in a place called La Maison de Normandie at a stop called B-o-s-g-o-u-e-t. Come and pick me up.'

'Hello to you too,' the voice at the other end replied.

'Look, Mucker, we'll do the small talk when we meet. Come get me.'

'Is your friend gone?'

'Fuck sake! Enough! Come pick me up.'

'Bosgouet S-u-d is it?'

'Hang on.'

O'Hare checked the service stop sign. 'Aye, what you said there is right.'

'Give me an hour.'

'Make it half that.'

O'Hare used the men's restroom at the service station to shower and put on a plain blue polo shirt he had brought along. By the time his contact drove into the service stop, he had pinpointed the six CCTV cameras dotted around Aire de Bosgouet Sud. Without looking up, he strode out and was in the 4 x 4 before his face came into shot.

8

MAC WAS ENGROSSED in a phone call when Kate arrived at his office at eight o'clock the next morning. He pressed his back into his new leather executive chair and nodded as he got an occasional word into the conversation. He indicated his new chair as if seeking her approval.

Very nice, she mouthed.

'Thanks for the offer but we're fine for air support.'

Kate tuned into the agitation of the caller.

'Peter, of course, three aircraft would be better than one but we will solely use our resources in our jurisdiction.'

He rolled his eyes skywards.

'Peter, I appreciate that your Home Secretary wants hourly briefings.'

Kate was hearing one side of the conversation. She scribbled 'Symons?' on a pad and placed it in front of her boss. Mac nodded and switched the call to the speaker. A petulant voice whined.

'Chief McEnroe, I cannot overemphasize the urgency of

finding that fucking boat. The media is already asking why the UK threat level has been raised.'

'Peter, when we have any news that's actionable on your part, we will be in touch.'

Mac slammed the phone down.

'Jesus Christ! Top brass breathing down my neck, now MI5 as well. Care to explain why we haven't located the MV Delia?'

'I've got a chopper today for the first time. Digger and I are going up in the bloody thing.'

The thought of spending hours being buffeted about in a fragile aircraft was already making her light-headed.

'When will you be airborne?'

'When we're done here.'

They reviewed the case to date. The key things were that the Carlingford operation was a well-planned and executed job; the Brits knew nothing about it in advance and O'Hare was the only known suspect from the group. More significantly, the trawler and its cargo were still at large.

Symons's air reconnaissance had managed to confirm that the MV Delia maintained a southerly course after it left Carlingford. They lost it as a thick mist descended on the Irish Sea in the late afternoon and had not picked it up since. Symons was convinced that the activity was a prequel to setting up a spectacular bomb attack in the UK. Anything on the scale of the Canary Wharf bomb blast in 1996 was a terrifying prospect. He had the UK terrorist threat level ramped up to critical, which meant an attack was expected imminently. Kate reminded Mac that the heightened security alert would send ripples across the English Channel. He agreed to talk to his French counterpart.

The drone of an approaching helicopter ended their conversation. Kate and Digger drove to the rendezvous and jumped on board. The craft was painted military green rather than the usual police markings. Kate donned a headset once she had been securely strapped in by one of the crew.

'Your chopper is being serviced,' the pilot advised. 'Will this one do?'

'Colour doesn't matter. I'm not mad about any of them.'

The aircraft hovered briefly and then swept out over Dublin Bay. Cargo ships and car ferries heading for the capital quickly disappeared behind them as they headed south. Digger handed Kate binoculars and she focused on the slate-grey Irish Sea beneath. It distracted her from the queasiness kicking off in her stomach.

Apart from refuelling stops, she spent the rest of the day in the chopper as the search for the MV Delia became more frantic. The hours slipped by as they scoured the coastline before fading light forced them back towards base. As Kate stowed the binoculars, the pilot's voice crackled in her headset.

'Our air traffic controller is patching a Detective Sergeant Duggan through.'

She acknowledged the pilot's message and listened intently as the call came on the line. She grabbed a pen and scrawled some notes, high-fived Digger, and put through a priority call to Mac.

'Zoom has located the Delia.'

'Where?'

'Rosslare Harbour.'

'Shit!'

Rosslare Harbour lay on the southeast tip of Ireland. Daily car ferry services operated from there to ports in the UK and France. Zoom had spotted the trawler as he walked from the harbour towards his digs for the night.

'Wait till you hear the rest,' Kate said.

As soon as she ended the call, Mac rang his French counterpart for the second time that day.

'*Re-bonjour* Mac,' came the friendly greeting.

'We need to talk,' Mac said.

'So let's talk.'

'Face to face in Dublin tomorrow.'

SIU's first real break in an operation Mac now dubbed, Cassandra, posed more questions than it answered.

9

A UNITED NATIONS of languages and dialects crams onto the Paris RER at morning rush hour. This morning was no different; Yves Fenaux's carriage on the C line was suffused with pungent human odours. When the doors opened at stops on the line the semi-fresh air that wafted in did little to refresh him.

At Pereire Levallois he pushed through the throng and stepped off. He raced up the stairs out of the station. He needed a cigarette. By the time he reached the street, he was dragging deeply on a Craven A. The vibration in his pocket alerted him that his phone had picked up a signal again and he had missed calls from his deputy.

Fenaux hit call back and waited for an answer.

'What's up?'

'The eggheads say they've got something,' Dubois told him.

'Trying to justify their existence. What is it this time?'

'A message on one of the sites. They think an attack is coming.'

The French Interior Security Service, la Direction Générale de la Sécurité Intérieure, (DGSI) monitored radical Islamic internet forums. Every country did it. The analysts tried to decipher the traffic. They triggered regular alerts, getting everyone worked up before minimal investigation proved their theories wide of the mark.

'*Merde*! It's just more bullshit.'

'This one's different, not a keyboard warrior, I think.'

'Different, how?'

'It's the tone, it's confident.'

'What does it say?'

'It begins with the usual stuff about the decadence of the Crusader; it's the final sentence that worries.'

'What precisely does that say?'

'*Always we have the will. Soon we will have the means. Soon we will strike at Satan.*'

'How do we know it's one of ours?'

'We've traced it to La Courneuve.'

Fenaux took a final drag from his cigarette and flicked it in the gutter.

'We'll talk about it when I get in. What time is my flight to Dublin?'

'Eleven o'clock. A car will take you to CdG.'

The DGSI Head of Intelligence wore a black leather jacket for the anticipated cooler Irish climes. He had bounded up the stairs from Pereire Levallois station and the humid Parisian air pushed beads of perspiration down his back. He shuddered involuntarily as he ended the call.

At Dublin airport's VIP lounge, the first thing Kate noted about Fenaux was that they were almost similar in height. He had jet black hair and a tanned complexion that was down to a Corsican mother rather than the Parisian weather. He had the darkest brown eyes she ever encountered. Something about him gave an impression of greater stature; not so much a swagger as an attitude.

Cigarette smoke wafted as she guided him through the corridor. Despite the ubiquitous no smoking signs, he had lit up immediately on hitting the terminal. Kate hoped the hospitality staff would turn a blind eye. Mac ensured his premium contacts received first-class treatment and wanted it to stay that way. Just minutes after stepping off the plane Fenaux stubbed out his cigarette and climbed into the Mercedes Viano Kate had brought along to blend in at VIP parking. He shook hands with Mac and slid the door closed as she jumped into the driver's seat.

'*Ça va*, Mac?'

'*Pas mal et toi*?'

'Forgive me Kate; I come in your country and speak French.'

'No worries, Mr. Fenaux.'

'Yves, please.'

'Okay, Yves. Speak whatever language you wish; I won't be joining in if it's anything other than English.'

'Do you mind if we speak French?' Mac asked her.

'Knock yourself out.'

Mac spoke the language fluently, a rare feature in a senior Garda officer. Years earlier he had established a liaison post in Paris, spending eighteen months there. He briefed Fenaux on what they knew so far, taking the opportunity to flex his linguistic muscles. Kate didn't know how he had learned it but as he began his accent took on a Gallic twist that left her feeling like a proper monoglot.

'Kate's crew did a great job given the intel we had to work with. When the van eventually moved, the last thing we expected was an offload to a boat. This is a first and the skipper of the MV Delia has never appeared on our radar.'

'Why do you think it happened in this way?' Fenaux asked.

'We can only speculate. To throw off surveillance, most likely. Taking the crate by sea was a stroke of genius.'

'How did you find the boat?'

'Twenty-four hours ago one of Kate's crew, Zoom, located it at Rosslare port. The Customs cutter he was on was tying up for the evening when he tagged it wedged between two other trawlers.'

Fenaux laughed. 'Zoom. I like this name.'

'A rugby man, not easily stopped.'

'Did you question the skipper of the trawler?'

'Customs questioned the skippers of all three boats, asking each the same questions. Zoom just listened; we didn't want to tip off the IRA.'

'What pretext was used to question them?'

'Customs told them that they were looking for a bigger boat, suspected of transferring packages to smaller ones off the south-east coast.'

'The IRA will swallow this?'

'Who knows?'

Mac told Fenaux that the harbour master had informed them that the crate was collected by a white truck, which was waiting when it docked. The next vessel to leave Rosslare Harbour that day was a car ferry to Cherbourg.

'The car ferry docked at Pier A in Cherbourg yesterday afternoon at three-thirty,' Mac explained.

Mac wrapped up by telling Fenaux about his inquiries with the Police Aux Frontières at Cherbourg. The border police confirmed that five white trucks had come off a Celtic Link ferry. SIU was already checking out the transport companies.

Fenaux elbowed Mac in the ribs as he switched to English. 'So you are letting terrorists come into my country.'

Mac winced. Up front, Kate grinned; Operation Cassandra was getting to him already.

Fenaux laughed aloud. '*Calme-toi* Mac, just kidding.'

As Kate drove into the restaurant parking area an edgy atmosphere overshadowed the prospect of a first-class lunch. Before they went inside Fenaux told them about the message the DGSI had picked up the previous night. Nothing connected the two events; it was simply the face of twenty-first-century terrorism.

10

AFTER LUNCH, the drive through the traffic-choked city centre delayed their transit back to base. While SIU was not a Security Service in name, their remit frequently propelled them into that realm. Everybody at SIU was aware that unfriendly Security Services knew where they were and what they did. The high walls and mature trees made hostile surveillance problematic but not impossible. Mostly, they did their work away from prying eyes.

Kate guided Fenaux out of the lift towards the conference room.

'Glad we passed on the wine,' Mac whispered as they strode along the corridor.

Assistant Commissioner Dominic Fox, the big boss at the Security Branch waved away apologies for their late arrival and focused on welcoming their visitor. Fox had surrendered most of his hair to alopecia before his twenty-first birthday. The smooth, jovial exterior concealed a serious and ambitious personality. He mostly left the management of intelligence-led operations to Kate and Mac. His insistence on attending this briefing meant everyone was on their best behaviour. Digger, Zoom, and Angie sat in on the meeting and Kate introduced them to Fenaux as Detectives Rooney, Duggan, and Harrington.

'You're familiar with events so far,' she began. 'These are photos of the interior of the shed.'

Fenaux studied them. 'Is there something I should look out for?'

'That's the point, there's nothing remarkable in them. The audio we managed to pick up is equally disappointing.' She slid stapled sheets across the table. 'Here's the transcript.'

'There was minimal conversation while they worked. There's a phrase on the second page you might find interesting - *they've done it before; they'll know what to do.*'

'Who are *they*?' Fenaux asked.

'That's what we need to find out,' Kate replied.

Fenaux looked around. 'Who found the trawler, please?'

Zoom raised his hand. 'What do you want to know?'

'Everything.'

'Here are some photos I took.'

Fenaux picked them up, scanned them briefly, and threw them aside.

'What else?'

'It was tied up between two other boats when I saw it...'

'Yes, yes I know about that part, but do you know why it was used in this way?'

Kate interrupted. 'We're still looking into the whys and wherefores. Let's move on.'

Digger checked a message on his phone which sat on the table in front of him. She picked up a signal that he needed a word but ignored it and went on to describe the meeting O'Hare had weeks before he vanished with a person unknown but believed to be a jihadi. When Kate glanced at Digger again there was a renewed urgency to his signals.

'Commissioner Fox, there's an urgent matter that needs my attention. Permission to pause the meeting.'

'Granted. Don't delay.'

'How do you see a joint investigation working?' Kate heard Fox asking as she left the room with Digger.

'Jesus, what's so urgent?' she asked in the corridor.

Digger handed her his phone. 'Read this.'

It was a text from Pete McNally, the base security officer for the day.

Peter Symons is at the entrance in a taxi. He wants to see Mac urgently.

'What the hell?' she whispered.

'This is no coincidence. Our comms must be compromised.'

'Let's not jump to conclusions. An unplanned meeting is not the norm though.'

'Symons must know Fenaux is here and that somethin's up. What do you want to do?'

'Go to the entrance, delay him, either Mac or I will call you.'

Kate resumed her seat in the conference room. She waited until Fox finished speaking to Fenaux.

'Give us the room,' she said to Angie and Zoom and the pair departed.

'Peter Symons has arrived at our front door unannounced,' she told Assistant Commissioner Fox. 'He wants to see Chief McEnroe urgently.'

Fox looked to Mac, his face not concealing his annoyance. 'This is not the way I like to conduct business.'

He turned to Fenaux. 'Our apologies for this mix-up.'

'I'll sort it out,' Mac said.

'Make it fast,' Fox ordered.

11

MAC TOLD Digger to escort Symons to his office. The stone-cold handshake offered by the MI5 liaison had dark portents. Mac studied him as he took a seat opposite. He did not remove the oversized black trench coat he wore and Mac did not encourage it. His foppish public schoolboy hairstyle was incongruous on a man well into his fifties. Digger departed and closed the door.

'Well, Peter, this is a surprise.'

A trace of a smirk unfurled across Symons's thin lips.

'I had embassy business in Dublin and decided to make a courtesy visit on my friends.'

Still within earshot outside the door, Digger muttered, 'Lyin' bastard.'

'Without even a phone call in advance. What's on your mind, Peter?'

'One of our surveillance planes took an interesting photograph yesterday.'

'Really? What was that?'

'It photographed everything in Rosslare harbour. We think

the MV Delia is there.'

It had slipped Mac's mind that he had given Symons the go-ahead for RAF surveillance aircraft to take a wide sweep as they turned northwards returning up the Irish Sea. Symons, it seemed, had transmitted an interpretation of Mac's goodwill gesture that flagrantly infringed sovereignty boundaries.

'We're aware of that.'

'When were you planning on telling me?'

'Peter, I am involved in a hot pursuit with another agency. I won't be distracted from that.'

'After all we've been through these last two weeks, after all that, you bring the intel to the French first.'

'What makes you think it's the French?' Mac asked.

'I'm not stupid!'

'Neither am I.'

'The fucking French!'

'To the best of our knowledge, there is a truck with the crate from the border shed in France. Locating it is our priority and DGSI had to be informed if we're to have any chance...'

'What truck? This is the first I'm hearing of a truck.'

'Peter, you know how it is when a pursuit is on, you focus solely on...'

'This is bollocks and you know it.'

'If that's your view; fair enough.'

Symons was red-faced, his voice getting louder all the time.

'Jesus fucking Christ don't you realize that London has always been the IRA's favoured target? A missing fucking truck and you didn't think it worthwhile to tell me?'

'Peter, is this getting us anywhere?'

'I can't believe you cut me out of the loop.'

Symons was now shouting and Mac was conscious that the ruckus would be overheard.

'Peter, you need to calm down.'

'My Home Secretary will freak if she hears this; fucking freak.'

'If you informed her, what would you tell her?'

'That the Irish Garda fucked up again.'

'In what way?'

They spent the next ten minutes discussing the outcome of events at the border shed. Mac explained the kind of evidence Irish courts required to sustain a terrorism charge. He outlined his belief that whatever had been crated up could turn out to be innocuous. By the end, Symons had simmered down.

Mac told him, 'We found scraps of angle iron, used welding rods and steel filings. A dossier is being prepared for you with a copy of everything we've got, photos included. Pick it up as you leave.'

'Mortar manufacture, do you think?'

Mac stood, indicating he was terminating the meeting.

'Whatever came out of the shed did so crated in a wooden box so I don't know.'

He ordered Pete McNally to drive Symons to the airport and ensure he caught his London flight. When he returned to the conference room Kate's briefing had concluded and the meeting had descended into small talk.

'Apologies,' he said, 'an unexpected caller.'

'So important, he couldn't wait?' Fox asked.

'Sir, Mr. Symons had not advised us he was calling today.'

Kate resumed the discussion on the operation. 'Where do we go from here?'

'Get the Americans involved,' Fenaux suggested.

'What agency?' Fox asked.

'Robin Jeffers is based in Paris, he's the FBI Legal Attaché for Europe. He's a good guy.'

'If Islamic radicals are involved, the CIA will want in as well,' Mac said.

'Our Anglo-Saxon friends will try to take the driving seat,' Fenaux continued. 'We need to ensure that, from day one, the investigation is an international one.'

Fox said gruffly, 'Let's not turn this into a pissing contest.'

'I agree,' Mac said. 'But the Brits see it solely as an IRA plot against the UK. There may be more involved.'

Fenaux rowed in. 'If, as we suspect, radical Islamists are part of the plot, anything is possible. We had no warning of the Charlie Hebdo attacks.'

'So when do we gather people around a table?' Fox asked.

'ASAP,' Mac replied.

'I would be honoured to host the first conference in Paris.'

Kate glanced at the boss as he considered the pros and cons of going to France for the first case conference. He was a pragmatic policeman but also a political animal. Fenaux was returning to Paris on the last flight out of Dublin and needed a decision.

'Gentlemen, let us proceed with the safety of our citizens foremost in our minds,' Fox began.

A big speech is coming, Kate groaned inwardly.

'The immediate threat which we cannot quantify rests, to the best of our knowledge, in France. It emanated from our soil. It seems logical that the Irish and French services take the lead. That we reach out to our allies for assistance, and,' he glowered at Mac 'keep them fully informed, is a given.'

At least he was making sense.

'So Mr. Fenaux, in this context, I request that our French colleagues convene the partners and we run this down fast.'

Her boss should be on the stage. Kate nodded in agreement and tried to keep a grin off her face. Mac studied Fenaux, wondering whether the final part of the boss's oratorical flourish had overpowered him linguistically. Not in the least.

Fenaux stood up, smiled, and shook Fox's hand. *'Que les Jeux commencent.'*

The boss looked to Mac for illumination, 'Let the Games begin.'

Pete McNally walked in carrying a tray with a bottle of 12-year-old Jameson whiskey in its centre surrounded by numerous glasses.

'Not now,' Fox barked.

Fenaux occupied himself scooping up reports from Kate along with photographs of suspected jihadists; all unidentified visitors to Nasri.

'Don't worry, Yves,' Fox said, 'when we break this case I'll crack open a better one.'

Fenaux nodded, locked his briefcase, and headed for the door. Kate exited ahead of him. Mac copped her grin as she shouted to Zoom that their visitor needed to get to the airport quickly. Zoom's pastime was car rallying. When SIU needed a new vehicle's limits tested he was their go-to guy.

'When I drive, no one misses their flight,' he bragged. The part he always omitted was his passenger's deathly pallor and unsteady gait on arrival. Fenaux was in for a treat.

12

O'HARE SPENT the night in a small hotel in a place that sounded like elbow, it was Elbeuf. When a 4 x 4 picked him up at ten o'clock the following morning they headed for Paris. The driver told him that finding the place he wanted would not be easy. It was a dodgy area and he didn't want his jeep wrecked.

'It won't be touched,' O'Hare assured him.

They drove in silence and followed signs for the A86 which kept them out of central Paris. O'Hare repeated the street name in Seine-Saint-Denis and was relieved when they eventually swung out of heavy traffic.

They drove to Montfermeil and passed an open-air market where trading was winding down. Stallholders were packing their leftover produce into waiting vans. While one worker loaded unsold produce another stood guard at the rear. The traders knew their customers.

'Parking is fucking shite around here,' the driver grumbled.

'Quit your moaning and drive on,' O'Hare snapped.

They snaked through the clogged traffic, O'Hare calling out left and right turns until they reached a T-junction. A battered shut-down garage sat across the street in front of them. To the right, O'Hare spotted the rendezvous location.

A red canopy over the entrance advertised it as a café, hotel, and restaurant. Chez Carima had two large black wrought iron gates to the right of a building that had seen better days. A child stood in the gateway.

'Follow the chisler,' O'Hare ordered.

The driver approached the entrance cautiously. The kid pushed the gates open and closed them again. While they parked he disappeared. The duo entered the rear of the building near the fire exit. A first-floor dining room was unlocked as they approached and they were guided inside. Red and gold were the predominant colours inside. Silver foil covered the windows. The light from the table lamps was gloomy and it was hard to see anything. The table furthest from the kitchen was set for dining. Two Pakistani men dressed in suits sat at it. On seeing O'Hare, they stood up. One walked to greet him.

'Come, you are late and there is little time.'

<hr>

The day following Symons' unexpected visit Assistant Commissioner Fox summoned Kate and Mac for an early morning audience.

The exterior of his office gave little indication that effectively, he was a Security Service Head. Inside, the corpulent senior officer sat on a leather executive chair behind his immaculately neat desk. A portrait photograph of President Higgins hung on the wall behind him. Two armchairs were positioned in front of a couch, separated by a mahogany coffee table.

One wall of the office had floor-to-ceiling bookshelves with publications on international terrorism and counter-terrorism.

Books on policing methods and lots of legal tomes completed the collection. His office reflected the prestige of his rank.

Mac pulled up one armchair and Kate the other. Their backsides had barely touched the seats when Fox began.

'Quite frankly, I am appalled. We looked like circus clowns yesterday.'

'I don't agree, Comm...'

'Chief Superintendent, I'm not done.'

'For Symons to gate-crash our briefing with another Security Service in that way was, to say the least, unprofessional.'

Mac prepared to speak.

'...but maybe he had good reason. Chief Superintendent, I am surprised that given the high stakes here, you seem to think we can afford a cavalier attitude to intelligence sharing.'

'That's not...'

'Not yet, Chief Superintendent. To a neutral observer, Symons might be seen as just doing his job. Now, I am fully aware that he took advantage of the situation to embarrass us. Do not give him that opportunity again.'

'Yes, Sir,' Mac said.

'Anything else?'

'No, Sir.'

'Good. Fenaux has set the Paris meeting for Friday. Both you and Kate will attend. That is all.'

<hr>

While O'Hare conversed with the two Pakistanis, the driver ate a meal with the kitchen staff. When they returned to the 4 x 4 he asked no questions. O'Hare gave him the address of their afternoon destination.

'That area is fucking worse than this kip.'

'Just get us there,' O'Hare barked. 'I'll need you with me.'

They drove out of Montfermeil onto the *périphérique*, the mid-afternoon traffic less frenetic.

'That's the place,' O'Hare signalled as they approached the sign for La Courneuve.

As O'Hare had been advised they ditched their transport in a supermarket car park and walked the final kilometre into the estate. They went directly to a tower block behind two larger ones. The group of yobs hanging around the steps out front grew uneasy when they realized they had company. This was their block. The larger ones in the group moved to intercept the approaching pair. A voice from the stairs shouted it was okay.

'*Ca va, ca va!*'

O'Hare and his driver walked confidently through the yobs into the building.

'*Troisième étage,*' the same voice called to the pair as they entered the foyer.

'Third floor,' the driver told O'Hare.

As they followed their guide the stench of urine and rotting food was unremitting. The guide rat-tat-tatted a signal on a grey door and it opened immediately. A young man wearing a white thobe stepped out.

He was not much older than twenty-one but his hewn hard face made him appear older.

'Greetings my brothers,' he said in halting English, shaking O'Hare's hand and inviting them both to enter.

13

CHARLIE RETURNED a day earlier than planned from his getaway with his mates. He told Kate that the wife of one of the guys had gone into premature labour and they all decided to return early. She had never met his friends. Charlie told her all they talked about was football and she would be bored. They had gone to London for a blowout, taking in a Premiership soccer match along the way. She was happy to have him back. When he was around they made love in the evening, delightful interludes to tension-filled days. He was due back to sea at the weekend and the Paris meeting would take two days away from their time together.

Kate woke early on the morning she was due to travel. She showered quietly and tiptoed from the bedroom to the kitchen where she poured herself a glass of orange juice. She had her travel bag packed and stowed it in the hallway overnight. Her car keys were on the countertop and as she picked them up she noticed Charlie's phone blinking. An unseen message. She tut-tutted as she unlocked the screen. 'Charlie's hopeless, no screen lock.'

The message was a WhatsApp from an Irish phone. Kate hesitated, about to put the phone back on the counter when she read the message headline; *cant wait for...* To read the rest, Kate would have to open it. She scribbled the number on an old newspaper, tore off the corner of the page, and put it in her bag.

Do I want to do this? she wondered. Charlie would know it had been accessed. She clicked open and the selfie that sprang to life overwhelmed her. The naked blonde seemed totally at ease sprawled on an unmade bed. She was petite apart from voluptuous breasts that seemed out of proportion with the rest of her body. The message read *cant wait for you to play with this again.* The image left little room for doubt.

Kate stormed into the bedroom and threw the phone at Charlie's sleeping head.

'Holy fuck!' he shouted as he jumped out of bed. He stared, open-mouthed at her, rubbing the back of his neck. 'Kate, what's wrong?'

'Get dressed and get out!'

'Why, wha...?' he stuttered, as Kate departed, slamming the bedroom door.

His bleary eyes took in the bedroom, trying to make sense of what had just happened.

The phone had bounced off his head and landed on the floor. He picked it up and after three frantic swipes unlocked the screen. As the naked selfie revealed itself, he groaned. His tired brain worked overtime to come up with something to say.

'Kate, Kate...' he shouted, 'it's not...'

The sound of the apartment door slamming made it pointless to finish the sentence. By the time he got clothes on, she would be gone. He rang her phone. It was powered off. He slumped back on the bed and pressed a hand to his head as a searing pain began its throbbing beat.

The early Dublin to Paris flight was cancelled and Kate arrived with Mac at their city centre hotel at eight o'clock in the evening. Mac switched seamlessly into French mode and chatted with the DGSI man who turned up later at their hotel apologizing for the missed airport pick-up.

'Would you like a coffee?' Mac inquired.

'*Mais non,*' Bruno replied, 'We can share a beer, perhaps?'

'I have calls to make,' Mac told him, adding that he planned on getting an early night.

He hadn't eaten the meal on the plane and chewed antacids for most of the journey. Kate, however, needed distraction. Bruno brought her to l'Empereur Café & Bar, just up the street. Its outdoor seating offered a close-up view of the chaotic traffic around the Arc.

'The boss, he is busy. Can I show you some of our beautiful city?' Bruno offered.

'Maybe,' she had replied.

The morning sounds of a new city always intrigued Kate. The noise that woke her the next morning was the reverberation of lifting gear tipping rubbish into Ville de Paris collection trucks. She opened her eyes and adjusted slowly to the room's dim light. The bedside clock glared five-thirty. She turned over and groaned.

Bruno grinned.

'Bonjour chérie!'

'Oh shit! Get dressed; my boss can't find you here.'

'Don't worry, chérie. I will be discreet.'

Mac planned an early breakfast so they could walk from their hotel in the 17th arrondissement to Place Beauvau at the other end of the Champs Élysées. While he was in tour guide mode, Kate was bewildered. How could her life have turned upside down so completely in twenty-four hours? How could she have been so stupid? She didn't screw around. Bruno had walked her back to the hotel and shared the tiny elevator to her floor. On impulse, she had invited him to her room.

She set out up avenue Carnot with her boss. Both sides of the tree-lined street were awash with delicate pale purple flowers. Mac pointed them out. 'Paulownias, the inner city heat brings them into bloom early.'

Kate did not respond.

'Don't get too worked up about the meeting. Enjoy the stroll.'

'I'm not. The blossoms are beautiful.'

They should have added to her perception of chic in the City of Light but she had hardly noticed. The Arc de Triomphe stood at the top of the street and most of the Eiffel Tower was visible from there. She was oblivious to the grandeur of it all. At the top of avenue Carnot, Mac insisted they cut through the tunnel that came up at the centre of the Arc de Triomphe where the eternal flame flickered in the breeze.

'Takes your breath away, doesn't it?' he said.

'What?'

He pointed down avenue des Champs Élysées towards Place de la Concorde and in the opposite direction up avenue de la Grande Armée towards the business district of La Défense in the distance.

'The view!'

'It's lovely apart from the suffocating exhaust fumes.'

They walked down the Champs Élysées and turned left onto avenue de Marigny. Mac pointed to the heavily guarded building on the right as they entered Place Beauvau.

'The Élysée Palace, the French president's gaff.'

They flashed IDs to the gendarme at the gate who consulted

his list and directed them to an arched walkway where Bruno awaited. Kate wondered, what the hell was I thinking? She tucked her portfolio under her arm. The walk from the hotel had cleared her head and she strode across the small cobbled courtyard ignoring Bruno's wink as he directed them to the meeting room.

'Cheeky bugger,' Mac muttered.

'Let's focus on what's ahead.'

'Remind me to show you a room here afterwards.'

Kate nodded.

The place reeked of history. The block had been the SS head-quarters during the Nazi occupation in the 1940s. One room was left untouched since that time and lest future generations forget to remember, the French government opened it for public viewing one day each year.

In the conference room, there were two chairs at the top table. Interpreters sat in a booth alongside and the meeting began promptly at eight-thirty. Fenaux opened with welcomes and a tour de table.

'Peter Symons, representing MI5 on behalf of Her Majesty's government of Great Britain and Northern Ireland; Daphne Clarke accompanying.'

'Dan Whatney, CIA, Paris Country Station.'

'Robin Jeffers, FBI Legal Attaché for Europe.'

'Colonel Pierre de Hautecloque, Direction du Renseignement Militaire, la DRM.'

Fenaux clarified that the Colonel's presence was down to the role the Army played in guarding key French installations and government buildings. He would observe only but as the meeting concluded later, the Colonel withdrew, indicating that the case was best left to DGSI.

Fenaux began by displaying the three photos Kate had given him.

'DGSI has identified three recent jihadi visitors to Ireland,' he said.

He explained that all three: Said al-Khayyan, Omar al-Haddad, and Ibn Saud had been to Afghanistan on numerous occasions and more recently to Iraq.

'We know they have all been trained in weapons and tactics. Saud has received training in manufacturing and deploying IEDs. We believe all three have engaged in attacks on American and NATO forces in Afghanistan. We assess Saud to be the most dangerous because of his specialized training.'

He nodded in Kate's direction. 'Next, we will get a scene set from the Irish side.'

'This is Jafar 'Hajj' Nasri, AKA the Money Man,' Kate began.

She filled in the profile picture of Nasri's twenty years in Ireland as a successful businessman.

'Nasri's status in this case is what?' Whatney, the curious CIA man, drawled. All that was missing was the Stetson. With that accent, Whatney would fit in at any ranch bunkhouse, at least in Kate's mind. His broad shoulders and muscled arms hinted at a gym bunny.

'We assess him as the linkman for jihadists who come to Ireland for rest and recuperation from hostilities.'

'An important player, d'ya' reckon?'

'We know Nasri provides money to those returning to the jihad. Beyond that, we've no idea.'

She updated them on Operation Cassandra. SIU confirmed the ferry transfer had been carried out by a legit haulier, John Glynn. Normally haulers require customers to open accounts with them and effect payment by bank transfer. Glynn claimed to have been lured into accepting cash on this occasion, by the size of the payment and the pressure of an imminent tax bill.

'Where did Glynn dump his load?' Jeffers asked. It was the

first intervention from the FBI man. His colloquialism threw her.

'Eh, eh... at a yard,' she replied. 'Under interrogation, he told us that he dropped it at a yard outside Cherbourg.'

'Have you pinpointed it?'

'Glynn claims his wife wiped the coordinates from his Sat Nav. So we're still checking.'

Fenaux intervened. 'Since DGSI got details of the truck we have inquiries going over an area within 200 kilometres of Cherbourg. It's early days.'

Mac opened up the meeting for questions. Symons jumped in.

'My team assesses that there is only one target here, the United Kingdom. Our analysis is that the biggest threat has to be against London.'

'Do you have specific intel that London is a target?' Fenaux asked.

'No, but it has always been thus.'

The exchange dragged on becoming fractious and inconclusive; old antagonisms simmering beneath the surface. Fenaux was not buying the British logic.

Mac invited comments from the Americans to break the tension. 'Any thoughts, Robin?'

Urbane and sophisticated, dark hair immaculately groomed, Jeffers seemed the polar opposite of his CIA colleague. He was the first African-American Kate had come across in a foreign posting.

'It's very early to be drawing hard and fast conclusions about the target.'

Whatney asked. 'Has a connection between the Paris suspects and the IRA guy been established?'

'No,' Kate said. 'We believe Nasri is a link but we don't have conclusive evidence beyond that.'

'We've had the three French suspects under surveillance for the past week,' Fenaux explained. 'They live in Seine-Saint-Denis just outside the city. To date, they've done nothing to attract attention.'

'We're re-working every angle on the trawler captain and truck driver,' Kate said. 'We expect they have more to give up.'

Symons wanted the next case conference to be held in London. The request was turned down on the basis that there were no leads in the UK at that time and it was agreed to meet in Dublin in two weeks.

Before departing, Mac brought Kate to see the former Nazi interrogation room. It was unspectacular but poignant. The names of loved ones were scratched onto walls by Resistance fighters awaiting interrogation at the hands of Hitler's secret police, almost inevitably followed by their execution. She traced the etchings with her fingers. True love.

Her apartment was filled with flowers when she returned to Dublin. The blooms were almost two days old and Kate was tempted to dump them instantly. She grabbed the card from the bunch of twelve red roses that sat on the coffee table in the centre of the lounge. It was Charlie's scrawl – *Kate, I need you, please turn your phone on.* She walked to the bedroom, threw her overnight bag on the bed, and changed into sweats. She had to dig around inside her shoulder bag until she retrieved her private phone. There were seven missed calls, five from Charlie, and two from her mother. She slumped into a giant bean bag, her favourite seat, and listened to all.

The first three were pleading calls from Charlie. He told her the picture was his mate's idea of a joke. They paid a lap dancer to pose and sent the pic to Charlie for a laugh. The fourth call had one of the jokers on the line apologizing and saying that the pic was never intended for Kate's eyes. In the final call, Charlie was at the airport catching a flight to London for an onward connection to Barbados.

'Kate, don't give up on us,' he said. 'It's a huge misunderstanding, that's all.'

Kate's mother's first call asked her to bring Charlie up for dinner before he went off travelling again. In the second, a day later, Margaret Bowen just asked her daughter to get in touch. Kate killed the messages, curled up, and within minutes was dozing. She dragged herself to her feet, crawled into bed, and fell asleep.

14

AFTER PARIS, Kate threw herself into work. Her priority was to take a fresh look at the haulier who ferried the container to France. Initial inquiries had been carried out by Special Branch. She was dissatisfied with the result. They had accepted his initial explanations far too readily in her view.

With Jack Quinlan's assistance, she arranged to get John Glynn inside a Garda station where she could interview him on her terms. Quinlan arranged for Glynn to call to his local public service vehicle inspector. If the PSV man deemed his truck not roadworthy it would put him out of business. Hauliers were always deferential.

When Glynn presented himself at the public counter Quinlan told him there was a change of plan. He steered him into an interview room and after introductions, Kate got straight to business.

'Why did you transport a single crate load to Cherbourg at the end of March?'

'You'll have to do better than that,' Glynn replied. 'What load are ye talkin' about?'

'The dodgy one. The one you did for cash.'

'I dunno what ya mean.'

The way he said it, it sounded like 'mane'. Kate was irritated. While she excelled at surveillance, she lacked the patience a good interrogator needed. Quinlan intervened.

'John, I know some of our lads have spoken to you on this before, so let's not play around here.'

Glynn switched his attention from Kate to the experienced detective.

'Take your time. Get a clear picture in your head of everything you can remember about the people who paid you to do the run. Then in your own time and your own words, tell us all you know.'

'Am I arrested?' Glynn asked.

'No, John, I want you to do your best to help us out.'

'There's nothin' to tell. A man asked me to do a run, I needed the money. I picked the load up in Rosslare and dropped where I was told outside Cherbourg.'

'Why did you do it for cash?' Kate asked.

'This lassie asks the tough questions,' Glynn said to Quinlan.

'Tell us about the boys that asked you to move the load,' Quinlan said.

'In my business, I don't mind the faces that much; gettin' paid is all that matters.'

'So you took the cash,' Kate said.

'Do you remember their accents, at all?' Quinlan persisted.

'All I remember was that they were northern boys, shippin' machine parts. I know no more than that.'

'Any idea of their age or what county men they were?' Quinlan came back.

'No clue in the wide earthly world.'

When they took a five-minute break, Quinlan brought Glynn a coffee and returned to the corridor to Kate.

'What do you think?' she asked.

'He's shit scared,' Quinlan replied. 'I think we're banging our heads off a brick wall.'

Glynn had admitted again to short-circuiting his usual system by accepting cash rather than the standard payment from the customer's bank account. That was old news. They knew he needed money for an overdue VAT bill.

'Cut him loose,' Kate said. 'I'll try a different tack.'

She rang Digger and told him to set up a meeting in Rosslare.

Kate and Digger drove there to meet Detective Sergeant John Casey, a friend of Mac's from his Dundalk days. Casey was in charge of immigration control at the port and Mac assured her that he was a tenacious investigator. There was the unanswered question of where O'Hare went when he left the trawler. Glynn represented a decent lead. Kate sought Casey's help in finding out what the haulier was reluctant to give up.

He was stocky, in his fifties and he caught Kate's glance as they shook hands. None of his fingers were straight.

'A souvenir of my hurling days,' he laughed.

Hurling, the fastest field game in the world was unique to Ireland. Played on grass, it coupled the skills of field hockey with the speed and intensity of ice hockey. Hugely popular, it was not for the faint-hearted. Casey had played it to a high level and captained his county team to win an All-Ireland title. He trained their current under-21 team.

She gave him a rundown on the case.

'The Cherbourg ferry comes in tonight,' Casey told her. 'I'll speak to the captain.'

'Do you think he will be able to help us out?'

'We get on well. If there's anything he can do, I'm confident he'll do it.'

'Are you busy in the port, these days?'

'Everything's a struggle. Management has little interest in tackling people smuggling.'

'What about hideouts? What are you seeing on trucks?'

'Everything and anything. Re-arranged loads creating hides in the middle, slings underneath trailers and compartments under cab bunks.'

'You must know a lot of the drivers who come through.'

'Most of the regulars anyway.'

'What do you reckon, are most of them okay?'

'You can never be sure. Though, if I catch anyone with human cargo, I see to it that he loses his PSV license.'

'Fair play, John. We'll talk later.'

The next morning Mac accepted a DVD from Casey at his office and cued it up on his PC. Kate and Digger were sitting alongside him. Casey had called after midnight with the news and Kate was eager to see the footage.

'I checked the passenger list which confirmed that John Glynn was the only paying passenger on his truck and in his cabin,' Casey said. 'You can thank our enforcement of immigration controls for all this footage. Because of the fines we impose, all the carriers have tidied up their acts when it comes to transporting undocumented passengers.'

Mac stared at his screen. 'Forward to 22:51, is it?'

'Exactly. And there he is, Mac, I remembered him from Dundalk. It was like seeing a ghost. O'Hare's got a bit older like the rest of us but there isn't a doubt in my mind, that it was him.'

Digger nodded in agreement.

'I was under pressure viewing this because the captain did not want to delay the ship's departure. So, the only sighting of O'Hare is as he exits the public toilets there on the upper deck and heads down toward the cabins. We've patched in footage from a cabin corridor camera next. It follows Glynn to cabin 37, a two-berth. He's carrying sandwiches and coffee. Five minutes after entering, he leaves again and heads to the bar. Now either he's a very fast eater or he's left the grub to someone else. He stays in the bar 'til closing, an hour and a half later. We didn't bother putting that coverage on the disk. It's there if ye want it.'

'That's brilliant work, John.'

'You're welcome. O'Hare was never like the rest of them; didn't show any aggression when you stopped him at the checkpoints, just cold and indifferent.'

'Do you have any thoughts on how Glynn got him through into France?'

'We have a pretty good idea,' Kate said.

'Really?'

'The Fishguard ferry arrived an hour before the one from Cherbourg. Glynn's truck rolled off it and John got Customs to pull him over. They took these.'

They scrutinized the photographs showing recent work increasing its length had been carried out on the compartment underneath the bunk. There were three blankets neatly folded at one end. Glynn told them he stored tools there.

'John, that's Trojan work,' Mac said.

'You know where I am if you need me.'

During the Dublin conference the following Friday, Kate briefed the partner agencies on their lead. The other agencies had stretched every sinew to unearth new leads in Operation Cassandra. The Americans reported trawls of databases that came up blank. Fenaux advised that the French had not traced the crate and there were no new leads on O'Hare in France. Symons informed the conference that MI5 had no reports of IRA suspects on the ground in the UK. Year-old intelligence led them to assess that the IRA had scouted targets in London's financial district. When queried on the strength of the sources, Symons simply elaborated that they were credible. When Kate asked him why SIU was only hearing about it a year later, Symons blustered that the reports were being evaluated when Operation Cassandra began.

15

BEFORE A CEASEFIRE WAS CALLED as a prelude to peace negotiations, the Provisional IRA Army Council had asked Sean O'Hare how long they could sustain the war. His view was that they could keep the fight going indefinitely. Dissenting voices spoke of battle fatigue among volunteers and tried to persuade him that the battle had always been about achieving political power.

What bullshit! It was supposed to be about uniting Ireland.

When the Army Council agreed to end the war, most of its members assumed a cloak of respectability and signed up to practice peaceful politics. Erstwhile comrades dumped him as surplus to requirements. If he was reading the signs correctly, nobody foresaw the scale of what he was planning. Fighting was something he did well and this time he would direct the campaign.

He felt exhilarated. Since leaving Carlingford weeks earlier, his travels had gone without a hitch. His return flight from Islamabad to Amsterdam had been in economy class. He had not slept during the fourteen-hour journey but that did not bother him. He forced himself to stay alert during the twenty-minute transit from Schiphol airport to Amsterdam Centraal train station. After paying cash for a one-way ticket to Paris he settled into his seat. He had written down the metro connections he needed to make to get from Gare du Nord to Porte Maillot and the bus connection to Beauvais. There a budget flight would take him to Shannon rather than Dublin and pick-up arrangements had been carefully planned. Only one volunteer knew he was coming. Between them, they would take care of a distraction that threatened his plan; an opportunity to renew old skills and send a deadly message to his new volunteers.

John Glynn liked where he lived. It was a great place to come home to after long runs on the continent. The yard at the rear was spacious. An old hayshed, no longer used for its intended purpose of storing winter fodder, served as a shelter for the truck he depended on for a living. He inherited the place from his grandmother. He and his wife Ettie, his childhood sweetheart, had taken care of Granny Reilly during the last five years of her life. She was a tough old bird and putting up with her daily demands was laborious. To her dying day, she held rigidly to her belief that Ireland belonged to the Irish and the British had no place in governing it. She made them promise that they would never turn away any of the 'boys' who needed a bed for the night.

Glynn knew the routine. As a child, he had spent summer holidays in Granny Reilly's house. He had seen her preparing what she called the settle bed in the kitchen. She laid out food and milk on the table overnight. As a child, he never saw who stayed but there was always an empty plate the next morning. While he did not agree with the killing that stained decades in Northern Ireland since the seventies, he held good to his promise. The settle bed was replaced by a fold-up camp bed and several overnight guests had come and gone since her death.

He was unsettled when the two Northerners visited him earlier in the year. He did not like either of them. What he was being asked to do seemed straightforward; pick up a load in Rosslare and transport it to France. The one who did most of the talking explained there was an added element to the job. Glynn was agitated by the whole thing. He only agreed when the talkative one offered him two thousand euros cash for the venture. The pair had inspected his cab and Glynn agreed to carry out the necessary work to enlarge the compartment under the bunk.

He was glad when it went without a hitch and he had breathed a sigh of relief when his unwelcome passenger left him in peace at a service stop in France. He hadn't introduced himself; never spoke on a phone in his presence and barely thanked him for purchasing the prepaid mobile in France.

Glynn was uncertain if any of the neighbours knew that his home was an IRA safe house. Such things were not spoken of openly. The run to France had brought Garda attention to him that he could have done without. First, the Special Branch and then Quinlan the detective from Dundalk tricking him into going to the local station for questioning. He did not care for any of it. He figured the latest pull by the Customs at Rosslare was a routine one for drugs. He would never try anything as stupid as drug smuggling.

Glynn wheeled the truck off the main road into his laneway. The hazel on either side of the lane almost met in the middle creating an archway. The summer evening was wet and blustery, swollen grey clouds bringing the night in prematurely. The lights were on in the kitchen. Ettie would probably have their solid fuel range burning to banish the evening chill. She kept a good house. He knew the kitchen would be cosy and she might even have something baked. Not having children to worry about meant he received her undivided affection.

He had rung her an hour earlier from the port and told her to expect him home around eleven o'clock. He drove the truck under the shelter of the hayshed, turned off the engine, and sighed. With a bit of luck, he hoped to sell the business in a year or two and devote his time to the love of his life. As he jumped down from the cab he expected their collie, Sheba, to come running but she was nowhere to be seen. He smiled at the image of the spoiled dog lying in front of the warm cooker. Ettie's going to ruin that dog having her in the kitchen, she'll stink the place out of it.

He walked to the back porch where he usually dropped his work boots. In the depths of winter, he hung his coat and cap there too. A glance through the porch's side window told him something was wrong. He ran straight through with no thought for his muddy footwear.

Ettie was tied to a chair in the kitchen with a slash of duct tape across her mouth. Blood from a laceration near her hairline had congealed on her forehead. As Glynn tugged at the ropes to undo them, her eyes darted maniacally back and forth. He carefully stripped away the duct tape.

'For God's sake, get out,' she screamed.

When Glynn looked up he saw a figure with a pistol pointed at him amble from the parlour. The intruder wore a boiler suit and balaclava. He froze in terror when another armed trespasser came behind him from the porch. He was incensed. A house belonging to a neighbour had been broken into in recent months. They had been roughed up also. Consumed with fury that the intruders had struck his wife, he reached out and ripped the balaclava from the gunman in front of him. O'Hare's face stared back.

'Here now, that wasn't such a bright idea.'

Glynn roared into his face. 'You did this? You? Cut her loose for God's sake and leave us in peace.'

Glynn felt the cold barrel of a gun press against the back of his skull.

'We need to talk first.'

'Cut her loose, she's no part of this.'

'She stays put.'

O'Hare and his accomplice twisted Glynn's arms behind his back. They pulled and cinched cable ties around his wrists as he looked toward Ettie.

'Don't worry Doll, it'll be alright.'

'Don't you hu...' she screamed at O'Hare as he roughly pulled the tape back in place.

They hauled him to a small outhouse beside the hayshed. Granny Reilly had reared pigs here over the years. Glynn had long since cleaned it out and used it as a tool shed. The smell of pig shit stubbornly lingered on the concrete floor. O'Hare's accomplice cut the cable ties from his wrists and forced him onto a chair. They lashed him to it with a blue nylon rope and Glynn glanced nervously as three square bales of straw were placed, one on top of the other in front of the closed doorway.

O'Hare whispered into his ear. 'We don't want our business here broadcast, do we?'

Glynn grunted through the tape in reply.

O'Hare laughed.

'By the bye, that aul' dog of yours didn't want to let us take any of his bedding. We had to persuade him.'

Glynn dipped his head to one side wondering what O'Hare was talking about.

'Let's just say his shepherding days are behind him.'

O'Hare stared at his prisoner without a flicker of emotion. Glynn tried to fathom why O'Hare had exploded into his life again. He had done nothing to warrant it.

As if reading his thoughts O'Hare said, 'All in good time. We'll get straight to business.'

He took an eight-inch carpenter's nail pincers from a pocket of his boiler suit. Glynn recognized it, it belonged to him; he used it for cutting wire and pulling nails from timber. It had grown rusty from storage in the damp shed over the years.

O'Hare grabbed Glynn's left hand in a vice-like grip. In rapid succession, he ripped the nails from his thumb and index finger. Skin tore from the top of the damaged digits and blood spewed from the open wounds. Glynn howled in pain. O'Hare pressed his face close to the demented truck driver.

'Now I'm going to ask you a question. Give me an answer I'm not happy with and we'll repeat the procedure. I'll keep doing it until I am satisfied. Nod your head if we're on the same wavelength.'

Tears streamed from his eyes. Glynn nodded slowly.

'Try to shout when I take the tape off and it's a repeat prescription. Do we understand each other?'

Glynn nodded again.

'What did you tell the cops?'

Glynn gulped air when O'Hare stripped the tape from his mouth.

'Nothing! I told them nothing.'

O'Hare pulled the tape back in place.

'We'll try again.'

By the time Ettie heard the men coming back, she sensed her worst fears realized. A dull thud moments earlier had sent shivers through her body. The man her husband unmasked appeared in her kitchen doorway; bloodstains on his boiler suit and latex gloves. His eyes, dull and cold, scared her as she tried to stare him down. She sobbed silently. A rivulet of green snot slid across the duct tape covering her mouth. It ran down her chin onto her brown cardigan. Her head bobbed up and down as she cried helplessly grieving her loss. O'Hare walked behind her. He pressed the pistol hard against her skull and pulled the trigger.

'Join him.'

16

PORTADOWN LAY thirty-two miles west of Belfast, on the surface another sleepy provincial town. The housing estates on its outskirts told a different story. Bitter Protestant versus Catholic confrontations blotted the town's past and divisiveness still simmered. In the estates, tribal colours painted on kerbs and gable ends marked territory. The tricolour green, white, and orange for Catholic and the red, white, and blue of the Union Jack for Protestant.

Detective Constable Harry Mitchell had dropped into the town's Meadows Centre to buy cigarettes. The centre's large car park was protected by CCTV and a mobile security patrol. The decent security level gave less opportunity for terrorists to target him with an under-car IED.

The warm weather at the end of May was short-lived. The June day had been punctuated by heavy downpours. The euphoria at the end of the Provo campaign of violence had given way to wariness. The ceasefire was holding, peace uneasily taking root. Dissident IRA groups still actively targeted individual members of the Police Service of Northern Ireland. Staying vigilant kept you alive.

Mitchell parked his Range Rover under the scrutiny of a CCTV camera and entered the bright and cheery mall. Syrupy piped music played in the background as the late Friday evening surge, if you could call it that, got going.

Something caught his eye. Alert to any 'new blood' tailing him, Mitchell used shop windows to check if anyone was taking an unhealthy interest. In a quick sideways glance, he saw a man pushing a family-sized shopping trolley toward Tesco. The father was playing with the little girl standing in it, the love between them plain to see. When the mother told him not to get her too hyper, he told the wee girl she could have one more twirl in their chariot.

Mitchell dropped his plans to go to the newsagents for cigarettes; instead, he trailed the family into Tesco. He picked up a shopping basket and kept his eyes on them. He put a small bag of onions, some carrots, four bananas, and a sliced bread loaf into his basket.

After five minutes he had seen enough; no point in pushing his luck. He strolled to the express checkout, paid for his purchases, and headed back to the car park. He checked underneath his jeep, threw his unwanted groceries on the back seat, and drove out. He went straight to Portadown police station where he called a Belfast number that connected him to MI5's Northern Ireland command post. He gave his name, rank, and serial number to the call-taker and left a terse message.

'Tell Mr. Symons that Sean O'Hare's back in town.'

Peter Symons was leaving London's Ravenscourt Park Tube station when his evening plans changed. The text message read:

Call please; he didn't need further information. He jumped on the first red bus that came along, it took him to Atherton Road, a stone's throw from his Battersea flat. He walked the rest of the way to the converted 1950s family home. He owned the top floor, its four rooms perfectly adequate for his needs. He paid a Portuguese cleaning lady a carefully measured weekly amount to keep the place spic and span. It freed him from mundane domestic chores.

He rang the Duty Officer from his secure landline who relayed the observant PSNI man's message. Symons's heartbeat quickened. He called Daphne Clarke and told her to meet him back at the office.

'O'Hare is home, he's ours. Those Irish arseholes will find out now who's in charge.'

He showered and changed into a rented tux. The old college chums were getting together for their annual reunion at Oxford. Most of his contemporaries this evening would be wearing suits they owned. In some cases, they would even have been laid out for them by their valets. It didn't bother Symons that he was different from most of them, what mattered was that he got to rub shoulders with powerful people. It had pushed his career along nicely. He had no hope of making the pre-dinner drinks but should arrive in time for the meal. He called a cab and met Clarke at his office.

'Get the Belfast office on the line. What are our dogs doing right now?'

'We're covering those two new bloods who dropped that stolen van across the border,' Clarke informed him.

'What are they up to?' Symons asked.

'Nothing exciting. They got into a brawl outside a Republican drinking club last Saturday night.'

'Fucking savages. Call the night shift manager and order me a car and driver for tonight.'

Clarke hesitated. In normal circumstances, Symons's rank did not qualify him for this privilege.

'What shall I tell him is the nature of the emergency?'

'Tell him it's none of his business. And get Belfast on the line now. I want a bells and whistles operation on O'Hare's movements, nothing spared.'

Clarke knew the surveillance operation her boss would demand on O'Hare would hark back to the early days of the Northern Ireland conflict. She had heard the stories. No method, no matter how bizarre went untried. Operatives spent days secreted in the boots of parked cars or attics. Bugs and cameras were drilled into unlikely places. When Symons was happy his orders were clearly understood he asked Clarke to check if his car was downstairs.

'The Passat had been sitting outside reception for the past twenty minutes.'

'Not the Lexus?'

'Can I go home now?' Clarke asked.

'Take an on-call phone with you. Contact me if anything substantial occurs.'

As London receded in the background, traffic eased. Symons gazed into the lush green summer beauty of the English country-side. He stretched and reflected on the twist in events that he believed would put him in the driving seat. His thoughts drifted back to his mentors.

Before the wall came down he had cut his teeth with the Service at the Berlin bureau. The unremitting East/West struggle that seemed to go on forever then ended abruptly. He revered the men who had trained him up. Back then a nuclear calamity always seemed only one nervous miscalculation away. Tales of derring-do during the Cold War era abounded. Symons lapped them up. Espionage was their stock in trade, their reason for being. The British did it better than anyone else.

As the University of Oxford came into view Symons's thoughts flashed back to the Paris conference. Fenaux, challenging his analysis; the Irish supporting the French man.

'Fucking amateurs,' he muttered.

'Excuse me, Mr. Symons,' his driver said.

'Just thinking aloud.'

'Not about my driving, I hope.'

He stopped the car in front of the Old Library. These days, the elegant room was used for intimate receptions.

'Back here for one o'clock,' Symons said and slammed the door.

17

YEARS OF EXPERIENCE had taught ex-Marine, Stan Graham, that maintaining precarious OPs in hostile territory was possible, but never easy. The MI5 surveillance team leader was restless, his crews struggling. Portadown was a compact provincial town difficult to sustain teams in for long.

'Prophet 1 to Blue team leader, target leaving estate, pick up on exit,' he ordered.

'Roger, Prophet 1.'

He listened intently to the radio chatter as O'Hare was picked up by a motorbike when he reached the main road alongside his housing estate. As the chatter became animated he intervened.

'Prophet 1 to Green team leader. Get ready. Target coming your way. Prophet 1 out.'

'Roger.'

The target acted like he was heading out of town. O'Hare had been using anti-surveillance tactics since they took up on him. If he was going elsewhere, he would have to use one of the town's exit roads. Graham covered them all.

'Grey Team leader to Prophet 1.'

'Prophet 1, go ahead.'

'Target has just passed us, direction, Garvaghy Road. New transport, new transport, white Volvo S40.'

The Grey team was on foot in the town centre.

'Prophet 1 to Grey team leader, calm down. Registration details, please.'

Graham passed it to the other units and controlled the pursuit until it finally exited the town. At first, they thought O'Hare was headed towards the A3 motorway, instead, he remained on a secondary road, which sent him in the Newry direction. He was heading south. The Green team took up the chase and there was palpable relief in Graham's voice as he rang Symons to tell him the target might soon cross into the Republic. The MI5 man was furious and kicked a chair across his squad room.

'Fuck, fuck, fuck!'

The dramatic effect was muted somewhat when the chair slid harmlessly to a halt by a workstation.

'Newry town is bypassed, Sir,' Graham explained. 'Once he's there, it's only a few miles to the border and he's beyond our reach.'

Symons had suggested to Mac at the Dublin conference that he embed some of his men with SIU crews but was met with a flat refusal.

'I'll call McEnroe,' Symons told Graham, 'here's what I want you to do.'

'Base to Tango Bravo 4.'

'Tango Bravo 4. Go ahead.'

'150 heading our direction from Newry; can you pick up?' Kate asked.

'Roger. Leave it with me,' Digger replied.

For radio comms, SIU designated O'Hare as '150'. Intel from agent 150 had pointed them in his direction.

When Mac called Kate she was in Dundalk checking reports from her crew tracking O'Hare's associates. Even with Jack Quinlan's help, progress was slow. They had tagged two clandestine meetings O'Hare had with Bob McElgunn in recent weeks. McElgunn was a former Sinn Fein town councillor who had resigned when the party signed up to enter government in Northern Ireland. Kate classified him as a close ally of O'Hare. She also noted that no prior warning of those particular border crossings was received from Symons. O'Hare was either dodging those tailing him or the Brits were ignoring the border and staying on him. Her reports came from one of Quinlan's touts.

Dealing with O'Hare's appearance in her jurisdiction was not going to be straightforward. Kate was reeling from the murders of John Glynn and his wife. The media was calling it another in a string of violent attacks on rural communities. She knew otherwise.

A neighbour had raised the alarm when Glynn's wife didn't show up as usual at her country market and wasn't answering her phone. The couple had been dead for at least ten hours by the time the first responders got there. Jack Quinlan had called Kate that morning. Mac cautioned that this early stage of the investigation was best left to the crime scene examiners. She ignored the advice and met Quinlan at the outer cordon.

The tiny shed scene seared brutal images into Kate's memory. John Glynn's slumped body was still tied to a chair. He had been shot, execution style, with a single round to the back of his head. Crime scene photographers worked, seemingly unmoved by the images they captured. Congealed blood was pooled on the ground around the victim where two severed fingers also lay. It was equally gruesome in the kitchen. She walked out and left the crime techs to do their work. The Commissioner had directed the national murder squad to take over the case. Nothing would be spared in bringing the culprits to justice he informed the press.

Before leaving for Dundalk that morning Kate had informed Mac that she had spoken to Glynn weeks earlier. He was taken aback.

'You did what?'

'It was when we were trying to find out if he had taken O'Hare in his truck; before John Casey got us that CCTV footage and proved he did.'

'Jesus Kate, you interviewed him in a Garda station. You should have discussed any approach with me first.'

'Look, it was just a chat, not a formal interview. There's no record of it. Only Jack Quinlan and I know about it.'

He ordered her to report the contact to the murder investigation team's senior investigating officer. To protect the integrity of Operation Cassandra, they agreed on a limited release of intelligence to the SIO on what they knew regarding O'Hare's contact with Glynn.

'If they nail O'Hare for it, it's the end of Operation Cassandra.'

'I would be surprised if forensics find anything to connect him to the scene,' she replied. 'Either way, he'll have his day. I intend to make certain of that.'

Kate sent details of the white Volvo S40 to her crew by encrypted SMS and they were ready to roll. A few minutes later Digger was back on the airwaves.

'They cut it fine tellin' us. 150 just passed Carrickcarnan,' he said. 'He's ours now. Doin' a steady 120 kilometres but very alert. I'm out next junction.'

'Roger that.'

Digger did not risk spooking their target by getting too close on the Honda 500cc he was riding. Kate had managed to get two cars ahead and ordered Pete McNally to link up with Digger when he ducked out. The trip from Dundalk to Dublin is fast on the M1 motorway, a new north/south corridor along Ireland's east coast.

'Tango Bravo 3 to Base.'

'Tango Bravo 3.'

'Target has just passed us doing 150K.'

'Roger that. Keep in sight as long as possible. Zoom, do not match his speed.'

Begrudgingly he acknowledged the order. Fast-slow driving was a favoured ploy for anti-surveillance. SIU anticipated it but O'Hare's use of the tactic on the M1 brought its risks. Drivers from north of the border, noted for their aggressive driving, always attracted attention. The yellow registration plates were magnetic for Roads Policing Units wanting to bring up their monthly tally of traffic offences.

In the first instance, Kate wanted to ensure that O'Hare did not end up having his borrowed car seized. Secondly, if she did not rein him in he might get suspicious or SIU could lose him. She rang Geraldine Cummins, a Roads Policing Superintendent, and officer training colleague. She outlined her predicament. Ten minutes later, a traffic car signalled O'Hare to the hard shoulder and an exasperated crew followed orders to the letter. They allowed the Northern gentleman to proceed with a ticking off and a warning on his future driving behaviour.

Having unwittingly dodged a bullet, O'Hare stuck to the speed limit until the signs for Dublin airport came into view thirty minutes later. Ger Cummins called Kate and confirmed that O'Hare was travelling alone. When he reached the M50, Dublin's outer ring road, progress became pedestrian. It was clogged at five o'clock most Fridays and today was no exception.

Kate had a crew on standby in the city centre to cover any possible meetings but O'Hare drove past the off-ramps that would take him there. When the wooded hills that form the backdrop to Dublin's sprawling south side came into view she redeployed her city centre crew. She told them to catch a Luas and head south. Had O'Hare other things on his mind? When he took the Sandyford exit she knew she had made the right call. By that stage, her city centre crew was cutting through rush hour traffic on the tram.

'Get off at Dundrum,' she ordered. 'Split into pairs, head to the shopping centre, and cover the entrances to the malls from the car parks.'

The Dundrum Town Centre was an ideal meet-up location. It was less than ten years old, built during an economic boom, and aimed at the wealthier citizens of Dublin's south side. It was difficult to cover if short-handed and today Kate had to make up the numbers. She got to the mall ahead of O'Hare and went browsing in Marks & Spencer. Its large window offered a good view and browsing in the lingerie department offered reasonable cover.

'Tango Bravo 2 to Base.'

Kate pressed the transmit button in her pocket.

'Go ahead.'

'150 parked up and walking. Entering at Level 1.'

'Roger that. Standby for contact.'

O'Hare walked directly into Marks & Spencer. Kate glanced

towards its small coffee shop. The after-school trade from the local all-girls secondary was clearing out, leaving two elderly couples sitting near the cash register. A lone blonde sat at a middle table with a weekend bag and a lime green jacket on a chair beside her. She sipped coffee and absentmindedly broke off a piece of muffin.

'150 entering M&S,' Kate relayed. 'Base to all units. I have eyes on target in M&S. Pull back and stand by.'

Nothing beats being on the ground. Seeing the target in the flesh for the first time changes perspective and makes it real. O'Hare was thinner than she expected and a full head of jet-black hair made him look younger. He was almost six feet tall and kept himself in shape. She relayed his description including his clothes. The sleeves of his pale blue polo shirt flaunted his biceps and the skinny jeans emphasized his narrow waist. Doesn't half fancy himself, she thought.

O'Hare was testing whether anyone was tailing him. She moved through the lingerie department into the women's fashion section. She took four tee shirts into the first cubicle of the women's changing room from where she could observe him in action. He was very good, and patient. He browsed through the menswear department for ten minutes, all the while observing the shop entrance, and beyond. Anyone taking even a cursory interest in him would set off alarm bells. He glanced momentarily in the direction of the daydreaming blonde.

'Tango Bravo 4 to Base.'

'Go ahead.'

'We have a problem.'

'Specify.'

'The cousins have shown up.'

'Roger that. Detain and wait for me. Tango Bravo 1 take up at M&S café. Target is currently in menswear. I believe he's meeting the blonde in the café.'

She handed her try-ons to the sales assistant.

'Maybe next time.'

She saw Angie pay for a coffee and settle into a chair, two tables back from the blonde. She pulled her knees up to her chin displaying blue jeans that had seen better days. She flicked pages of a well-worn copy of New Musical Express as she sipped her coffee. Angie was twenty-five but passed for seventeen. She was petite, with black hair, today styled like Julia Roberts' Tinker Bell. O'Hare passed her without a second glance. The blonde looked up and smiled as he approached. He bent and kissed her before settling into the seat opposite.

Kate was furious. The fucking cousins! Her foray on the ground that got her close to O'Hare had to be put on hold. The dangerous distraction pissed her off.

DIGGER BRIEFED her in the shopping centre car park as Pete McNally guarded a middle-aged man in the back of the van. He sported a green bucket hat. The daftest headwear she had ever seen on a surveillance operation. He looked so out of place that if he had gotten within a hundred meters of their target he could have jeopardized the entire operation. When Digger came at him from behind, the prisoner seemed convinced it was one of O'Hare's crew. By the time he grabbed the phone from his hand, it had registered a *'message sent.'* No content; most likely a distress alert.

'Report,' Kate said.

'This is 'Jim.' We've checked his phone and downloaded what's on the SIM. Too soon to know what any of it means.'

When Mac rejected Symons's request to embed his personnel south of the border he warned Kate to expect the unexpected. Symons was brass-necked, always requesting one risky concession or another. Mac's orders were clear, if anyone showed up they were to be detained and taken to the SIU base.

Jim clammed up, unimpressed with the fact that a woman

seemed to be in charge. He doggedly refused to answer any of her questions. She needed to be certain that there weren't any more 'sophisticated' operatives on the scene who might screw with her operation. Jim suggested calling a Belfast number to resolve the matter.

'Cuff him and stow him in the front between the two of you. Meet me back at base.'

'No worries. You go on ahead. We'll see you there.'

Whatever Digger's exaggerated calm tone was supposed to convey went straight over Kate's head. He drove the van back through the city centre but detoured into a run-down flat complex. As neighbourhoods went, Hanratty Gardens on Dublin's north side was as rough as it got. Endemic drug problems had resisted all efforts to find solutions. The crime level and living conditions reflected as much. A small courtyard lay at the centre of the flats complex crisscrossed by lines stretched between steel grey poles. Some had clothes, the rest whipped in the wind that swirled around the drab concrete square. Three floors of apartments surrounded it. Vulture-like youths with carefully pulled tracksuit hoods concealing most of their faces peered over balconies at each level.

When Digger tossed Jim from the van, certain salient facts were not lost on this cousin. This was not a friendly neighbourhood, someone with his British accent could not survive long here and he needed to make a fast decision.

Before driving away Digger told him, 'Nod when you're ready to talk.'

When Jim heard a stampede of feet pounding down the concrete stairways his mind was made up. He nodded vigorously and Digger reversed hard. When he braked alongside him Pete McNally threw open the van door and reached out. He caught the unlikely spook's arm and swung him inside. A volley of rocks thundered off the van's back door as they sped away. Most of the colour drained from Jim's face. Digger grinned.

'Talk!'

'There's five of us.'

'How many vehicles?'

'Two cars.'

By the time they reached the SIU canteen, Jim had coughed up everything. Digger forced him onto a chair.

'Sit.'

Mac and Kate arrived. The prisoner had kept his green hat clamped tightly on his head. Mac clipped it off as he took a chair opposite. His expression gave nothing away as he eyeballed the Englishman.

'Get this man a coffee.'

'No thanks, I'm fine.'

'We're not trying to poison you. Kate, bring the pot.'

She filled three cups. Mac took a mouthful. Their unwelcome guest relented, dumped two spoons of sugar into his cup, and took a sip.

'You'd think by now your boss would have been in touch?'

Jim's eye contact failed and his head dropped.

'If you don't mind Sir, I cannot tell you anything further. You have my name, rank, and serial number.'

Mac sideswiped Jim's mug and sent it crashing to the floor. 'I don't have time for this bullshit.'

Jim winced. 'Sir, I was following orders.'

'So were Hitler's generals.'

'You know in this game distractions cause failure and anyone distracting us is no friend of ours; your boss needs to speak to me.'

'What will happen to me?'

Mac stood up.

'Well let me see, an incursion into a sovereign State to carry out spying activities on behalf of a foreign power. What do you reckon if I were in your shoes?'

Jim looked up at him.

'I guess you're going to charge me then.'

'You wouldn't last one night in Mountjoy Prison if word got out. No one could save you.'

'Sir, just tell me what I need to do.'

'Go back to where you came from and tell your boss we need to talk.'

'Yes, Sir.'

'Anything to add?'

'Sir?'

'Do you have anything further to say?'

'I don't understand, Sir.'

'No apology then?'

'Sir I was...'

'Yeah, yeah, following orders. You need to get to hell out of my country.'

On cue, Pete McNally appeared and led the failed surveillance operative from the room.

Kate ribbed Mac as they walked back to his office. 'Don't expect Hollywood to come calling anytime soon.'

'That fucking idiot! I want that little weasel, Symons, to squirm before I let him off the hook. This kind of bullshit helps no one.'

Pete and Digger took Jim to Dublin's Connolly Station and bought two tickets for the Belfast train. Digger would jump off at the last border stop if satisfied they were not being followed. At Dundalk, no one batted an eyelid as the two mates stood up and said their goodbyes. Jim came to the carriage door to wave goodbye.

'Next time I'll come to visit you,' Digger yelled.

A whistle blew, the guard jumped back on board the last

carriage and the train slowly shifted out of the station on its journey north.

Kate's intuition proved accurate. O'Hare left the shopping centre with the blonde and cut back towards the city where traffic flowed freely. Thirty-five minutes later he parked at a hotel in Ballsbridge. Angie badged the manager of the upper-class establishment and requested his cooperation. It required some tactful verification for him to accept that someone of her demeanour was indeed Police. She played the major drug dealing investigation card to get him onside and discovered that 'Mr. and Mrs. McArdle' would be staying for two nights. The room next door to theirs was available if required. She took it.

Things settled down. The night crew reported nothing unusual. The couple ate in the hotel restaurant and kept to themselves in the residents' lounge. While they dined, the SIU crew drilled. The hotel manager would have been horrified if he'd heard the faint whirring sound as a discreet entry point for audio cover was made between the two rooms. Kate decided not to risk putting a camera in place. Unsurprisingly, the audio feed captured the intimacies of the illicit affair.

What surprised her was the couple's shared history. They reminisced about their childhood. They had lived on the same street. When O'Hare was six years old his family home was burned out by a Protestant mob and ordered to leave the area.

Another incident had separated them before the trauma of his forced exile. O'Hare spoke of his confusion when her pals called him a dirty *Taig* and he ran home to ask his mother what that meant. Prods and Taigs, abuse as old as the conflict itself. Extremists on the Protestant and Catholic sides flung the slang terms liberally at each other during confrontations. His mother warned him to 'stay away from that crowd'.

A chance meeting on a Belfast street six months earlier brought the childhood friends together again.

Insight into the target's background helped round out his personal profile.

Michelle McKittrick felt renewed as she walked toward the bus stop on Saturday morning. It was a beautiful August day and she was holding hands with someone she loved. She knew he was married. He told her he would have to hang in for a few more years because of the wee one. Meeting Sean after all these years seemed like destiny when they bumped into each other in Belfast. She had moved back home when her English husband turned out to be an asshole and they divorced.

It was her first trip to Dublin. The bus took them through leafy suburbs into the city centre. She snapped a photo of an old bridge as they crossed over the main one spanning the river. She was enchanted by the place.

Streets thronged with smiling faces, so many people chatting; there was a real buzz about. She liked the photo Sean took of her sitting at the street sculpture of the two old ladies chatting, 'the hags with the bags' the girl in a coffee shop told them. Sean feigned shyness when she asked a passer-by to take a picture of both of them. She understood.

She loved the open-air market they strolled through when they crossed the Halfpenny Bridge to the other side of the river. They spent an hour browsing through the stalls and Sean bought her chocolates. They walked on toward Grafton Street.

It was hopping, so crowded in the early afternoon. Sean was tired. He snapped at a waitress who struggled to understand his accent when taking their order. She kissed his hands to reassure him. They sat outside to soak up the sunshine and she needed a cigarette. He apologized and said he'd take a few minutes away to clear his head while lunch was being prepared. Fixing her hair in the café window, she laughed and waved him on his way.

Kate's crew had tagged along while O'Hare and his lover spent the morning on the tourist trail. Something altered after O'Hare argued with a waitress. They were unaware of what it was about but once out of Michelle's view, his radar switched to high alert. The SIU crew sensed the change.

He walked down Grafton Street towards Trinity College going against the flow of Saturday shoppers. Halfway down, a short winding alley led to Clarendon Street. He dodged into it trying to smoke out anyone following him; classic anti-surveillance tactics. Kate ordered her crew not to follow but to pick him up as he exited onto the parallel street.

They waited. Five minutes later she requested sightings but got nothing.

'Tango Bravo 2; check Saint Theresa's.'

Zoom tagged onto the back of an American tourist group following their guide down the narrow alley leading to the church. He dropped off halfway and nipped in through the tiny courtyard of Saint Theresa's, which had been a haven of tranquillity for Dubliners for over two hundred years. Inside, their target was nowhere to be seen.

An elderly woman was cleaning the altar. Zoom approached her.

'Are they hearing confessions today, Ma'am?'

'Not until six this evenin', son.'

'Pity! You didn't come across a mate of mine, I suppose, said he'd meet me at the entrance.'

'Ah Jaysus, you're after missin' him.'

'A Northern lad, right?'

'Dat's him, ye just missed him. A few minutes ago, he asked me was der another exit. I showed him the Clarendon Street door.'

She pointed towards the car park across the street. 'He went over der.'

'I'll catch up with him. Thanks, Ma'am.'

'No bother, son.'

Within just five minutes of switching modes, O'Hare had dropped his pursuers. He could have walked through the Brown Thomas car park and been two streets away before Zoom approached the church. It was serious but not fatal. They still had Michelle covered at the café.

Kate spread her crews through the side streets. Grafton Street was bustling; visitors and locals jostling in the bonhomie prompted by the sunny weather. Seriously pissed at the ease with which O'Hare had dropped them, Angie was in hyper mode. Keeping calm was key to getting back in the game. She sat slouched near the entrance to Captain America's restaurant, her head moving from side to side, eyes semi-closed listening to her music.

The headset, however, was connected to her SIU radio and her eyes were fully alert. She was scanning shop exits when the jerky movement caught her eye—something being dumped rapidly into a litter bin fifty meters away. In the window across the street from it, Angie picked out O'Hare's reflected image.

She called it in and Zoom followed him until he re-joined his weekend lover. As diners left the Captain America restaurant they shot glances at the junkie poking through the contents of a litter bin down the street. They had no idea that what Angie retrieved would prove invaluable. Kate picked her up nearby and assessed her find.

SIU's luck had changed. O'Hare missed the fact that as well as being printed underneath the battery of every cell phone the IMEI number was also printed on the box. With the International Mobile Equipment Identity number SIU found out the phone number within minutes. A judge signed an intercept warrant an hour later. He had to interrupt his Saturday morning round of golf to do so and was unimpressed at the intrusion. When the number came online Kate breathed a sigh of relief. All was quiet, O'Hare had not used the phone.

19

HE AND MICHELLE spent the rest of the sunny Dublin day as tourists. They queued at Trinity College for over an hour to see one of Ireland's national treasures from 800 AD, the Book of Kells. Alongside droves of American visitors, they marvelled at the single decorated page of the illuminated gospel manuscript on view. In the late afternoon, they jumped off an open-top city bus tour near the five-star Shelbourne Hotel. Kate hoped this diversion would yield something of intelligence value. Three of her crew followed inside and watched as the targets each drank a cocktail in the Horseshoe Bar before jumping in a taxi. Michelle said she was hitting the shower when they arrived back at their hotel. O'Hare shouted that he was ducking out for a walk before they ate. Kate's crew would keep him company.

He strode out in the direction of Dublin Bay and exited onto the seafront where the twin candy-striped chimneys of the old Pigeon House power generating station came into view. He crossed the road and swung right, heading south taking in the full vista of Dublin Bay.

Digger was monitoring images from cameras he had mounted in bicycle lights Angie and two other SIU members of the unit were using on the operation. The command van was parked at a nearby exhibition centre out of public view. He looked up from the screens.

'O'Hare's lookin' for somethin'.'

'He slowed down when he saw the last phone kiosk,' Kate agreed. 'Why would he need one if he's just bought a phone?'

'This guy leaves nothing to chance.'

O'Hare did not use the first payphone but remained wary. He seemed to have a route mapped out in his head. Kate needed to get someone ahead of him before he reached the railway level crossing.

'Tango Bravo 1, cross the Dart line and find a spot where you can observe the target.'

'Roger,' Angie replied.

O'Hare waited when he arrived at the level crossing. Angie veered into a convent school car park and observed him through binoculars. An alarm sounded and the level crossing gates began to close. Signs flashed warnings not to cross.

'Tango Bravo 1 to Base.'

'Go ahead.'

'This guy's nuts. He's just skipped between the level crossing gates seconds before the train passed through. He's on the coast road now.'

'Roger.'

'Tango Bravo 1 to Base; I'll stick with him as long as I can.'

Digger watched as Angie's jerky footage showed the target entering a payphone kiosk, close to St. Vincent's University Hospital.

'Tango Bravo 1, return to base,' Kate told Angie. She could not risk anyone getting picked up by O'Hare's hyper anti-surveillance antennae. Would their wire get them a break-through?

The speaker Digger had set up in the rear of the van crackled into life.

'Write this number down and call me back in five minutes.'

O'Hare's curt instructions as he recited the callback number elicited no response.

Before the target disappeared from her view Angie reported: 'He's smashed the phone.'

Kate was downbeat when she checked the number. The non-speaking end of O'Hare's call was Jafar Hajj Nasri's private number. SIU was monitoring it but he was unlikely to use it to call back.

'Dammit to hell.'

Digger ignored her petulant outburst. He had the knack of constantly staying ahead and today was no exception. Technology absorbed his attention.

'What gives?'

He smiled and handed her a headset.

'Oh, ye of little faith! Listen and learn.'

Anticipating a target's next move is a surveillance skill learned through experience and Digger had been busy. During the afternoon, using a phone company van as cover, he had placed a discreet transmitter in each of the six public phone kiosks within walking distance of O'Hare's hotel. Kate would have to authorize overtime to enable him to retrieve his toys later in the night.

One ring and the phone answered.

'Is everything arranged?' O'Hare asked.

'You visit us,' Nasri said, his accent clipped.

'Is everything arranged?'

'Soon in transit.'

'To where?'

'Near the City of Flowers.'

'We'll need to check.'

'This can be done. My brothers grow anxious. When will you show us what we need to know?'

'Tell your brothers to look after their side. When the goods are inspected I'll contact you.'

'They need reassurance your tools still work.'

'Tell them to keep watching the news.'

'I will pass this message. Inshallah, your work goes well.'

Kate didn't play favourites with her crew but if she did, Digger would surely get the lollipop. He looked at her as the call ended. In an instant, he was on his feet shaking the command post from side to side. Angie arrived back and asked what was going on.

'I love it when a plan comes together,' Digger laughed.

'Stop! You're showing your age.' Kate groaned at his cheesy A-Team reference.

They clued Angie in on the confirmation of the link they had suspected; a verified connection between O'Hare and Nasri.

'Where's the City of Flowers?' Angie asked.

Digger sang: 'Tulips from Amsterdam.'

'Dunno what that means.'

'Not heard the song?'

'Never. You think Nasri's talking about Amsterdam.'

'Until someone tells me differently, it's as good a guess as any,' Digger replied.

Proving the link lifted Kate's spirits. If Digger was right, something, likely weapons, would be delivered soon possibly for pickup by O'Hare. Subject to certain unknown conditions being met. It confirmed her suspicions. She looked forward to seeing how Symons reacted. He was perpetually sceptical. Digger's off-books caper had yielded gold-standard intelligence that gave the case a turbo boost. Intercepting the phone call in the manner he did was outside the law. Proving that IRA dissidents and Islamic radicals had negotiated some kind of deal was momentous. She would find a workaround to share it with international partners. Stopping the plot would be the biggest challenge of Kate Bowen's career.

PART 2

20

AS THE TRAWLERS converged Phelim O'Leary's stomach heaved, a mixture of travel sickness and anticipation. September squalls blew up as they left the Scottish fishing port hours earlier and the Irish Sea crossing had been rough. O'Hare observed him through binoculars as they neared the agreed rendezvous south of Kilkeel, the largest fishing port on Northern Ireland's east coast. At Crawford's Point, the trawlers drew alongside and O'Leary emerged from the wheelhouse, reached over, and drew his boss toward him.

'Welcome aboard,' the twenty-something said.

O'Hare wore a fisherman's waterproof bib and brace. He fixed him with a stare before moving past him. 'Below deck, now.'

In the cabin, the younger man slid into a seat and opened a bottle of Paddy whiskey.

'A drink!'

'No drinking, I told you that a year ago.' O'Hare reproached.

Rebuffed, the ginger-haired revolutionary screwed the bottle

123

cap back in place. O'Hare had appointed him as Officer Commanding his British sleeper unit when he completed months of covert training a year earlier.

'I thought you'd like to mark the occasion,' O'Leary said, his accent now with an acquired London twang.

'You look a bit green around the gills, are ya' alright?'

'Fine.'

'Is everything on track?' O'Hare asked.

'Just give us the target.'

'Any problems?'

'The lad you sent across to do the setup was a bit wobbly.'

'How d'ya' mean?'

'He took a lot longer doing the set-up than he said he would.'

O'Hare's irked expression told O'Leary that the bomb-maker had been selective in his report.

'Did ye have the mix ready for him?'

'Ready and waiting, as ordered.'

'The work is done, though, isn't it?'

'He got it done eventually. We're loaded and ready.'

O'Hare grabbed the young man's right hand in a crushing grip. O'Leary tried not to wince as his boss searched his face for any sign of weakness. The young OC held his stare.

'You've done alright.'

He passed a folded sheet of paper across the table.

'Here are your orders, follow them to the letter.'

'Count on it.'

O'Hare pushed out of the seat and ascended the cabin steps. The vessel that had brought him to the meeting returned alongside. He quickly re-boarded and as it disappeared from view, the OC unfolded the page from his pocket. The target location was written in large bold print across the top, *the Queen's House*. His heart skipped a beat until he read the directions and realized that this royal palace was in east London.

***

Five days later, Barbara Moorehouse was coming to the end of her late shift at Broadcasting House in Belfast. As a British Broadcasting Corporation receptionist, she had dealt with her fair share of bizarre telephone calls and today had been no different. With no full moon, she hoped the weirdos were tucked up in bed by eleven o'clock.

She planned to stroll from the Ormeau Avenue office in the city centre, pick up a pizza and catch a late-night bus home. She had worked with the BBC for over twenty-five years while a sectarian terrorist war waged around her and was not unduly worried about the late hour.

She picked up her private phone and chucked it into her handbag before fishing out the money-off voucher a workmate had given her for a six-inch Margherita pizza from a nearby Italian restaurant. She called in the order as she unclipped her security swipe card and pushed her chair towards the desk. All that remained was to unplug her headset and activate the message minder. She groaned as the light blinked on her console. With any luck, she would be able to redirect the caller.

'BBC Belfast. How can I help you?'

'Listen very carefully,' the voice began.

Barbara's instincts kicked in, she recognized the tone, sat back down, and picked up a pen. This was not going to be a routine call. She knew the drill. *Listen, clarify and record*, she repeated silently to herself.

'We are the Saor Nua volunteers of the Real IRA; the true torchbearers of the flame of Irish freedom kindled by Padraig Pearse and his comrades at the General Post Office in Dublin in

1916. Until Britain disengages from Ireland, members of the British establishment cannot sleep peacefully in their beds. Our code word is Neptune.'

The use of a recognized code word was vital information. It motivated a stronger reaction from police in clearing areas under a bomb threat.

'Sir, can you tell me if there is imminent danger?'

'Darlin', you need your ears washin' out.'

'I'm sorry Sir, can you repeat the code word.'

'The code word's Neptune. And remember this; while Britain interferes in Ireland neither the British government nor the Royal family can rest easy.'

'What about tonight?'

'I told you, you're not listenin'.'

'About tonight, Sir? Is there an imminent threat against the Royal family?'

'You've kept me talkin' long enough darlin',' he said. 'Remember this now, they've to be lucky all the time, we've only to be lucky once.'

Barbara's strict Christian upbringing prompted her to wish even this menacing caller a 'good night' but it went unheard. She rang her supervisor and was relieved that Charles Worthington hadn't retired for the night. He told her to call the Police number they had for such an eventuality and inform them. It was up to them to pass it along their line of command. BBC Belfast would pass it to journalists in the morning.

'Any thoughts, Barb?'

'Sounded genuine but weird. The caller gave the new code word but refused to confirm any immediate threat.'

'I'll have a listen back in the morning. Nighty-night for now.'

21

GREENWICH ROYAL PARK was a perfect fit for the BBC Proms in the Park final concert. The Proms series of concerts celebrated classical music and were embedded in the consciousness of some Brits as an essential part of summer. Prince Charles and his Duchess would be the royal cheerleaders for this one. Tickets for the cultural, end-of-summer high point, sold out in record time.

Greenwich Park had been a roaring success as a venue for the equestrian three-day eventing competition at the London Olympics, but security had been challenging. A similar level of security would be required for the Proms concert. The organizers decided that a combination of mobile patrols and static checkpoints was the best solution. Among the controls to be set up, a checkpoint would monitor access to muster stations where contractors for the event stored equipment overnight.

Greenwich Council hired as much security as its budget allowed. On-site security guards, like Delroy Dixon, were constantly on the move. His easy-going manner and latent power made him one of the company's most requested employees. The company that employed him required time-stamped patrol reports during his ten-hour night shift. He had done this faithfully the night before the concert and clocked off at six the next morning. He was due back at two o'clock the same afternoon, it was all hands on deck for the big night. He cancelled his daily bodybuilding session at the gym and reported for duty precisely on the hour.

The early part of the afternoon was all about getting contractor junk out of sight before concert-goers arrived. Coming up to seven o'clock, two white vans approached Delroy's checkpoint from the Vanbrugh Park Gate direction. The Irish crew said they had been working backstage and told him they needed to leave one of their vans at the muster station. He gave them a key that allowed them to re-open it and urged them to get a wriggle on and depart. The driver parked the van and locked up the enclosure before re-joining his mates. They returned to Delroy, handed him back the key, and drove out of the park.

O'Hare drove to Bob McElgunn's house in Dundalk to watch the Proms concert. Classical music was not one of his life's pleasures and his wife would be suspicious if he watched the Friday night spectacle at home. When he arrived the opening notes were streaming from a fifty-five-inch screen in the sitting room. McElgunn ripped the plastic cover off a slab of beer and as O'Hare sat down he tossed him a can of Amstel Gold. Teezie, his partner was out with girlfriends for the night.

'You cheap bastard,' O'Hare laughed. 'Cheers!'

They settled down to watch the action. Sir Terry Wogan, compère for the evening strode onto the stage when the opening music died. Wogan had been Britain's favourite Irishman for decades and began by welcoming his Royal Highness, the Prince of Wales, and the Duchess of Cornwall to the event.

McElgunn threw an empty can in the television's direction. 'Fuckin' Brit.'

O'Hare pulled the ring on another beer and sniggered.

'At least he'll go out with a blast.'

As expected, Delroy Dixon, Leon Malcolm and the rest of the security team supervised an incident-free evening. The respectable middle to upper-class Proms crowds all but guaranteed as much. Their bosses would be delighted that the evening's security arrangements had protected the concertgoers. As the crowd dispersed, a departing reveller gifted the duo a half bottle of champagne.

Delroy and Leon tossed a coin to decide which of them would get some shuteye for the remaining night hours while the other covered the bases. Leon won the toss and downed most of the champagne. Delroy was nonplussed, not wanting to disrupt his training regime. He waved his friend good night as he wandered off along a path toward a portacabin behind the Pavilion Tea House.

Delroy did a final walk about and time-stamped his patrol reports with a mix of his and Leon's electronic swipe cards. He returned to his cabin and was barely settled when his world exploded. The force of the blast wave that hit the cabin tossed it violently onto its side. His world went dark. When he revived he had to kick out a perspex window to climb free. How long had he been out? He stumbled to his feet and tried to work out what had just happened. He stared in the direction of the Tea House. It was on fire. He took off running towards it. He raced along Great Cross Avenue towards the ornamental fountain shaking his head to clear it. It pounded in pain and sweat pumped from every pore.

Something was burning in the muster station. That made no sense. Delroy fought a rising panic. He tried to raise Leon on the radio but got no response. They had been jubilant when they landed the security jobs and planned on using their wages to fly home for a break in Jamaica. Escape the madness of London for a while. He hadn't signed on for this shit.

The London Emergency Plan was triggered when nearby residents dialled in urgent calls. A blaze of blue lights and sirens at full pelt shredded the tranquillity of the park. Smoke was thick and the heat intense as Delroy tried to pinpoint the porta-cabin. He ran toward the Pavilion but a Chief Fire Officer's car cut him off.

'Stay back,' the Chief shouted. 'Is anyone in there?'

'No mate,' Delroy replied. 'The Pavilion's closed, but my friend's missing.'

'Where was he when the fire broke out?'

'He's in the portacabin.'

'Where's that?'

'Around the back, I was trying to find it but I can't see it.'

'Get the medics to check you out, I've got a fire to fight.'

22

TWENTY CRUSHED BEER cans lay strewn around McElgunn's sitting room floor. As the evening wore on, the pair had grown uneasy. The tenor and soprano gave performances that drew rapturous applause from an appreciative audience. The BBC Concert Orchestra and Choral Society performed. O'Hare's head began to ache from the cheap beer. As the realization hit home that a year's planning had come to naught he thought his head was going to explode. McElgunn flicked through the channels but there was no breaking news.

'The stupid little shite,' O'Hare shouted, 'he fucked it up. If that weapon's seized, I'll hold him guilty of treachery.'

'It's early days to think like that,' McElgunn replied.

'Don't tell me what to fuckin' think.'

'Do you want me to contact our doomsday man?'

'No, wait a while yet. Turn the sound down on that fuckin' yoke, will ya.'

'Do want it off altogether?'

'No just do what I tell ya and turn the fuckin' thing down.'

'I'll make coffee.'

'Make it strong.'

When the Fire Chief's unit arrived from East Greenwich station, it battled the Pavilion blaze. Firemen using oxygen tanks ventured to the rear of the burning building to search for the missing security man while two London Met police officers interviewed Delroy.

'Maybe Leon took a different route; maybe he's lying out there on the grass injured or unconscious.'

'If he is we'll find him and look after him.'

The fireman leading the search radioed his Chief. The Chief could not hear him and ordered anyone nearby to stop what they were doing.

'Repeat your message, please.'

'Body around the back; it's in bad nick.'

'Roger.'

He turned to a police officer, 'Keep everyone back. You better come with me.'

Officers restrained Delroy from going to see with his eyes what he knew in his heart. His stomach heaved and dumped its champagne contents over the boots of the two constables.

As he paced McElgunn's sitting room in silence, O'Hare kicked beer cans out of his way. His head thumped as he worked out how best to get O'Leary back from Britain. McElgunn suggested the ferry but O'Hare did not want to take any chances and said trawlers were the only way to go, more secure. He stood, pulled on his jacket, and was about to leave when he stopped in his tracks and stared at the mute television screen.

'What the fuck? Turn it up, turn it up.'

The ticker tape of breaking news on Sky reported an explosion in Greenwich Park, London. The pair listened to the early reports from outside New Scotland Yard and then from the scene. Smoke billowed from a building. O'Hare scanned the screen minutely and then shook his head.

'No, no, that's not right; that's the wrong fuckin' target entirely. And it's three hours too fuckin' late.'

***

'Holy shit! Are you getting this?' Charlie said suddenly.

His ship was docked in Miami and he and Kate were having another catch-up. She relented in the face of a tsunami of apologetic text messages and flowers. While his explanation for the mystery naked selfie message seemed a tad convenient, they had kissed and made up on Skype. Her guilty conscience from Paris played a part in giving him a second chance.

'What?' she asked.

'CNN is reporting an explosion in London.'

'Hang on, I'll turn on the telly.'

A sick feeling hit her stomach when Kate saw the footage from the Sky News helicopter.

'I've got to go.'

'Call me soon, Babe.'

'Okay.'

23

KATE FOUND out in the early hours that initial police inquiries made substantial progress. The London Met investigation team reconstructed key events. It determined that two white construction trucks had travelled in convoy earlier in the evening, approaching Greenwich Royal Park from the Lewisham direction. The vans drove past the police station near Blackheath Gate, turned left onto Maze Hill, and entered the park at the Vanbrugh Gate on the warm evening.

The IRA plan was uncomplicated but clever. The identical trucks encountered Delroy Dixon at the major checkpoint near the junction of Bower Avenue and Great Cross Avenue. The driver with the Irish accent told the security guard that they were dropping off one truck at the muster station and heading straight out again. Delroy instructed the driver not to bother taking off the tarpaulin cover on the truck they were leaving in. The ginger-haired driver thanked him as Delroy stripped back the tarpaulin from the truck they said they were parking in the muster station. It contained the expected construction tools.

Delroy explained that without noting the registration plates he couldn't tell the difference between the two trucks, they were both Mercedes models, the same colour; same tarpaulin covers. The CCTV images confirmed the deception; the second vehicle contained the explosives and the men left the park in the truck Delroy had searched.

When the burning truck was discovered, police extended their cordon to take in the entire park. Around the same time, Peter Symons took a call from Daphne Clarke, his number two.

'Switch on Sky News.'

A ticker tape headline ran across the screen: *Explosion Greenwich Royal Park. Warning phoned to the BBC.*

'I was right, I was right!

Clarke held the shriek away from her ear.

'Get everyone into the office,' Symons ordered.

'On my way.'

'And I want the latest from Scotland Yard on the investigation by the time I get there. Also, get me a full report on that warning call to the BBC.'

'I'll do my best.'

Later, as he took his seat at the head of the small rectangular table in his conference room, Symons felt rejuvenated; in command of all he surveyed. A small team admittedly, but tonight's events put him in the spotlight. He was now squarely in the driving seat of Operation Cassandra.

Despite reservations from his analysts, Symons had advised higher management that the altered code word media outlets had received earlier in the year was another indicator of advanced planning for an attack. The *critical* national state of alert generated months earlier by Symons's knee-jerk reaction to the missing trawler had been scaled back to *severe*. Severe meant that an attack was highly likely and the bosses chose to leave the state of alert at that level.

As the meeting began, Daphne Clarke stepped out to take a

call. Police had pinpointed the attack firing point as muster station number two.

'Harks back to earlier times, I'm told,' she said when she resumed her seat.

'The attack?' Symons asked.

'The weapon.'

'In what way?'

'Most of the weapon is intact. Here's what I have from the scene.'

Clarke put the phone camera snapshot of the burnt-out truck up on the screen. Symons left his seat, stood beside Clarke, and speculated on the obvious.

'Mortar tubes?'

'Looks like homemade gear, like the PIRA used in the past,' Clarke replied.

'When will we know about the explosive used?'

'The Prime Minister has demanded a report for his morning eleven o'clock meeting.'

'Make sure I know before he does.'

'I will try my best.'

'Don't just try.'

He pointed to the screen.

'Irish stupidity and French arrogance got us this. *I'm* going to lead this case from here on in.'

As Symons barked out orders, she wrote them on a whiteboard.

'You know, none of the leads from Operation Cassandra pointed to London as a target. I reviewed the file before you got in.'

'My dear naïve Daphne; London has been the IRA's favoured target throughout their campaigns. You should be aware of that. Even since the ceasefires, they've had people targeting in the City.'

'What do you want me to do?'

'Talk to McEnroe first thing tomorrow. Get him over here to discuss this mess.'

The meeting petered out with a discussion on further attack scenarios. Symons called another meeting for 6:30 the next morning before allowing his team to disperse.

By the morning meeting, police had traced the trucks to a building site in Lewisham.

'Our research puts two home-grown Islamic radicals working on the same site,' Clarke informed him.

'What difference does that make?' Symons asked her.

'Operation Cassandra is considering Al Qaeda/IRA collaboration; I thought we should check them out.'

'Daphne my dear, that angle is bullshit. As I've tried to tell people all along, London's been the target. Look at the photographs from that border shed that I forced McEnroe to hand over.'

'What about them?'

'The metal looks identical to the Greenwich device.'

'I suggest waiting for the ballistics report.'

'Thank you for suggesting the obvious. Nobody listened when I tried to warn them.'

'What about the contact between O'Hare and Nasri, the Dublin jihadi suspect? If this attack is their doing maybe we should look at radical Islamic groups as well.'

'You know I wonder...' Symons began. 'McEnroe is cagey about that contact.'

'I've read the transcript. Maybe if you rang him he might clear up any uncertainty.'

'Leave that to my judgment, will you Daphne? And sit down, will you, the tasks are done for the morning.'

Clarke resumed her seat directly opposite Symons.

'What response did you get from him?

'Chief McEnroe assured me that he will assist us in any way he can and didn't bring up our unresolved issue.'

'The border misunderstanding? Oh for God's sake, that's history. Did he at least acknowledge that last night's explosion was linked to his fuck-up?'

'We discussed possible connections with the untraced crate from the trawler. His view is that it's way too soon to make such assumptions.'

Symons pressed both hands flat on the table and leaned across. His thin lips tightened as he spoke, staring directly at Clarke.

'Well, that's convenient for him.'

Not flinching, Clarke replied, 'he feels it's best to let the police carry out their investigation. You know, collect the data before starting to theorize, and twisting the facts to suit theories.'

Symons began pacing the top of the tiny conference room.

'Meantime, what? We wait for another bomb to go off. It's time he realized that the direction this operation takes is no longer his to call. This meeting is over.'

24

THE EXPERTS ROLLED out on television news channels described the Greenwich explosion as a botched attack. O'Hare reacted quickly; he rang Nasri early the morning after the explosion to arrange a meeting. He was greeted by silence and an immediate hang-up. He redialled and got the same result.

Since their first meeting, he had accumulated intelligence on his Dublin key contact. He knew where his business was located, what car he drove, where his children went to school, and much more. It was time to dip into that font of intelligence and deliver a message.

The following Monday morning Bob McElgunn felt conspicuous as he sat in his car, parked in a street close to Nasri's business. He watched the fat businessman arrive at the small industrial estate at eight-thirty dressed in a navy pinstripe suit. By a quarter past nine, he had observed Nasri's two delivery vans leave the warehouse and the remaining workers settle into daily routines.

McElgunn drove to a nearby petrol station, picked up a coffee and returned to a new parking spot directly behind the warehouse. He tried the rear door but it was locked, so he walked around the front. Inside the warehouse, he slipped past three workers busy stacking shelves. He continued to the glass-panelled office at the rear and entered without knocking.

'My boss is feeling unloved. Why aren't you answering his calls?'

Nasri jumped to his feet.

'What is this about? I owe nobody nothing.'

McElgunn closed the door behind him.

'Do you want to recheck that?'

The foreman walked slowly in the direction of the office. Nasri beckoned him away with a dismissive hand gesture.

'Who are you and what do you want?'

McElgunn smirked.

'You know who sent me.'

Outside, Nasri caught workers casting glances in the direction of the unusual visitor. He leaned out his office door and told the foreman to give everyone a ten-minute break. All three walked out of the warehouse in the direction of a coffee shop but only two got there.

The third walked around the block out of view of his co-workers, took out his phone, and dialled the number he kept locked in his head. When his brief conversation ended, he wiped the call history from his mobile. Detective Gerry Grealy rang Kate immediately.

'Nasri has company this morning. He's going at it hot and heavy with some dodgy-looking customer who walked straight into his office.'

'Are they still there?'

'Up to five minutes ago, anyway,' Grealy replied.

'What do you think? Is it just business?'

'He sent everyone out when his visitor arrived. Our man won't be ringing again.'

'Thanks, Gerry. Appreciated.'

She briefed Digger and jumped into the only vehicle left in the garage, a white beat-up service van. They hared it out of the SIU base and within twenty minutes were parked down the road from Nasri's warehouse. Digger pulled on a boilersuit and grabbed a toolbox from the rear of the van.

'Time for a nosey.'

He quickly disappeared beyond the industrial estate's high wall. A young tyre company employee directly across from Nasri's warehouse was struggling with a truck tyre as Digger approached. He was using a crowbar trying to detach the tyre from its rim.

'You've got a problem with the heatin',' Digger said, walking toward him. 'I'm here to fix it.'

The young worker grunted as he relaxed the metal bar.

'Not us, boss. Try next door.'

'Thanks. I'll call the office instead,' Digger replied

He scanned across the lot into Nasri's warehouse. A worker was dumping cardboard boxes into a skip near the entrance. He could make out two figures in the office at the rear. One was short and fat, the other taller. He walked back and re-joined Kate.

'Anything?'

'Someone's still there. I couldn't see enough of him to ID him. That's a long meetin', wouldn't you say.'

'If it's O'Hare or one of his mates, we're too close for comfort.'

She drove cautiously away from the immediate area as Digger climbed into the back and began working on a laptop.

'What are you doing?' she asked.

'Tryin' to connect into the traffic feed from Command and Control.'

'You can do that from the laptop?'

'Know the right codes and you can do most things these days.

The screen flickered into life.

'Okay, we're up.'

Kate reversed into a new parking spot, streets away from the industrial estate entrance.

'What are you picking up?'

'Traffic coming out of Nasri's estate has to exit onto Harold's Cross Road. That's what we're seeing, best of all the cameras are set up to capture the reg plates. We can check them as they exit.'

Fifteen minutes later Kate was looking over Digger's shoulder when he shouted, 'Bingo!'

Neither of them required a computer check on the registration number when they saw Bob McElgunn's car exit. It turned right onto Harold's Cross Road.

'Tell the Dundalk team to expect company,' Kate said. 'It's going to be a long day.'

In both jurisdictions, there was intense political pressure to find out who was behind the London bombing. Most of Kate's crew was in Dundalk and the surrounding border area searching for O'Hare's acolytes.

That evening, they put McElgunn to ground at an address in the Slievemish housing estate in Dundalk where he met with O'Hare for an hour. Kate considered hitting the place and arresting them both but assessed the chances of finding any material evidence to support a terrorism charge as low.

Later, she executed a U-turn and headed back toward Dublin when they tracked O'Hare's car to a slip road for the M1 motorway. It disappeared northwards. Shackled by the invisible border, she pulled her team back and contacted Daphne Clarke with vehicle details and the direction of travel.

Symons spent the week following the bombing trying to copper-fasten control of Operation Cassandra. He hastily arranged a meeting in London that Mac and Kate attended. Rather than Fenaux, a French liaison officer based in London was invited. Symons tried to sell the notion that the mortar device most likely came from France.

'A strategy based on investigative outcomes rather than guesswork is the only way to go,' Mac retorted. 'Let the Met work the clues.

Symons regarded him with disdain.

'This is likely the start of a sustained campaign on the UK mainland. Preparing for that eventuality will be my priority.'

'Do you have the intelligence to support that assessment?' Mac asked.

'That's my analysis based on previous murderous campaigns.'

Kate stayed out of the back and forth. Wherever the truth lay, proving Symons's preconceptions wrong would be an uphill task.

25

O'HARE ORDERED his active service unit to leave London. When O'Leary received the word, the ginger-haired OC dispatched the ASU immediately. Four travelled separately on car ferries from Hull to Zeebrugge in Belgium and transited to Dublin on cheap flights from Zaventem airport outside Brussels.

He hung back. His job in financial services was good cover, he tried to convince O'Hare. It made sense for him to stay. Forty-eight hours after the explosion, the Met blew his argument out of the water. It published a close E-Fit resemblance of him and O'Leary instantly quit the city.

He made his way to Oban, a west coast Scottish fishing port, and waited for word. After spending a chilly night in a fish market shed he boarded a trawler for Northern Ireland. On arrival, another message directed him to a decrepit farmhouse deep in a remote valley on the edge of the Mourne mountains.

Two hellish days and nights followed. Food was meagre, bread, cheese, and water. He was sorely tempted to disregard his orders and bug out. There was no electricity, no mattress to sleep on, and only threadbare blankets for warmth. In any case, the scuttling rats would have kept him awake. By the third night, the batteries in the camping light supplied were running down.

There were no introductions when two men walked in without warning at dusk. O'Leary stared into the gloom and shifted nervously on his chair. He could barely make out their shapes. Both wore balaclavas and made no move to remove them.

O'Leary recognized Bob McElgunn's voice. Because of the constant shadows north of the border, O'Hare gave his sidekick the task of debriefing the ASU. He dispatched a trusted volunteer, Nutser Treacy, for company.

'I thought the bossman would want to talk.'

'Other fish to fry,' McElgunn replied.

He pulled up a chair and faced the young man. Treacy remained standing.

'Well?'

'Well, what? We got them yokes to fire, eventually, didn't we?'

'Let's talk about that a wee bit more.'

Sixty minutes later O'Leary had been over the story five times. McElgunn listened as the OC swore that the active service unit had diligently followed O'Hare's instructions. When the device didn't go off at its intended time, O'Leary tried to get back into the muster station to check it, but security prevented him. When the crowd thinned out he had slipped in and corrected the problem.

McElgunn grinned when the story finished at the final telling. In the dusky light, the toothy expression took on a menace that chilled the young revolutionary.

'That's quite the tale. You know, none of your ASU can account for what went wrong. They said the mortars were properly set up before you drove it in. You were the last one in the van, you changed something, didn't you?'

'They're talking shite.'

'One last chance.'

'I done nothing but followed orders.'

'It's time you met my associate.'

O'Leary glanced over his shoulder as Treacy trapped his arms. With McElgunn's help, he secured the prisoner to the chair, lashing each leg with black plastic cable ties.

'Go to work,' McElgunn told Treacy dispassionately.

Treacy grabbed a fistful of O'Leary's hair and yanking hard, tilted the chair backwards. He laid it flat, slowly unlaced the prisoner's left boot and removed it. Beads of perspiration dripped from O'Leary's forehead when Treacy righted it again. He shivered when his bare foot touched the freezing flagstone floor. In the semi-darkness, Treacy swung a lump hammer onto his foot. O'Leary screamed in pain as toes crunched and squelched and blood flowed freely as a nail from his little toe hit the floor. By the time Treacy finished working him over, tufts of ginger hair were strewn around the chair. For a grand finale, he slammed the hammer's handle hard into the prisoner's chin. Blood and saliva cascaded down his tee shirt. O'Leary spat two teeth out, to avoid swallowing them. His howls of pain went unheard except by the six sentries posted near the entrance to the dark valley. Treacy's breath heaved when he paused and looked toward McElgunn.

'He's all yours.'

Later, as he finished noting down a full confession from the prisoner, McElgunn rubbed his right wrist to relieve the ache. It was the most writing he had done in a long time.

The Queen's House, the Royal Museum in Greenwich, where Prince Charles attended a pre-concert buffet had been the target. O'Leary accepted that members of the royal family were fair game, as IRA targets. There were a hundred and fifty people, apart from the Prince and Duchess, at the Queen's House reception and thousands of concert-goers nearby. He could not live with the blood of women or children on his hands.

The hapless prisoner confessed that he parked the van in a position to avoid the intended target. He altered the long delay timer to eleven fifteen to be certain innocents did not die.

'You're in the wrong business,' McElgunn told him as he walked out into the silent valley.

Intermittent sobs from the farmhouse punctuated the peaceful ambience. McElgunn blocked out the noise and shifted about trying to pick up a signal to contact O'Hare. Before the call connected, a single shot rang out. McElgunn ducked and ran back indoors.

Treacy stood behind the chair, calmly snipping the cable ties from around his slumped victim's legs. Blood streamed from the cavity in the back of the victim's head.

'What the fuck?' McElgunn demanded.

Treacy answered without a hint of emotion.

'What's left to talk about, eh?'

26

FENAUX READ a report on Symons's London meeting an hour after it concluded. Most of the anger he felt at being excluded had dissipated. Mac called him from his London hotel room. When Kate heard the conversation begin in French, she scribbled a note that she was returning to her room.

Mac said: 'The idea of the French contribution being relayed through an emissary rather than by you is ridiculous,'

'I ordered our liaison officer to listen and report back. If Symons was interested, he would have invited me,' Fenaux replied.

'It beggars belief.'

'Do you believe that weapon was assembled in France and transported to London?'

'Highly unlikely.'

'We haven't exactly been sitting on our hands. We've made hundreds of inquiries to try and locate that crate.'

'I know that.'

'Covered all routes out of Cherbourg with a drone and spent countless man-hours analysing the images. We've looked at yards, lock-ups, garages, and warehouses and still have very little to go on.'

The London Eye loomed in the distance out of Mac's window, each pod packed as it began another panoramic revolution. He stood up and stretched his back.

'At least we know about the toll booths.'

Fenaux's inquiries confirmed that Glynn's truck had gone through the *péages* at Douzlés and Beuzeville on both sides of the A13 motorway on the day he arrived from Rosslare. The A13 connected Caen and Paris. This was much further than the driver had hinted at; Beuzeville was almost one hundred and ninety kilometres from Cherbourg.

Fenaux ran facial recognition software on the hundreds of hours of CCTV images his investigators retrieved from the service stops along the motorway to try and pick up traces of O'Hare and Glynn. When he heard they had scored a hit at Aire de Bosgouet Sud for both Glynn and his truck, Fenaux was elated. When he saw the images his mood changed. The footage showed Glynn placing a spare tyre onto the trailer and securing it with ratchet straps. The rest of the trailer was empty; the crate had been offloaded elsewhere.

Even so, Fenaux mapped a fifty-square-kilometre area around the toll booths and divided it into search grids. The searches had yielded nothing to date.

After he ended the call with Mac, he scratched the itchy stubble on his chin. He had not shaved today and a salt and pepper growth had sprouted. He threw a report he had finished reading onto his desk. He snorted in disgust and stared out the window of his Levallois office in the Paris suburbs.

London's Evening Standard had run a story suggesting that the IRA had smuggled the Greenwich Park weapon into Britain from France. It confirmed Fenaux's impression that his exclusion from the London meeting had been a ploy to embarrass him.

After weeks of stalemate, his surveillance of Said al-Khayyan, Omar al-Haddad, and Ibn Saud had begun to yield results. All three suspects lived in Seine-Saint-Denis and were experienced jihadists who had seen action in Afghanistan. Early on, Fenaux's team had struggled to even establish a connection between them. Then they zeroed in on a sixteen-year-old friend of Ibn Saud.

He turned out to be the runner, the conveyor of messages between the clandestine group. DGSI intercepted his mobile phone and the intelligence picked up worried Fenaux. All three were on standby for another player in whatever drama was about to unfold. Desperate to push his advantage, Fenaux rang an old friend and arranged to meet the next day for lunch.

27

THE LITTLE RESTAURANT in Roissy village, close to CdG airport was ideal. It had ample parking at the back and a *patron* who recognized that sometimes his police clientele required extra privacy. Their table gave them a view of the door and through the window, they could see every car that drove into the car park. Christophe Reynaud was chatting to the patron when Fenaux arrived. He had changed little over the years. His face was a bit fuller but he kept himself fit.

'How are things with you?' Fenaux asked his long-time buddy.

'As always Yves, in the *merde*, just not as much as usual. You're making headlines I see.'

'The radical Imam? What did you read about it?'

Fenaux had to cancel summer holidays to deal with the case.

'Is it true that a priest tipped you off?'

'It was just a throw-away remark to one of my men after Sunday Mass,' Fenaux explained.

The *curé* at Saint Dominique's parish church and Chaplin at

Fresnes prison told the cop that the numbers asking to see him were falling.

'Père Martin assumed it was only a reflection of what was happening outside the prison walls. We became interested when he remarked that some prisoners had switched to seeing Imam Mahmoud.'

'*Incroyable!* The papers are well informed.'

'Too well,' Fenaux replied.

By the time the DGSI investigation concluded, they knew Imam Mahmoud had been visiting the prison twice weekly for twelve months. They estimated he had radicalized twenty-five prisoners to spread the message of Islam through Jihad. A special repatriation flight delivered the radical preacher back to Pakistan.

The patron arrived and took their order; Fenaux selected mussels with fries, and Reynaud chose the steak tartare.

'How are things going with the club at La Cité these days?' Fenaux asked.

For six years after he graduated as an officer, Fenaux had managed the thankless job of trying to keep the proliferation of social problems at La Courneuve in check. The experience toughened the young officer. Most days, a single incident could send the wafer-thin veneer of social cohesion up in flames. La Cité was just one estate of tower blocks that backed onto the A1 motorway leading to CdG airport and northwards to Belgium and beyond.

By the time the twenty-first century rolled around, *Les Grands Ensembles,* the high-rise apartment tower blocks built during the seventies in response to acute housing needs, were identified as indicators of social failure, isolation, and segregation. Today, a staggering 38,000 people live at La Courneuve, with over 4,000 crammed into La Cité.

Reynaud replied: 'We're still there if that's what you mean.

The council pulls their people from time to time when their budgets are shot but we cover the holes and get on with the job. It's always a struggle.'

Fenaux nodded recognizing the daily problems his friend faced.

'Worthwhile still, do you think?'

'Worth the effort. It's the only time the kids get to see us in a positive light.'

Back in the early nineties, Fenaux had seized on a police reform initiative of François Mitterrand's government. He set up a youth centre on the ground floor of one of the tower blocks and delineated it as a police-run club. He picked a team of young *agents* to get it up and running.

The local council's social services department pitched in. They coached sports, organized outings, and tutored their young charges in using emerging information technology. There was an after-school service that helped kids do homework, frequently before returning to disruptive homes. The club operated and flourished in its drab surroundings for ten years before moving to a new purpose-built centre as the new century dawned.

'Do you see any of the old members?'

'Of course, many live in the area. We even persuade some to return and help out with the after-school activities. It's great when that happens.'

'We need more of it.'

'I agree.'

The patron served the cops their meal. Reynaud looked up briefly as two other customers were seated by the patron a discreet distance away. He mixed the finely chopped onions into the egg yolk at the centre of his plate of raw steak mince. He seasoned it to his taste with Tabasco, salt, and pepper, and anticipated the unique flavour of the classic French dish. He checked over his shoulder for the other customers. Out of hearing range, he decided.

'Now my friend, I know you, and you didn't bring me here to talk only about the club.'

Fenaux regarded him with a mock offended look.

'I always make time for my friends. I do have a question I'd like to ask.'

'Go on.'

'You remember Omar al-Haddad?'

'Little Omar, that's going back a while. He was in the first group at the new clubhouse, a polite boy, highly intelligent.'

'Also deeply religious,' Fenaux's voice dropped almost to a whisper, 'what I am going to tell you is classified. Not to be discussed with anyone.'

Reynaud shifted uneasily.

'Little Omar is radicalized and has been to the Jihad in Afghanistan. He's part of a group that is planning something. We don't know what it is, where it will happen, or when it's coming. It will almost certainly involve an attack on our soil.'

Fenaux paused to let the information sink in.

Reynaud placed his cutlery on either side of his plate. He refreshed Fenaux's glass and then his own from the *pichet* of red wine. He picked a piece of bread from the basket, tore off a crusty mouthful, and chewed it slowly. He raised the glass but put it down without taking a sip.

'*Merde*, that's more information than I needed to hear.'

'Christophe, I wouldn't come to you if my back wasn't to the wall.'

Reynaud spread his hands on either side of his plate.

'What can *I* do for you?'

'Send Omar word that you want to meet him at the club.'

'And tell him what?'

'Just let me play this scenario for you and then you can give me your thoughts.'

Reynaud nodded and resumed eating the patron's excellent steak-tartare, though the edge had been taken off his appetite.

'Omar graduated from the Université de Paris with a 1st in Chemistry; did you know that, Christophe?'

'His mother told me her son was studying a science subject, I didn't know which one.'

'Do you know her well?'

'She has a stall in the market selling cheap clothes. She seems to know most of what goes on in her block and fills my ear from time to time about who sells televisions or game consuls at knockdown prices. I don't want anything to fuck that up.'

Reynaud ran a community policing unit at La Cité. Although essentially neighbourhood police, when they received a crime report they were tasked with investigating it. His was the best detection rate in the district.

'Don't worry my friend, play it right and what I am asking will not come back to bite you on the ass.'

'What do I have to do?' Reynaud asked bluntly.

'I've arranged an offer of an internship with one of the big chemical companies, I want you to pass on the word to Omar and persuade him to take it.'

'That's it. I tell him I've got him an internship and wish him good luck?'

'Not exactly.'

'I thought there might be a catch.'

'Gain his confidence. Perhaps, ask him to help out at the Club. From the sound of things you need all the help you can get.'

Reynaud didn't like the direction the conversation was taking.

'Then what?'

'Christophe, you know I won't ask you to do anything that puts you in danger or puts your work at risk.'

Reynaud nodded.

'I want you to give Omar a contact number, it can be yours, or mine, as you wish. I want you to tell him that if he ever has anything playing on his mind, anything he needs to share, he can call either of us. Will you do that?'

'You're trying to recruit him as a tout.'

'No, he's past that point. I don't want to scare him off.'

'So you think by tugging at some of the better memories he had growing up you might get him to come across in a crisis.'

Fenaux shrugged.

'Fuck, you are desperate. What the hell, I'll do it for *you*.

'It's fucked up, but this case goes beyond our shores. I've got to exploit every angle.'

Reynaud mellowed on hearing Fenaux's passion.

'If it can be done, Yves, you're the one to do it.'

The patron suggested a *pousse-café* and they enjoyed a generous glass of Armagnac before heading towards their separate vehicles at the rear of the homely restaurant.

'*Bon courage, mon ami,*' Reynaud shouted from the window of his car. Fenaux tooted in response.

Neither took notice of the black Kawasaki scooter with green trims that followed onto the A1. On the short hop back to La Courneuve, Reynaud was preoccupied with the job Fenaux had tasked him with and failed to notice the Kawasaki at all. Both the rider and pillion passenger only had eyes for him.

28

A WEEK on from the bombing, Kate worked through an evening debrief with Mac. He wanted to re-evaluate every angle on Operation Cassandra. Despite the Northern origins of the bomb plot, it stung that he had not seen the London attack coming. SIU had no intelligence that O'Hare had an active service unit in Britain. It seemed Symons was similarly unaware.

Kate's phone rang; Quinlan.

'Can I call you back, Jack? I'm in the middle of something here.'

'I thought you might like to know, I've located that ginger from London.'

'Great! Steer clear until we get up to help you watch him.'

'This one's quiet enough.'

'How do you mean?'

'He's dead.'

Kate and Mac drove to the isolated road near the South Armagh border where the victim had been dumped. Quinlan drove them to the scene which had been cordoned off to traffic. They donned white suits and ducked into the white forensics tent. Kate moved around the body. It did not take long to find the evidence of torture.

'Did you know him?'

'No,' Quinlan replied. 'His name is Phelim O'Leary. What I'm hearing across the border is the family is decent with no militant republican background. Understandably, they're distraught.'

Kate inspected the evidence of torture.

'Who did this?'

'I'll give you one guess,' Quinlan replied.

'Same killer as Glynn?' Mac asked.

'Similar brutality,' Quinlan said.

'O'Hare is desperate if he's killing anyone he thinks might give up information,' Kate said. 'London's only a beginning.'

Quinlan drove his detectives hard in the days immediately following the discovery of O'Leary's body. They scoured the homes of Saor Nua suspects for evidence that might connect them to the crime. As they parked their cars around the corner from Bob McElgunn's house in Slievemish, Quinlan reflected on the length of time they had been adversaries. It seemed like forever. McElgunn had been an elected Sinn Fein councillor in Dundalk before a disagreement over the Peace Agreement saw him lose his seat.

He had learned from the political game to maintain a facade of respectability. He helped some neighbours get social welfare entitlements and agitated to keep the local bus service running. All matters that made him popular in the locality and he made sure that no one ever saw his other side. Since the Peace Agreement, Special Branch had largely left him alone which was why, when he opened his front door and saw Quinlan, his face turned puce.

As the door opened Quinlan pushed inward: 'Stand aside, Bob.'

One of Quinlan's colleagues pressed a search warrant into his hand.

'This is outrageous.'

In the kitchen, McElgunn's hairdresser partner was cutting an old age pensioner's hair. She shouted at him to keep the noise down.

'Running a business from your house, Bob,' Quinlan said. 'Does Revenue know about this?'

'Do yer dirty work and get the fuck out,' McElgunn replied.

Detectives were already searching the upstairs rooms. Two hours after arriving, they carried out ten evidence bags full of material meriting further scrutiny. By that stage, the coiffed pensioner had finished her cup of coffee and left the house without any money changing hands. The search party was on the point of leaving when Quinlan asked McElgunn to stand aside from the storage area under the stairs. He emptied the cluttered cupboard and located a battered computer. An attempt had been made to break it up.

All spit and fury, his face inches from his adversary's, McElgunn told Quinlan: 'Ye'll get nothin' from that yoke, it's fucked.'

'In that case Bob, you've nothing to worry about and we'll have it back to you in jig time.'

Quinlan brought the computer to Detective Ollie O'Brien, a forensic IT specialist in Dublin, and requested a rushed evaluation. The following evening, he called to Mac's office with O'Brien in tow. Kate was waiting for his report.

'Before you ask, I'm just back from Malaga,' O'Brien said to her, pointing to his shoulder-length curly hair.

'Suits you, Sir! The bleached blond, I mean.'

He laughed: 'The Guardia Civil seized laptops from some Irish crims down on the Costa. I got the job of harvesting the data.'

'Nice work if you can get it.'

'About that pile of crap Jack brought in; it was in bad nick,' O'Brien began. 'I did my best with the hard drive which had a problem with the MBR.'

'Less jargon, please, Ollie,' Kate said.

O'Brien had completed a Masters in Digital Investigation and Forensic Computing at University College Dublin. He was the top dog in his field and much in demand. When Kate discovered Charlie's laptop in her apartment, she brought it to O'Brien and requested a favour. He unlocked it but found nothing suspicious on it. He gave her a code for future use if she wanted to check it again. She asked him to keep the job between the two of them and off the books.

He continued. 'MBR is the master boot record, I fixed it. The next big thing was analysing the partition structure and recovering the lost partition tables.'

'Jeez, some man for one man,' Quinlan laughed.

'Ollie, I'm not kidding on the jargon,' Kate said. 'Get on with it.'

'We got lucky, the owner tried to break it up after he erased the files.'

'What's lucky about that?'

'It meant the PC was permanently switched off.'

'So?'

'With erased files, they're flagged for deletion; you need to recover them ASAP. Every second the computer is switched on afterwards means there's a chance the files will be overwritten and then they're gone.'

'Show us what you got,' Mac said.

'These look like some kind of payment records,' Ollie began pointing to the Excel spreadsheet on the screen.

'Payment records?' Kate said.

'Weekly wages going out, by the look of it.'

'Who's getting paid?' Mac asked.

'That's something you'll have to figure out yourself. Limited details, I'm afraid, first names only, *Pat, Bob, Liam, etc.*'

Kate glanced at Mac.

'What justified these payments?'

He shrugged.

Next Ollie showed a budget pie chart showing 'travel' and 'procurement' that ate up seventy per cent of available funds.

'There seems to be a steady income stream in place; I've no idea from what source.'

'I hear whispers across the border that he could be into smuggling through the business he runs,' Quinlan said.

'The haulage business?' Kate asked.

'Aside from the fuel laundering he has a couple of trucks on the road. Does continental runs. So, plenty of opportunity.'

Ollie O'Brien interrupted.

'Sorry folks, I'm due in CAB in an hour. To wrap up, what you're seeing on screen are all recent records. The older stuff can be retrieved later if you want it.'

'We'll need it all for the investigation,' Kate told him. 'Great work!'

'No bother.'

'Keep in touch on your progress on the rest, won't you?'
Ollie folded his laptop.

'No problem, *Ciao* for now.'

'That's Italian, and it means hello.'

'And goodbye, or so I'm told,' Ollie laughed, as he closed the door.

'Do the names mean anything to you?' Mac asked Quinlan.

'They're all O'Hare acolytes,' he replied. 'Bob is McElgunn, Pat could be the fella that drives him around, Wilson is his name. I know four Liams, so take your pick.'

'This evidence is an indicator of organized crime,' Mac said. 'Why not use it to bring a charge against McElgunn?'

'Give O'Hare something to react to,' Kate said. 'Flush him out into the open.'

'He's been the one making us jump through hoops,' Quinlan chipped in.

'The computer records indicate organization as a structured group,' Kate said. 'How do we prove their main purpose or activity is the commission of or facilitation of serious criminal offences?'

'We'll work with Customs to link him to fuel laundering, maybe illegal importation of cigarettes as well,' Mac replied.

'I can testify about his daily routines,' Quinlan said. 'How does a man on the dole have a full-time driver?'

'Essentially, we pick him up, charge him and turn the investigation over to CAB,' Mac said.

The Criminal Assets Bureau was set up in the nineties to seize criminals' assets. It was a multi-agency unit of Police, Revenue, and other government departments.

'I like the sound of that,' Kate replied. 'The CAB investigation would keep McElgunn and O'Hare worried. A smokescreen to allow us to dig into his real intentions.'

'I'll talk to the DPP,' Mac said.

Early the following morning he told the Director of Public Prosecutions.

'We won't get a better chance to test the new legislation.'

'From the evidence you're telling me you've got,' the DPP replied, 'we could go with a holding charge of directing activities of a criminal organization.'

'I agree.'

'I will need to see it all in writing before I sign off on it *and* robust evidence to make it stick.'

By late afternoon the paperwork had been processed and Quinlan had scooped up McElgunn at his house. He charged him before the non-jury Special Criminal Court in Dublin, normally reserved for terrorist cases. McElgunn was remanded in custody.

29

O'HARE WORKED FURIOUSLY to get everything back on track. The loose ends from London were tidied up when the OC was dealt with for his treachery. The initial hesitation by the Dublin contact to re-engage after London was overcome following Bob McElgunn's visit. His second-in-command described Nasri's indignation as he placed photographs of the Nasri family in front of him, one by one, like playing cards. McElgunn hadn't rushed the encounter. He gave each item time to sink in, as he disclosed one piece of data after another on the Nasri family. They knew where he and his family lived and much about their daily routines. By the time McElgunn finished, Nasri was willing to talk. When O'Hare rang him, the greeting was minimal and chilly.

'Your demonstration was unusual,' Nasri said.

'It worked, didn't it?' O'Hare replied.

'My associates have questions.'

'Let's hear them.'

'There were problems with one of the items. Is this correct?'

'Yes; a technical problem that won't happen again.'

'What about losses?'

'None; all my salesman have returned.'

'Good.'

'We proceed as agreed?' O'Hare said.

'It seems, it is written,' Nasri replied.

O'Hare smiled contemptuously and hung up. He rang McElgunn to share the news. To his surprise, the number was answered by his partner.

'Put me onto himself, will you Teezie.'

'Och no, I can't, have you not heard?'

'Heard, what?'

'He's in prison tonight.'

O'Hare called to the house and quizzed Teezie about what had been seized. He raged at his ally's sloppy mistake when told of bags of paperwork and a broken computer being taken away.

He set about getting McElgunn out on bail but had to wait two days for the next court sitting. On Monday morning, Digger observed him from a distance as O'Hare had an animated conversation with a Dundalk garage owner.

The businessman fronted up as a bailsman later in the afternoon and O'Hare provided the €10,000 cash required. Despite strong objections by Quinlan to McElgunn being released from custody, the court took the view that as a former elected politician, he was likely to show up for his trial.

Digger rang Kate in London to tell her the news.

'How did he manage to get the garage owner to go bail,' she asked.

'Laundered diesel, I'd imagine. O'Hare's gang likely keeps his forecourt pumps workin'.'

Diesel for agricultural use was marked with a green dye because it sold considerably cheaper than the standard. O'Hare's gang removed the dying agent and sold the resulting product at selected stations around the country. After forty-eight hours behind bars, McElgunn emerged through the gates of Port-laoise's high-security prison into the garage owner's waiting car.

When Kate and Mac returned from Symons's conference they briefed Assistant Commissioner Fox. It was the second meeting in a fortnight. Fox wanted every detail. Mac expressed the view that the meeting had served little purpose apart from boosting the MI5 man's ego.

'The explosive used was ANFO.'

'ANFO! Jesus, that's a blast from the past,' Fox replied. 'Pardon the pun.'

ANFO was ammonium nitrate/fuel oil. When the Provisional IRA refined its homemade explosive capability during the eighties, ANFO was the result. They used commonly available agricultural fertilizer, calcium/ammonium nitrate, and crushed it into a powder. This gave it greater density and diesel oil completed the mix.

'Any ideas on what was used as a booster?' Fox asked.

'Semtex,' Mac replied. 'I suggested to Symons that a mixing plant for that amount of explosive would have to be located in Britain.'

'How did he react to that?'

'All but dismissed it out of hand.'

'Hard to expect anything else.'

Fox's interest switched to the intelligence retrieved from the seized McElgunn PC. He was pleased to see a suspect before a court considering the amount of his annual overtime budget that had been devoured by Operation Cassandra.

'I'm turning the case over to CAB,' Mac said.

'Why do that?' Fox asked.

'Because we believe O'Hare is putting together an underground army,' Kate said. 'Stopping that has to be our goal.'

'What evidence do you base that conclusion on?' Fox asked.

Kate painted the picture. O'Hare's successful insertion of an active service unit into the UK, the evidence of payments to volunteers, and finally, a record that travel and procurement had eaten up a large chunk of available funds.

'Can you be sure the records on the computer refer to O'Hare?' Fox asked.

'Bob McElgunn owned the PC. We know he meets O'Hare regularly.'

'And O'Hare didn't waste time in getting him out on bail,' Mac said.

Fox stood up and walked to the largest window in his office.

'Sounds more like the organized criminal gang, Quinlan told the court about.'

He stared out over an old parade ground, now filled with parked cars.

'Why aren't other Security Services sounding alarm bells? Do you think another London attack is inevitable?'

Mac replied: 'MI5 is sounding the alarm, but Symons is not seeing the full picture. On further attacks, the statistics tell us another is unlikely to come from an IRA source.'

'What stats are you basing that on?'

'Kate and I have looked at the attack patterns from the seventies to the nineties. It's hit and run. The IRA hits and then waits for the increased security to scale back before going again.'

'We believe O'Hare has plans that involve France,' Kate said. 'We just don't know what they are yet.'

'Nobody believing Cassandra's foresight. Ironic!'

30

BACK IN MAC'S OFFICE, Kate threw her raincoat over a chair and parked her overnight bag behind it.

'Let's assume Symons is talking bullshit about the weapon coming from France. That means there's probably another device out there.'

He nodded.

'Well, it's not something you slip in your pocket and smuggle across a border. Some kind of homemade weapon was hoisted onto the MV Delia. Someone will likely have to assemble it. That means surveillance opportunities in France.'

Mac agreed.

'Then there's this.'

She slid a conversation transcript across the table. Mac picked up the loose pages.

'What is it?'

'Exactly what it looks like, a transcript.'

'From where?'

'Digger persuaded the Chief Officer in Portlaoise prison that McElgunn was high risk and he switched him into a fresh cell on

Saturday night, with a pal, Sean Fitzpatrick from Dundalk, for company.'

'And?'

'Digger got in and out ahead of the switch and put a bug in the cell.'

'Jesus Christ, Kate! You'll get me sacked. Did *you* authorize it?'

'A Prison Service initiative.'

Mac arched an eyebrow.

'Anything that gives us an edge, can't be bad, can it?'

He flicked the transcript pages.

'What's in it?'

'Digger ignored the crap. What's there is anything he thought might be relevant to the case.'

Mac skimmed through the part of the transcript where the pair talked about the Quinlan raid on McElgunn's house that resulted in his court appearance. Then he read a highlighted section:

McE: Everything's moving ahead.

Fitz: You mean we'll soon be able to bring the fight to the enemy.

McE: More and more, brother.

Fitz: Ye should have heard the cheer that rang along the landing when we heard about the London bomb.

McE: I'm glad I didn't. But here, you've seen nothin' yet. When the Celtic cousins surface, we'll truly announce ourselves to the world.

Fitz: What do you mean?

McE: Fuck off and go asleep. I'm sorry I said anything.

Fitz: How's that wee missus of mine behavin' herself?

McE: Fuck off will ya? I need to sleep.

End

Mac threw the transcript back across his desk.

'Celtic cousins surface – what's that supposed to mean?'

'No idea. Maybe Fenaux can tell us if he ever gets his finger out and stops obsessing on Paris.'

'I'd probably put it differently, but let's ring him now.'

They exchanged pleasantries in French and Mac asked him for an update. He transferred the call to the speaker and replaced the receiver.

'Kate's here.'

'*Salut*, Kate! So we target some people at the fringes, and now we know that the three are interacting. We're intercepting a phone they are using to pass messages.'

'How did you identify the runner?' she asked.

'We got the metro police to do a control for us.'

'Risky strategy, don't you think?'

'Not really, they're normal here in Paris. Every day police on the trains do hundreds of stops to verify identities.'

'Are you pulling anything off the phone intercept?' Mac asked.

'The runner is conveying messages between the three suspects. They are waiting. They talk about staying calm, being patient.'

'What about outside Paris; any leads on the Cherbourg crate?' Kate asked.

'Nothing.'

They told him about the intercepted prison conversation. He didn't offer any insights.

'Has Jeffers come up with anything at all?' Mac asked.

'I talk to Robin every week. The FBI isn't picking up anything that connects to either France or Ireland. And the CIA isn't interested if the intel's not about the Middle East.'

'What about a case conference?'

'Symons doesn't invite me to his London conferences.

Instead, he leaks allegations to the press about the IRA using France as a base. Why bother?'

It was a sore point. Mac and Kate had attended both.

'If something comes from the intercepts, let's work together on it,' Fenaux said.

Mac didn't reply one way or another.

'I'm going to Boston next week for the FBI National Academy Associates dinner,' he said. 'I'll talk to some people while I'm there.

Fenaux and Mac had met for the first time, ten years previously at a leadership course in the FBI National Academy in Quantico. The FBI National Academy Associates organization kept the global graduates in touch.

'Sorry, I can't make it,' Fenaux replied. 'Enjoy the trip.'

***

Despite the London foul-up, O'Hare remained focused. His conversation with Nasri after McElgunn's visit reassured him that he remained in control of events. He was jolted by his sidekick's court appearance; unsure what to make of it. The ever-present shadows around Portadown were easy to spot. He dropped their surveillance whenever he crossed the border.

The wee boy, Nutser, had done well for him. He had developed into an able operator; someone ripe for another mission. McElgunn whined about the fact that Treacy delivered the ultimate sanction on the London OC without seeking his permission. O'Hare acknowledged to his second-on-command that the young lad was a wild one who needed careful grooming.

He drove from Portadown to Dundalk and parked in a shopping centre car park before ignoring the mall and walking directly out of it. He paced the streets in the Slievemish estate, checking for a tail before dodging into the rear garden of a terraced council house. The householder had disappeared for the morning. He retrieved a key from under a flower pot close to a makeshift shed. Nutser arrived on time and assured O'Hare that he hadn't been followed.

'I traipsed around that shopping centre for a good half hour,' he said.

'Good lad.'

'Are we gettin' busy again?'

'We are surely, boy. This time you'll need your passport.'

By the time Nutser left the house an hour later he knew what exactly he had to do. The Big Man kept it simple and made him feel good about himself. Nutser would not let him down. O'Hare waited for forty minutes after his protégé left the house. He walked through the estate and crossed the busy road to the shopping centre. He sat in his car for a further half-hour observing all movement in and out of the busy centre before heading back across the border.

31

MAC FLEW into Boston's Logan airport with four other Garda officers at three o'clock, local time. This year's annual meeting of the FBI National Academy Associates was special. The Irish-British chapter had been invited to Boston for a knees-up. Getting together was vital for renewing old acquaintances. Mac valued the contacts he nurtured through the world's largest law enforcement network as if they were gold dust. The Boston chapter had also invited along their New York brethren as special guests, citing the Irish connections of both cities.

The guests stayed in a Back Bay district hotel. The building had been headquarters for the Boston Police until the late nineties when a $60 million refurbishment transformed it into a luxury hotel. The Chapter dinner was set for Dillon's restaurant not too far away.

When they arrived Mac threw his case on the bed and rang home. The babysitter who answered reminded him that his wife was on a 'girls' night out. It had slipped his mind. The hours he was racking up on Operation Cassandra were dicing his family time and Mary had gotten tired of cancelled dinner dates. He asked the sitter to let her know that he had called. He heard music playing in the background.

'Try and get them off to bed by nine-thirty, won't you.'

He figured the chances of either of his daughters getting to sleep before midnight were slim.

In late afternoon September sunshine, Mac drank coffee and mingled with other early arrivals on an open patio near the bar. He seized the opportunity for a sidebar on the Greenwich attack with some London Anti-Terrorist Squad detectives. They told him nothing he did not already know. The latest intelligence was that the rest of the gang who carried out the attack were back in Northern Ireland. Mac updated them on the investigation into Phelim O'Leary's murder. It was early days and there hadn't been any breakthroughs.

The group was coming together for pre-dinner drinks as Mac returned to his room to grab his jacket. He was pulling it on when he heard a soft knock on his door.

'Come in,' he shouted.

A cheery face leaned in and quipped: 'Any whiskey drinkers in here?'

'Harris! How the hell are you?'

'Dude, couldn't be better. I just wanted a quiet word before the night gets rowdy.'

Jim Harris was a New Jersey native who retired a year earlier. When they first met, Harris's accent struck Mac as reminiscent of Tony Soprano, the TV mobster. With his bald pate and heavy jowls, the rotund detective even looked a bit like him. They had hit it off immediately when they met in Quantico years earlier. Even though Harris was Drugs Enforcement Administration and Mac's speciality was terrorism, they shared a common belief that fraternity among Police officers should extend beyond national borders.

'What's on your mind, Jim?'

'Dude, I miss the DEA.'

'Yeah? Well, a wise man told me once that you need to get on a twelve-step program when you retire from the police. That's what it takes to get it out of your system.'

Harris slapped him on the back.

'Ya haven't lost it, Mac.'

'Have you been doing anything apart from sweeping your yard?'

'Give a guy a break, will ya; I've got a family to feed. Don't say it too loudly but I'm just back from Afghanistan.'

'Jesus! We're too *mature* for that kind of shit.'

'Needs must, buddy, needs must. My son goes to college this year and those fees ain't going to get paid from a cop's pension.'

'How are Jim Junior and Sarah doing?'

'Jeez, you and your memory! They're fine. Older and bolder, ya know how it is. Look, I got something that I think might interest ya.'

'Shoot!'

'I'm contracted with one of our electric companies here in the US. They have contracts in Afghanistan to restore the national grid.'

'Sweet!'

'I take care of their security over there; just back from a six-month stint. What a beautiful, fucked-up country. If it wasn't for the war I mightn't have come home.'

Mac loved the no-holds-barred way Harris had of putting things.

'Any who, I accompany the engineers when they reconnoitre the provinces. As things stand I'll be back there in two months.'

'Must be interesting, all the same.'

'If ya thought too much about it, you wouldn't do it. IEDS and all that shit but yeah, ya get to see stuff.'

'Have you been to any of the hot spots?'

'About a month before I came back we were up near the famous Khyber Pass.'

'That connects Kabul to Pakistan, doesn't it?'

'Yeah, via Peshawar, that neck of the woods.'

Mac laughed.

'I remember some of my school geography.'

'The Darra people live in the region. They're wonderfully resourceful; ya should see it. They collected all the military junk the retreating Russians left behind. They've fashioned most of it into guns, they sell them in the bazaars as if they were pears or potatoes.'

'Christ Almighty!'

'I travelled with an interpreter who brought me round the back of one of the bazaars. If the company knew I was doing it on their clock I'd be canned.'

Mac had moved his case onto the floor. He retrieved a bottle of Jameson whiskey from it, poured two generous measures, and handed a glass to Harris.

Mac clinked.

'Sláinte!'

'Cheers!' Harris replied. 'So, we're chatting to one trader and he takes us out the back. He invited me to test-fire some of their homemade weapons. Not one misfired.'

'Now that's impressive.'

'Many sons and lots-a-guns is how the locals say it,' Harris laughed.

Mac downed his glass, grimacing as the neat whiskey hit his stomach. He hoped Harris didn't notice.

'We should make tracks.'

'First, take a look at these.'

Harris walked to the hotel room's table and moved some of Mac's belongings to one side. He pulled two folded A4 pages from his inside pocket and flattened them on the shiny mahogany surface. Mac looked at the pages and from them to Harris. Maintaining a poker face came as second nature to him, but Harris picked up the slightest reaction.

'Ya know these dudes. I can tell.'

'How the hell do you have their photos?'

Harris whooped.

'I knew it! In the private sector, the bosses tell us, that we have to switch off our curiosity when we reach a certain point during inquiries. Know when to stop poking around; in the company's interest, of course.'

'That must go against the grain.'

Harris drained his glass and put it on the bedroom table.

'Like ya wouldn't believe.'

'So, what about the photos?'

'I got these the day at the bazaar. I gave the owner a tip for allowing us to fire his weapons. Just as we were leaving, I asked him if he saw many Westerners in these parts.'

'What did he say?'

'He told me some come to buy guns from time to time. I could see the guy was hungry for more money and I figured what the hell.'

Mac walked to a wardrobe mirror and ran a comb through his hair.

'Keep talking.'

Harris patted his bald pate.

'What? Are ya tryin' to rub it in?'

'Mary gives me grief about photos from these nights. She says I look like the Wreck of the Hesperus in them.'

'So, I coughed up a few more bucks to the trader and he showed me his phone with these pictures on it. While he chatted to the interpreter I sent copies to my cell.'

'Risky!'

'Good opportunity, though. I knew I'd be seein' ya pretty soon and could tell ya about it.'

Mac noticed a tremor in his hands as Harris refolded the pages.

'Did your bazaar guy say what this pair did while they were there?'

'Said they test-fired a few AKs and handguns with him, and then were brought deeper into the mountains. The trader's job was to hold their passports until the entourage returned from their trek into the hills.'

'Why would they go deep into the mountains?'

'I didn't push him on that but a guy from Military Intelligence told me that the only reason Westerners are brought into that region was if they are in the market for more serious weaponry.'

'Bigger weapons? Like what?'

'Sniper rifles, anti-aircraft weapons; that kinda deal. The area connects to the Peshawar Valley in Pakistan and is controlled by local tribes. Ya could test-fire pretty much anything in there without anyone knowing, short of a nuclear bomb.'

Mac laughed and unfolded the passport-sized photos again. Harris was an able operator. He had run ops for the DEA in Central America. Pushing the boundaries to get this intel was well within his capabilities. Although the names were different, there was no doubt in Mac's mind that he was looking at pictures of Sean O'Hare and Bob McElgunn.

'Why don't you give these to the FBI and let them pass them on to me?'

'Ya fuckin' kiddin' me, Mac? Did ya hear anything I said? This could land me in deep shit with my bosses if they ever find out.'

'Sorry Jim, I wasn't thinking.'

'Screw the Feds – overpaid and over-hyped. Ya got the photos now I trust ya to deal with them.'

Mac smiled and clapped him on the back.

'What can I say, these tie into an active operation. They're a huge help.'

'Well, I'm glad. I hope ya get a result.'

'I owe ye, buddy. This gives us big impetus.'

'Payback starts tonight with a Guinness.'

'Let's get going.'

<hr>

Mac called Kate early the next morning.

'How's your head?' she asked.

'Fine,' he lied.

It was afternoon back home as he briefed her on the break-through. Without warning, Kate whooped.

'This explains it!'

He winced and pulled the phone away from his muzzy head.

'Explains what?'

'Why we've been living off scraps over here. Harris's intel confirms that serious action was happening on the other side of the world. Can you send me the photos?'

He retrieved them from the bedroom safe and placed them on the bed. He struggled to keep his phone steady enough for a clear copy, but eventually clicked and sent her both images.

'Harris says the area's awash with guns.'

Kate suggested she talk to Jack Quinlan and task him with looking into McElgunn's travels.

'Tell him to do it discreetly. We don't want to tip them off that we're on to them.'

'Trust me.'

When she called Quinlan and asked whether he had heard

anything about McElgunn being away, she was surprised to receive an instant answer.

'He was in Thailand.'

'How do you know?'

'His latest squeeze, Teezie, is a hairdresser, and she's been telling everyone how cheap it is to holiday there. Why do you want to know?'

'I'll fill you in the next time I see you,' Kate told him.

She filled Mac when he got back two days later.

'So, McElgunn likely hopped on a flight from Thailand to Pakistan and linked up with O'Hare there.'

'Well, if Harris's intel is to be believed, they were in remote mountains in Pakistan at the same time,' Kate said.

'Jim was told that three armed tribesmen travelled with O'Hare and McElgunn in a truck. Four others followed in a jeep.'

'Does that sound heavy?'

'Harris said they're paranoid about Western spies in the region. That kind of escort is normal practice.'

'All the same, the tribe must have something worth protecting.'

32

KATE CHATTED with Charlie on Skype. He was in George Town in the Cayman Islands and working an early morning shift on a luxury liner. Because of the time difference, he was five hours behind; she was speaking to him on her private mobile from her office. Time seemed to have flown by since they were last together. Meantime, much had happened and since making up, they had been in touch most days. Texts or emails mainly, but whenever possible they chatted on Skype.

'Just six more sleeps,' he teased her. 'I can't wait to see you.'

'Me too.'

'Can you book a few days off?'

'Hopefully.'

'Let's get out of Dublin for a while.'

'Do you have somewhere in mind? I can't go abroad at the moment.'

'Just let me know the dates you're free, and I'll take care of the rest.'

'Mysterious!' Kate said. 'I love it.'

As they chatted she tried to read him. Were there any tell-tale signs he was hiding something from her? Was she being paranoid? At Symons's first London conference, a throwaway remark by Daphne Clarke had cast fresh doubts in her mind when small talk over the lunch table drifted to football.

'I'm a Gunner,' Clarke admitted.

'What does that mean?' Kate had asked.

Clarke laughed.

'Arsenal supporter!'

'My boyfriend too,' she said. 'He loves Arsene Wenger; even got to a game here earlier in the year.'

'Who were we playing?'

'I don't know. It was the second weekend in April.'

Clarke had tilted her head and thought a while.

'You sure? I don't think there were Premiership games in London that weekend. Club players were away on international duty.'

'Maybe I have the date wrong,' Kate replied. 'I know zilch when it comes to boys kicking around a bit of leather.'

This had drawn good-humoured boos and hisses from the rest of the lunch table and she changed the topic of conversation.

When Detective Gerry Grealy rang her later that day he asked for an urgent meeting. It was Friday and she arranged to see him at SIU. Grealy was in a jovial mood; it was his last call before heading to his local watering hole for the first pint of the weekend. He plonked himself into a plastic chair in the canteen, indicating with a nod that he would take a coffee.

'Mr. Nasri is buying phones,' he said. 'Strictly one per shop.'

'That's interesting.'

'He has six already.'

'Six! Please tell me you've got details.'

'Every time the agent made a purchase, he clicked a photo and sent it to me,' Grealy said, smiling.

Kate swiped through his images of cheap Nokia phones with their batteries removed, the IMEI number visible on each one. 'This is good work,' she said.

Grealy acknowledged with a grin and sipped his coffee.

'That fat fucker is up to something; I won't ask you to tell me what exactly.'

'You're getting good at this game.'

'Just don't have me walk my man into harm's way.'

Kate promised that his agent's security would receive proper priority. She spent the rest of the evening preparing warrants to intercept each phone as it went live.

The first phone was activated the following Monday evening with the usual welcome to the network text. SIU was on high alert; through the night coverage ensured they missed nothing. Already Kate's annual overtime budget was shot to pieces. She had also mined most of the goodwill quota from her team. With Operation Cassandra nobody moaned.

On Tuesday morning at three o'clock, a sleepy Nasri answered the first call. Tracing kicked in instantly; a satellite phone originating in Asia.

'Sir, the man from the mountain, he comes.' The voice accented, Indian or Pakistani. 'I am to tell you that your order is on its way. All is well.'

'Thank you, goodbye,' Nasri replied.

Tangible intelligence linking Nasri to an en-route illicit arms shipment excited MI5's interest. In the wake of the Greenwich bomb, any initial impression Symons tried to create that he was going to orchestrate the future course of Operation Cassandra quickly dissipated. He was grasping at straws within a fortnight.

He knew that history gave the British an advantage in the region where the call originated and tried to muscle in. He cited Pakistani intelligence assets he could activate to get a tracker beacon onto any identified consignment. Mac turned down the offer. Trying to identify a consignment was a high risk but the possibility of a tracker being located was more so. They needed to be patient to complete the big picture. Fenaux agreed with the need for forbearance. Symons reluctantly backed off when the Americans rowed in behind Mac's analysis.

At the end of the week, Nasri's second phone was activated with a call from a payphone in Istanbul. He was informed that his delivery was en route and on time. Again, Nasri replied curtly and immediately dumped the phone.

He followed the same pattern after the third phone call from a truck stop outside Essen, Germany. It was the same caller from Istanbul who told Nasri that the delivery had been made, the load was secure, and friends were watching over it.

Dealing with separate countries with different legal systems would be complicated. Arms trafficking was only one facet of a much bigger picture. They would have to keep knowledge of the operation tightly controlled and keep local law enforcement onside, a tough balancing act.

Nasri activated the fourth handset immediately and sent an SMS to a British mobile. Symons's people confirmed it pinged in the South Armagh region.

The message read, '*tools ready for collection.*'

An hour later Kate snapped on a headset as a call flashed up on SIU screens. Bob McElgunn was playing it ultra-safe. The payphone he called from was located in a hotel at Crossmaglen. Although only a fifteen-minute drive from his Dundalk home, it lay in another jurisdiction.

'Your tools are within reach, our part of the bargain is sealed. Now is time for final settlement,' Nasri said.

'You're getting a bit ahead of yourself there, my friend, we'll need information and verification.'

'This can be done.'

'Location?'

'Not on this,' Nasri snapped.

'Then how, my good friend?'

'I will send someone, tell me where.'

'I'll text the location details.'

Fifteen minutes passed before Nasri's phone received the awaited message *Today – Old Bridge – 2 ladies – 8 o'clock*.

He acknowledged and killed the phone.

Kate knocked heads together to try to figure out a location for the meeting. Initially, they figured somewhere close to McElgunn but nothing fitted. Digger solved the puzzle. Proximity to McElgunn was not the key. It should have been obvious. One of O'Hare's photos taken during his Dublin weekend featured two old women. If he was right, the meeting was set for Dublin city centre.

By late afternoon, Digger had gotten access to a vacant fourth-floor apartment that overlooked the little plaza near Dublin's Halfpenny Bridge. Almost thirty thousand people used the Liffey's best-known pedestrian crossing every day. His camera was set to capture anyone coming through Merchant's Arch onto the bridge. He scanned the street sculpture of the two old ladies on their bench, handbags at their feet, as they sat in frozen chat. Digger's OP would double as Kate's command post for the evening.

Everything was set. Department stores would remain open

for late-night shopping and by eight o'clock the place should be buzzing. Digger opened his flask of hot water, poured it into his tub of Pot Noodles, and stirred. 'I love this job,' he told the empty space.

Gerry Grealy called at six o'clock as Kate joined him in the command post.

'Our man has been told to go into town tonight.'

'Do we know what for?' she asked.

'Nasri told him to go to a city centre shop where he would be given a message.'

She listened as he confirmed what they already knew.

'Does he know what he has to do with the message?'

'Pass it on.'

'Do you have time?'

'Eight o'clock.'

'Thanks for the heads-up, Gerry.'

As the appointed hour drew close, the crew was well-tuned into the ambience of the area. Beggars, shoppers, lovers, and street performers competed for space in the tiny square where they expected their targets to show.

Nasri's runner arrived by tram at 7:40 p.m. and got off at the Abbey Street stop. SIU was watching. Being a paid agent didn't earn him their total trust. Angie reported that he had walked up Abbey Street, crossed O'Connell Bridge, and gone into a shop on the quays. He bought twenty cigarettes.

'Standby,' Angie said.

Angie had rumbled something; Kate waited with bated breath.

'Boss, he was given something extra with his change.'

'Clarify.'

'He was given a slip of orange paper. He's heading up the quays now, we'll keep him company.'

She listened as her crew communicated locations and directions of travel. When he exited the shop he walked up the south quays, heading in her direction. Angie confirmed they had enough people to cover him.

'Target crossing the Halfpenny Bridge.'

Three minutes to rendezvous.

'He's dumped something in a litter bin,' Angie said.

'Do *not* attempt to retrieve until after the meet,' Kate ordered.

The agent walked slowly with the throngs of late-night shoppers across the metal bridge. He waited patiently for the lights to change at the pedestrian crossing on the opposite side. Before he reached the footpath, he delved into his right pocket and tapped a cigarette from a packet. Cigarette in mouth, he patted his jacket pockets before approaching the stranger nearest the 'old dears' sculpture. The exchange was innocuous.

The guy who produced a lighter and lit the agent's cigarette wore a white baseball cap. When Digger zoomed in he couldn't get a clear shot of the stranger's face. The logo on the cap read *I love Phuket.*

'It's McElgunn,' Kate said.

'You sure?' Digger asked. 'All I have is a side view, I can't make his face.'

'Zoom in on the cap.'

'*I love Phuket* – so what?'

'McElgunn was in Thailand earlier this year.'

An SIU member verified his ID on a street walk past. Kate ordered her crew to let him go. There was nothing to be gained by following him and when he was well clear of the area, she gave Angie the go-ahead to retrieve what the agent discarded. Dressed in a yellow high-viz vest, which said *working safely for Dublin city* on its rear, at a cursory glance, Angie was another city corporation worker doing her job. She retrieved the bag of trash and put a fresh one in its place.

Back at base, nobody volunteered to sift through the debris discarded in a few hours of city life. Since it was her razor-sharp eyes that caught the exchange, Kate told Angie she would have to go through the foul-smelling heap.

Digger held his nose and hummed *my old man's a dustman* as he headed out the door. Angie pulled on latex gloves and covered her mouth with a surgical mask.

'Gee thanks, Boss, next time I'll keep my mouth shut.'

Angie spent thirty painstaking minutes separating materials that were never intended to bond. Kate's phone rang as Angie's tweezers carefully unpicked the piece of flimsy orange paper attached to a discarded banana skin.

'Got it!' she triumphantly held aloft the orange-coloured paper scrap.

Kate hung up her call.

'Rotterdam?' she said before Angie could reveal the fruits of her labour.

'How the hell do you know?'

'That was Gerry Grealy. The agent just rang him.'

Angie brought over the orange scrap and placed it on Kate's desk. The words *Rotterdam port* were written on it. She pulled together the four corners of the plastic sheet, picked up the rubbish, and walked toward the door.

'Hitting the shower!' she said. 'Eileen will puke if I come home smelling like this.'

'Thank you,' Kate shouted. 'We had to be certain the agent wasn't duping us.'

Angie waved an acknowledgement before the squad room door closed. Kate called Mac and briefed him on the outcome.

'What's our next move?' she asked.

'We'll bring the partners up-to-date in the morning. The boss can parley with the Dutch.'

The intercepted conversation between McElgunn and Nasri was solid evidence of a *quid pro quo* between the two groups.

Apart from Nasri and the Paris suspects that Fenaux was watching, Kate had no idea how many others were involved or what level of threat they presented. It was by a stretch her most diverse case ever. Managing its myriad elements was like spinning plates.

PART 3

33

KATE WATCHED ENVIOUSLY as Charlie's chest rose and fell in restful slumber. Her sleep pattern was all over the place. She slipped quietly out of bed and tiptoed to the window of the five-star hotel. Moonlight streamed through a chink in the curtains and she peered through it at Lough Atalia and Galway Bay. Boats bobbed in the water as night breezes rippled the surface. In the idyllic moonlight, the place seemed perfect for an autumn weekend getaway.

A sleepy voice jolted her.

'Shouldn't you put something on?' Charlie grinned.

Her movement had woken him and propped on one elbow with the bedclothes askew, he was watching her. Weeks cruising in the Caribbean had given his body a dusky hue that she found sinfully arousing. She nipped across the room and slipped between the sheets.

'Sorry! Would you like something?' she teased. 'I can make you a cup of tea if you like.'

He drew her close and they kissed passionately.

'Hold that thought.'

She rolled him onto his back as a chink of moonlight through the curtains cast their skin tone into relief. Her pale white was a stark contrast to his deep tan. She wriggled and leaned on his chest, caressing its smoothness with her fingers.

'Why did you wax?'

'Anything for milady's pleasure. You mentioned you liked the idea.'

'Did I? I don't remember.'

'All that pain for nothing.'

She bent and kissed him; her arousal heightening as he explored her body; their rhythm, slow, luxurious and in tune late into the morning hours.

Nagging doubt kept her from sleeping later. She never asked him to change anything about himself. Once again she had caught Charlie out. Why fib about small stuff like chest waxing? What lay behind it?

Room service woke them and Kate pulled on a robe to let the waiter in. They ate in bed, hungrily devouring breakfast from the hotel's award-winning restaurant. Daylight hours were limited so they planned to browse the city centre in the morning before heading to Connemara for the afternoon. Her phone beeped a message as they jumped in the car.

'I better check this.'

Charlie concentrated on driving.

'Do what you gotta do.'

Mac had left a message asking her to call him urgently. She needed privacy, so Charlie dropped her at Eyre Square in the centre of Galway. The compact urban square was busy. Traffic streamed around its edges and she headed toward the corner where buses waited for passengers at the train station. She sat on an empty bench and dialled Mac's number.

'No rest for the wicked!' he remarked.

'For me neither it seems. What's up?'

'I need you back here now.'

Her heart sank. A weekend shredded before her eyes. How would she break this news to Charlie?

'Kate, are you still there?'

'Yes!'

'You know I wouldn't...'

'Yeah, yeah I know. I'm going to have to call you back.'

'We really need to...'

'Ten minutes.'

'We've got to talk - urgently.'

She was irate. In the aftermath of the London bomb, it had been non-stop. She needed the break and felt she'd earned it. Charlie had arrived home a week earlier and they needed time together to sort out their relationship.

As he crossed the square Kate studied his carefree expression. 'Work to live – not live to work' was his motto. It endeared him to her. The problem was her world did not work that way. He had no inkling of the imminent news.

She bought two coffees from a market stall at the top of Shop Street and handed over one as they strolled down Galway's main thoroughfare.

'Hey Bashful, I love you, you know,' she said, on impulse.

He nudged her in response.

'Now I'm one of the Seven Dwarfs, am I? The love just keeps on coming.'

'The one with the long lashes.'

They strolled hand in hand. He whispered in her ear.

'Love you too, Grumpy.'

She jabbed his ribs.

'Surely I'm your Snow White.'

'Right now, Grumpy fits better. Are you going to tell me the bad news or do we have to stroll to Connemara before you bring it up?'

'You know me better than I thought.'

'I know that frown.'

'I have to go back,' she said, eyes moistening.

He hugged her.

'Pity but we'll get over it,' he soothed.

'What do you think about moving in together?' she asked.

'Kate, you work in a job with crap hours.'

She frowned.

He laughed. Her frown deepened.

'Hold on; your hours are crap, I work in a job where I'm away for weeks on end. What an idea!'

She thumped his shoulder.

'Is that a yes or a no?'

'Yes,' he replied, kissing her. 'Let's get a place together.'

'Or, you could just move into my place.'

'Only, if we split everything fifty-fifty.'

'Let's worry about the details later.'

At the end of Shop Street, they dumped their paper coffee cups in a bin. Fishy odours from trawlers unloading their catch in the nearby harbour drifted towards the city on a stiffening breeze. Kate looked longingly at the local fish restaurant where they had planned to eat lunch.

'Grab the car and I'll meet you back at the hotel.'

'Sure.'

They kissed goodbye and she retraced her steps up the busy street. She called Mac and used the walk back to the hotel to process the scant details he passed over the phone.

Four hours later she was sitting in his office hoping that her expression reinforced the fact that she was not ready to forgive him.

'Better be good.'

His tone revealed the excitement of the chase hotting up.

'We've got movement,' he replied.

'Tell me the full story.'

'Whatever O'Hare sent to France is still there, we're almost one hundred per cent sure of that.'

'How do you figure?'

'Fenaux got a tip-off.'

'Okay. Explain.'

'He has a holiday home in Normandy where he spends any weekend he can out of Paris. That's how he got the word, from a former colleague, who lives in Pont de l'Arche.'

'Is that in Normandy?'

'Close enough. It's on the way from Paris. A builder's merchant in Pont de l'Arche passed information to Fenaux's mate.'

'What information?'

'The informant owns a DIY business. Fenaux's mate is ex-RG, you know like Special Branch here. He told him about an Irishman they used to keep an eye on. This guy lives fifteen kilometres from the village. He's married to a French woman and works for the Forestry Service in Normandy.'

'Has he form here?'

'We came across John Strain in the eighties when he was suspected of carrying out armed robberies for the Provos. He dropped off our radar until a trace request from the French.'

'Was there any specific reason for inquiring back then?'

'Just the French being French,' Mac explained. 'When Fenaux bought a house nearby, he kept his eyes and ears open.'

'To be expected.'

'*Listen to the river and you're going to catch a fish.* Learn the patterns and if they change, find out why. Fenaux knew Strain's routines like the back of his hand.'

'So, what changed?'

'Strain bought three packets of welding rods earlier this week.'

'What?' Kate asked.

'He works in the forestry as a labourer. He has no use for welding rods?'

'You brought me back to tell me that! Maybe he was buying them for someone else.'

'Patience!'

'What did Fenaux do?' she asked.

'He arranged 24-hour surveillance on Strain. Had his home phone and cell tapped, intercepted his internet, and generally threw everything at him.'

'Did they come up with anything?'

Kate wondered whether her weekend had been cancelled for a wild goose chase. She was also curious as to where she fitted in the picture Mac was painting.

'They figured they had everything covered until one of Fenaux's crew saw a postman doing his rounds and realized they hadn't included ordinary mail in the intercept warrant. They went back to the judge and corrected it the same day. Three days later this was intercepted.'

He handed her an A4 page. It was a copy of a postcard seemingly sent from Germany signed by Nutser. To the casual reader, it was like any other postcard.

'*Buddy,*

Passing your way soon. Our pal will meet ya for a coffee at the Porky Pig place. Here, did ya do our lucky lotto numbers lately? In case ya forgot them here they are 14 12 25 09 10 30. See ye soon brother.

Nutser'

It was evident that the writer intended any unwelcome eyes viewing the card to believe that Nutser and Strain were friends.

'I haven't heard of any other Nutser, other than Treacy. If that's the case, there's your connection to O'Hare,' Kate said. 'Quinlan says he's one bad bastard.'

'Looks that way,' Mac replied.

'Postcards for communications though; that sounds very old-school.'

'Maybe it is. But maybe it's clever too.'

'How do you mean?'

'Hiding in plain sight. There isn't a chance in hell that anyone in Germany or France reading that postcard would report it as suspicious.'

Kate had tuned out of work. She yawned and stretched. It took all her energy to switch on again.

'Maybe so.'

'We think the numbers indicate a date, time, and place for a meeting.'

'Really?'

'We think the action will be in Northern France, Côte d'Armor département to be specific.'

'Where's that?'

'Roscoff, where the car ferry arrives from Ireland, that's Côte d'Armor département. Morlaix is a big town nearby.'

'What about the numbers,' Kate asked.

'The first two indicate a road number – N12.'

'How did you come up with that?'

'We think the number 14 indicates the fourteenth letter of the alphabet: 'N'; the next number:12 indicates the route number, so N12.'

'I presume the N12 exists.'

'It connects Paris and Brest. It's 562 kilometres long.'

'What's about the other four numbers?'

'Date and time for a meeting; all of which means the

planned meeting is somewhere on route nationale twelve on the twenty-fifth of September at ten-thirty.'

'The day after tomorrow! What about Porky Pig? What's that about?'

'The French analysts started on the premise that if they were meeting along the N12, then a service stop was a likely venue. So we looked at ones close to Strain's home and came up with nothing. I asked Fenaux to send me a list of all service stops along the route. That's when I had my *Eureka* moment.'

'Which was?'

'As I checked down through the list it hit me – Porz an Park.'

'Porz an Park – Porky Pig,' she laughed. 'It's the way it sounds. What did Fenaux say when you suggested it could be the place for the meeting?'

'He laughed too.'

'He's discounting it?'

'No, he's going to give it a shot.'

'Where do I come into all of this?'

'I'm sending you over with a small team to assist Fenaux's people.'

She was excited by the news but tried to conceal it.

'Good,' she replied. 'What about the language issue?'

'Fenaux assured me he has people who speak good English.'

'Yeah, but you know from experience...'

Mac held up both hands in surrender.

'Yeah, I know that the English spoken mightn't be all that coherent, so I'm giving you McManus.'

'Okay, fine.'

As well as being a sworn officer with ten years of policing experience, Tom McManus was an accredited interpreter. He had worked at the Dublin conference and was superb at what he did. He was also one of the calmest people on the planet.

'By the way, you're getting an exclusive ride.'

'Ryanair, I suppose.'

'No, seriously, the Air Corps are going to drop you.'

Kate and crew would hitch a ride on an Army Air Corps AW 149 helicopter. It was due to fly to the Westland Helicopter plant at Yeovil in the south of England for its annual overhaul. G2, the Army intelligence wing assured Mac that getting clearance for a hop across the channel would not be a big issue. They would be dropped into a tiny airport close to Cherbourg. The chopper would refuel there and resume its original mission.

Mac relaxed, his hands cupped behind his head, chuffed with his plan. Kate felt nauseous at the thoughts of a bumpy low altitude flight across the Irish Sea but did not have the heart to puncture his upbeat mood.

Their mission was planned to start first thing the following morning. When the briefing concluded Kate left to break the travel news to the crew she had already selected in her head. The DGSI emailed shots of the service stop at Porz an Park. It was similar to hundreds of others dotted along France's main transport arteries.

The problem was it was tiny. Just five picnic tables and benches on a grassy patch in front of the car park. There were three similar units perched on a slightly elevated stretch of green. This area was screened off by bushes and small trees. The central parking space was reserved for trucks. There was a small timber cabin for tourist information, one public toilet block, and a restaurant offering basic nourishment. Eight fuel pumps completed the picture.

It was a well-chosen location that made mounting a surveillance operation difficult. SIU's role would be to identify the players that showed up. If the action moved on, Kate would decide on how far her team would go.

34

BY FIRST LIGHT, Digger and Kate had double-checked every aspect of the mission. Angie was in charge of equipment, and McManus took care of his requirements. Zoom drove them to the Air Corps base and a front gate sentry pointed them toward a briefing room where the helicopter crew was expecting them.

The pilot was at the door for a formal meet and greet. He nodded over Kate's shoulder towards McManus who was helping Angie unload the equipment for a final check.

'Superintendent Bowen, you're a team of three plus equipment, is that correct?' he asked.

'It's Kate, and we're a team of four, plus equipment.'

'My Op Order states three, plus equipment,' he replied with no invitation to informality.

'Well, someone's screwed up because there are four of us.'

The pilot was a man not fond of surprises. At least that was the way he played it for the benefit of four aircraft mechanics, already sitting in the briefing room.

'We're going to have to weigh,' he said.

'Individually or collectively?' Kate joked.

'Everyone and everything.'

Zoom and Angie repacked everything into the van. They all hopped on board and followed the discommoded pilot's directions to the weighing room.

'Shouldn't have eaten that pie last night,' Digger quipped.

'Let's get this done,' she said.

Lieutenant-Colonel Shaw from G2 introduced himself to her. Tall and angular, he tagged along with the group towards the weighing room. He said security on the operation was his brief and explained that before the SIU request, the Air Corps had planned to drop some of their aircraft mechanics at Westland's Yeovil plant to complete training courses on transmissions and blades. Because they had been bumped from the flight, the weigh-in was a ruse for their benefit to cut out speculative chit-chat.

'Your cover story is that you're a SWAT team heading to the UK on a training exercise.'

Kate nodded.

The morning was dull and dirty with a gusting westerly wind lashing rain against the chopper as they taxied along the apron. Kate sat beside Digger with McManus and Angie opposite. Their gear was stowed; night sights included. Angie brought a personal set of binoculars. She hated the ones the Job gave her, too big and cumbersome. She had spent an entire week's wages on getting a top-of-the-range model. She never loaned them out.

They steadily gained enough power to hover and set out on a route that took them towards the east coast. The rain gradually cleared and cloud cover lifted. The Wicklow hills and valleys spread out beneath them in a breathtaking panorama as they headed south hugging the coastline.

McManus appeared on top of his brief as he systematically leafed through pages of vocabulary lists he had prepared with

Digger's assistance. Surveillance has its terminology, technical and otherwise, and getting a grasp of it absorbed his attention.

Onshore breezes buffeted the helicopter and Kate tried to conceal her discomfort. Off-shore wind turbines on the country's east coast appeared and disappeared quickly. The engine growled as the pilot increased speed and gained altitude. Kate tensed, all that lay beneath them as they headed towards Europe was the steel-grey Irish Sea.

She reflected on her relationship's exciting new direction. Charlie arrived at her place the previous evening with a suitcase. Since college, Kate had always lived alone, and it seemed strange to be making room for someone else's clothes in her wardrobe.

She didn't want to start a new phase of their relationship with a big secret lurking and came clean about her dalliance in Paris. She confessed it was a spur-of-the-moment thing that meant nothing. She was relieved to get it out in the open, although surprised he forgave the indiscretion so readily. Charlie wiped away her tears.

'Everyone does stupid stuff.'

Their first night together as a couple in her apartment had felt right. She had gotten less than five hours of sleep but felt energized.

When they landed at Maupertus airport Bruno greeted them. Kate smiled and offered a professional handshake. He seemed chuffed to have escaped Paris for a while. Everyone jumped into the waiting cars and headed west.

As they reached the airport limits Kate asked, 'Will we be using these cars during the operation?'

Bruno asked the driver and then replied, 'Probably.'

'Let's not travel in convoy then,' she suggested.

'*Bonne idée,*' the driver agreed and radioed his colleague to shoot ahead.

Experience taught Kate that the IRA did not do things haphazardly. McElgunn's cryptic reference to 'Celtic cousins' remained unexplained. Someone might be scouting for unusual police activity. A tingle of anticipation was palpable with the crew; would their targets use this route?

Four hours later, when they arrived at Morlaix commissariat, the driver punched in a code at the entrance barrier and parked out of public view. Kate hoped the building might turn out to be ancient and full of history just like Paris. However, the modern building they were entering had little architectural appeal.

Fenaux greeted Kate and Angie, Gallic style with a peck on each cheek; Digger and McManus settled for a handshake. Inside, Kate took in the surroundings of the *bureau de la Police Judiciaire* – squad room for the detectives. Fenaux had commandeered it from the local P. J. Commandant. The grey desks had a well-worn look to them. The brown leatherette seats on the chairs were just about fit for purpose. Mac had talked about the movie posters in P. J.'s squad rooms. Here, Alain Delon's classically French *visage* looked down on them from a poster for *Un Flic*. A young Mel Gibson and Danny Glover glowered from the publicity shot for *L'Arme Fatale*.

Fenaux began the briefing as the strongest coffee Kate had ever tasted blew away the cobwebs. She was wide awake. McManus kicked into action with interpretation.

'After the postcard, we've picked up no communication of any kind between the two suspects, Strain and Treacy. Today we've had some domestic action – a big bust-up between Strain and his wife.'

'What was that about?' Kate asked.

'Strain's wife found a hidden phone in a garage beside the house. He grabbed it from her. She accused him of having an affair.'

'Is she right?'

'No, we think he uses it for more clandestine reasons. Nothing has come on his other phones.'

'Did the wife calm down?'

'No,' Fenaux smiled. 'She loaded the children into the family car and drove to her mother's house, twenty kilometres away.'

'Is Strain still at the house?' Kate asked.

'Still there.'

He turned to his number two, Bertrand Dubois, and asked him to brief everyone on how the Porz an Park operation would run. Everything about Dubois was neat. Not a single hair on his grey head was out of place. It was cut short and his deportment hinted at an army background. Dubois was at least five years older than Fenaux, a reserved character like a flip-side to his boss's gregariousness.

He laid out his plan to station a truck overnight in the central parking area of the Porz an Park service stop. They had a camera mounted on the roof of the restaurant for the past two days and knew that trucks parked up there each night.

'Can the camera remain in place?' Kate asked him.

McManus interpreted for the room.

'Too risky,' Dubois replied.

'How many people will you put in the truck?'

'No more than three; probably just two.'

Dubois's finger gestures rendered McManus's translation redundant.

'Any of us?' Kate asked.

'Either way, two or three, we'll use one of yours in the truck. The cab space would be crowded with three.'

'Don't use the cab,' Angie suggested.

'Why not?' Dubois asked.

'It's the first place I'd check; and if I suspected there were two people in it, it would make me wary.'

'But it is normal at stops for the driver to sleep in the cab.'

McManus was facing the two undercover squads but most hardly noticed him as they focused on the exchange of tradecraft needed to make the operation work.

'Having more than one in the cab could put whoever comes along on edge,' Angie repeated. 'The bunk is the only place you can keep out of sight. One is the max that can go in there, in my view.'

'Someone must stay with the truck,' Dubois stated.

'What if the truck gave the appearance of being empty?' Kate suggested.

'*En Panne* perhaps?'

'Out of Order, broken down,' McManus interpreted.

'Worth considering,' Kate replied.

'It would give us greater scope to stick cameras in the trailer and cover the entire parking area,' Digger said. 'It'll be a hard shell I presume?'

'A hard shell, yes,' Dubois confirmed. 'You've done this before?'

'Just a few months ago against a well-armed criminal gang.'

Digger explained how using a trailer on that occasion gave them the element of surprise for the arrests. Here they needed to preserve the element of surprise beyond the service stop. They wanted Strain to lead them toward whatever was planned.

'Does the trailer have a trading name on it?' Digger asked.

'What do you mean?'

'A company name. Is there any company name written on the sides or rear of the trailer?'

One of the French squad confirmed that there was a company logo.

'Is there an 'O' in the name?'

'*Comment?*'

McManus looked directly at Digger and asked him what he meant.

'What I want to know is, does the letter 'O' appear in the company name?'

A perplexed Dubois threw his hands in the air.

'Why?'

'The centre of the 'O' makes a grand cut out for a night camera.'

Delayed laughter filtered through the room on McManus's translation.

Kate butted in.

'Let's settle the question of whether holing up in the trailer is a go or not.'

Dubois turned to the guy sitting on the chair he had vacated. He had similar grey hair to Dubois but in a crew cut. Hardly ideal for surveillance, Kate thought, but then again this was France.

'Patrick, what do you think?'

'*Pourquoi pas,* why not? There is no 'O' in the name on the trailer, but there is a big Q,' Crew-cut smiled.

'Just the job,' Digger replied, and laughter trickled around the room.

The rest of the meeting was taken up with positioning teams. Digger insisted on being out in the open. He and two of Fenaux's men would dig in at a field that gave them a view of the service stop.

Angie would go in the trailer with two of Fenaux's crew. One wheel of the truck would be deflated. The restaurant owner would overhear an irate driver report to his employer that the spare tyre was also punctured.

Kate and McManus would remain with Fenaux and Dubois at the command post, or 'Poste' as they called it here. Vehicles would be stationed at points to take up the chase no matter which direction the targets went. Everyone would get a personal copy of the operation plan with call signs and contact details before deployment. It would outline where to go for safe haven in the event of becoming detached or isolated. It would even supply a map showing how to get to the nearest hospital. Kate was impressed. When questions about the plan petered out Dubois checked with the surveillance team covering Strain and was told that all was quiet. Fenaux announced that they should eat before deployment.

'We would like to host you in a restaurant outside,' Fenaux said 'but we don't want to take the risk. It's police canteen food I'm afraid.'

The basement canteen was reserved for their exclusive use. Compared to home, Kate and her team marvelled at the choice.

'There's even a salad bar,' Angie said. 'With a choice of dressings!'

'No chance of a full Irish breakfast, I suppose,' Digger grumbled.

By the time they finished, Dubois had received word from the team at Strain's house that he had packed tools into his beat-up 4 x 4 and extinguished all the house lights.

'Let's not hang about,' Kate said to Fenaux.

He clapped his hands to get everyone's attention.

'*On y va,*' he shouted.

Coffee cups were rapidly drained as crews began streaming out of the canteen.

'Here we go,' Kate whispered to McManus.

35

THE AFTERNOON MARKET at La Courneuve was its usual chaos of colour and noise. The car park, set out with stall covers by local municipal workers the previous evening, was now massed with shoppers, browsers, and thieves. Anyone naive enough to leave a car overnight generally regretted it the following morning. Crime was a perennial feature and cars made easy pickings.

Before heading into the mayhem, Sergeant Christophe Reynaud put a smile on his face. This was his domain and he loved it. He had patrolled this market for so long that most of the traders could have been on first-name terms with him. They chose to keep their distance by addressing him always as *Monsieur Reynaud*. He was strict; no unlawful act went without sanction and there was grudging respect for him among the trader community. He had his finger on the pulse of the area and remained at *Brigadier-Chef* rank because it kept him in frontline policing. Senior management relied on him for accurate temperature readings of the neighbourhood.

Reynaud and his fresh-faced *Sous-Brigadier* conducted their way through the shoppers. Fabrice was a recently promoted Sergeant, new to the area and Reynaud knew his attitude needed adjusting.

'Must we talk with these common people all the time,' Reynaud overheard him remarking once, back at the station, '*We're* the Police, after all.'

'These *common people* are our bread and butter,' Reynaud reminded him. 'We live or die by what we hear or don't hear. So be civil and chat.'

He had the best sources of information in this neighbourhood. Today, he had tasked Fabrice with a specific job and Reynaud went over it again to make sure his junior knew what he had to do. He was to engage the stallholder beside the target and keep her distracted for as long as it took Reynaud to kickstart Fenaux's attempt to get a line into Omar al-Haddad.

When the pair rounded a corner into the market square, Reynaud greeted a stallholder, almost hidden behind small mountains of nuts.

'*Bonjour Ali, ça va bien?*'

He bought two hundred and fifty grams of pistachios and continued the ambling patrol through the stalls. The market always struck Reynaud as more African than French. The pungent odours from the dazzling displays of spices punched through the fumes from the adjacent M1 motorway. The fragrant and colourful stalls took him back to his honeymoon with Yvette in Marrakesh and their trips to The Souk. Thankfully donkeys and their shit were absent here.

Aromatic spices gave way to more familiar smells as they wound their way through the market. Chickens cooking on a rotisserie made everyone think of dinner. Charcuterie stalls had mouth-watering displays of hams and salamis. The varied and pungent cheeses were also much in demand.

Early morning sunshine had been replaced by a grey drizzly

sky. Madame al-Haddad's stall was located at the perimeter of the market where the traders selling clothes and footwear were clustered under covered stalls. Keeping their merchandise dry would be a challenge until the market wound down at four o'clock.

'*Salut Madame al-Haddad,*' Reynaud said. 'Business is good today?'

She smiled.

'When it rains people don't buy, they just want to keep dry.'

Fabrice chatted to the 'old crow' running the stall beside Madame al-Haddad. She was unsure what to make of it. She had seen this one before and he seemed to be one of those Police who treated her kind like something you wiped off your shoe. Now he was all chat, quizzing her about the footwear she sold and asking about a warm pair of boots for the approaching winter.

During her ten years in the market, she had seen very few cops buy anything from the stalls. Reynaud bought stuff occasionally from her neighbour, cheap tee shirts for his summer holidays in the South, but little else. Were the Police trying something new, ingratiating themselves with the traders?

After five minutes Reynaud wished Madame al-Haddad *au revoir* and the young Sergeant quickly lost interest. Reynaud asked him if he found what he was looking for and he replied, 'Not this time.' The 'old crow' turned to her neighbour and hiked a thumb in the direction of the departing cops.

'*Connards!*' she spat contemptuously, annoyed that her efforts had been wasted.

Aline al-Haddad smiled inwardly at her neighbour's disgust at not making a sale, even to a cop. She hoped Omar would take up Reynaud's invitation to help at the Club he had enjoyed so much growing up. If he did, she wouldn't worry about him so much. She told Reynaud she would pass on his request, but clarified that Omar had left on a trip earlier that morning without telling her where he was going.

Reynaud and his apprentice left the market to continue their neighbourhood patrol. Neither noticed the green Kawasaki scooter that shadowed them all the while.

The night-time weather in Brittany was as anticipated; drizzly and cold. The command post was not quite as high-tech as Kate envisaged. It was cramped, fitted out to accommodate three people with an array of equipment that lined two sides. McManus was pinned into a corner trying to remain inconspicuous. He passed the time reading a local newspaper that one of Fenaux's crew had given him. His ear was tuned to the routine bursts of radio traffic, which he interpreted for Kate. Surveillance required split-second decisions, a mixture of instinct and experience. When the action hotted up, she needed to be clued in.

Mac called with details on Strain that had been dug out of archived files.

'He disappeared in 1987. Suspected of being one of three men who robbed £128,000 from a bank in Cork city.'

'What about the other two?'

'They disappeared as well after the raid, no trace.'

'They all got clean away?'

'I don't think so. Families of the two we haven't heard of since were in contact with the Victims' Commission.'

The Independent Commission for the Location of Victims' Remains was set up as part of the Belfast Peace Agreement. It sought to obtain information that might help locate the remains of victims of paramilitary violence, mainly suspected informers.

'The families of these two suspects have demanded that their sons be included in the Commission's work,' Mac told her.

'Do you think Strain played a part in disappearing them?'

'If they are dead; I'd strongly suspect so.'

'Okay to share this with our colleagues?'

'Of course! Call me if anything happens.'

'Will do.'

Kate told Fenaux the news on Strain and she examined the photos of his house and surroundings from the briefing. It was an impressive Normandy dwelling. In Kate's opinion, it had to be way above Strain's Forestry Service pay scale.

'Are they loaded?' she asked.

McManus clarified and without a second thought, Fenaux replied in French.

'Not at all. His wife works in a local bar. Her father works on the boats transporting new Peugeots and Citroens from Paris to Le Havre along the Seine. Nice work but a bit like a cop's salary, you won't be poor but it won't make you rich either. Strain bought the house twenty-five years ago, no mortgage, no loan, nothing in France.'

'Mac thinks there's a good chance Strain killed his associates and kept the money.'

'*C'est valide* this theory. A house like Strain's is not cheap.'

Mac's intelligence cast Strain in a whole new light; ruthless and connected. Kate messaged Digger and Angie by secure text with Strain's updated profile. It appeared Strain owed the IRA a debt that O'Hare was calling in.

Chit-chat at the command post quickly dried up. It boasted an espresso machine but Kate stopped using it when caffeine overload induced a thumping headache. She focused on the thirty-minute radio checks with Digger and Angie into the night. All was quiet as the clock tiptoed into the early morning hours.

Traffic on the N12 eased after one o'clock as the damp cold of the night seeped into the dig-in team. Digger was bored. The only things moving in the countryside were scavenging rats.

At 6:15 a.m. a sullen sky lightened and radio cackle began in earnest. McManus's sleepy brain kicked into gear admirably quickly. The truck team called in the registration number of a dark Citroen C5 that had made its second drive-by the service stop. It had to be checked out.

Dubois ran the plates, then looked at Fenaux and smiled.

'Alors Yves, on va boucler la boucle aujourd'hui.'

Kate looked to McManus.

'We're in business – we complete the picture today.'

'The car belongs to a local Breton Libre sympathizer,' Fenaux said.

'The Celtic cousins,' Kate replied. 'Are they active at the moment?'

'Not especially, but militant protest is always strong around here.'

'I wonder is this what McElgunn was talking about? It seems a nice easy job for them.'

'He is O'Hare's closest ally?' Fenaux asked.

Kate nodded.

'I guess we're going to find out what the Celtic cousins are up to now they've surfaced.'

The picture quality was poor but they could make out what was happening. The Breton drove into the service stop and parked in front of the restaurant. The owner shook his head indicating he was not yet open for business. The Breton made a hand gesture that Kate took to be uncomplimentary because Fenaux and Dubois both laughed. The suspect jumped back into his car and drove off.

Fenaux's phone intercepts confirmed that the Breton was a scout. Strain received a call on his mobile telling him all was clear, just one truck in the parking. Strain had slept for four hours after turning off the lights at his house. He got up at 3:30 a.m., drove the 4 x 4 out of the garage, and was en route. Fenaux's team was tailing him and the phone call confirmed that he was headed in their direction. Kate flashed Mac a text – *action imminent*.

Strain drove his battered dark green Toyota Land Cruiser into Porz an Park service stop at 7:30 a.m. There were a few other cars dotted around the parking area.

'Why so early?' Kate wondered aloud.

'What do you mean?' Fenaux asked.

'He's not supposed to meet Nutser until 10:30, he's way too early.'

McManus's simultaneous translation made communication flow seamlessly.

'Maybe we read the code wrong.'

'Maybe! If Nutser shows, we'll know for sure.'

'Any thoughts on Strain's mode of transport?'

'Not the vehicle I would choose to drive 400 kilometres in,' Kate replied.

'Maybe he needs it for where he's going.'

They watched Strain for ten minutes as he took in his surroundings; a cool customer. Finally, he got out and used a key to lock up. He had mousy-coloured, greasy hair. He wore it long like he couldn't let go of the seventies and the dark workman's coat he wore had an oily slick on its collar. A few inches over six feet, he was heavyset, as if he had enjoyed years of good French cooking. He walked to the restaurant, en route throwing a cursory glance at the flat tyre on the truck.

'Is he meeting Nutser somewhere else?' Kate asked.

'Can't be sure,' Fenaux replied. 'His 4 x 4 can drive cross-country though; difficult to follow.'

'Maybe it's because of the row. Perhaps he had no choice of transport; his wife took their other car to Mama's house.'

'Maybe.'

'Do you think there could be another reason?'

'We know he intends to be away from home overnight. We know he has purchased welding rods. Any work he has planned will surely be in an isolated place. We need to be prepared for this.'

Dubois said something that Kate didn't understand.

'Air cover,' McManus told her.

'Remind me why we haven't put a tracker on this vehicle,' Fenaux snapped at his second-in-command.

'Because of the dogs, we didn't want to spook him.'

'Do it now,' Fenaux commanded.

Dubois ordered two crews to the service stop. Both were mixed, male and female, with three members each. They worked fast. One team parked on the opposite side of the car park from Strain's while the other entered the restaurant in case he decided to exit. Their job was to run interference, distract or delay him, if necessary.

The tracker crew did their job swiftly. They were exiting the car park when Angie texted Kate a 'heads up' message. Almost simultaneously the dig-in crew called it in. A motorcyclist and pillion passenger were arriving. Dubois acknowledged the sighting and told those in the restaurant to order more coffee. Much to Kate's frustration, the command post had no visuals inside the restaurant.

The bike was a Honda 750 CC, burnt red colour, old enough to be a classic by the look of it, and in super condition. Dubois had to silence admiring radio chit-chat from the teams that could see it. He was only interested in the riders.

They parked in the bay occupied minutes earlier by the beacon crew.

'The rider's female,' Kate said.

Fenaux chuckled.

'We can see that.'

The camera shot of the pair was not very clear. The rider helped the pillion passenger remove his helmet. She moved confidently and stowed the helmet in the rear pannier. The camera caught the passenger's image as he rubbed his face.

Fenaux sighed.

'What?' Kate asked. 'I mean *who*?'

'Little Omar.'

'Our Omar al-Haddad from Paris?'

'The same.'

'He looks different from the picture you showed at the conference back in May; older.'

'That picture was two years old. The beard changes him.'

'It's not just the beard, he looks harder somehow.'

The pair walked separately towards the restaurant. Angie told Kate the rider was buying cigarette papers and tobacco. Omar queued for coffee fidgeting nervously at the patchy beard on his chin. The rider paid for her purchases, used the restroom, and exited through the rear door, pulling her helmet back on before leaving at speed. The bike was listed to a local woman with no previous terrorist traces. Fenaux ordered that she be let go. He would investigate her later.

'Another Celtic cousin?' Kate asked.

'Maybe,' Fenaux replied.

'What about air cover?' Dubois reminded Fenaux.

'I'll ask the Gendarmerie to get a fixed wing up,' Fenaux said. 'I spoke to the Colonel last week and told him we'd be operating in his neck of the woods. He told me to call if we needed assistance but I didn't expect to be requesting it so soon.'

'The plane can bounce the signal to us and we'll stay well back until they go to ground,' Dubois told Kate.

She agreed it was the best solution.

The restaurant crew reported that Omar had joined Strain at his table and they were chatting in French. Snatches of conversation were overheard. Strain asked him if he had been tailed. The young passenger replied that on the final leg, he was too busy holding on for dear life to notice. Strain laughed, telling him that using the bike was a good idea. Strain spoke of getting hands dirty and a long night ahead.

For us too, Kate thought.

36

WHEN THEY LEFT the restaurant Strain did not hang about. Once on the motorway, he pushed the 4 x 4 to its limits, maintaining a steady hundred and thirty-five kilometres per hour until Morlaix came into view.

Fenaux managed to keep two teams ahead and two to the rear. Two more were keeping pace on parallel roads. Angie and Digger quit their observation posts and were part of the chase crews. The 4 x 4 stayed on the N12 past Morlaix before veering onto a side road heading in a westerly direction. The command post kept pace, five kilometres to the rear.

The switch to rural roads altered the tempo of the pursuit. The long straight stretches of road cast Kate's mind back to a childhood camping holiday, with her mother driving their beat-up car between the ferry port and campsites; a trip that seemed never-ending.

They passed a green oval sign with an image of an animal resembling a weasel. Kate asked Fenaux what it meant.

'*Les Parcs Naturels Régionaux*, this is their symbol.'

Up ahead another sign indicated that they were entering *Le Parc Naturel Régional d'Armorique.*

'What the hell is in here?' Kate asked.

Fenaux watched the blinking dot on his tracking screen.

'Trees. He's heading for the forest.'

It made perfect sense. Strain knew how forests in the region functioned. It was mid-week, the weather was inclement, and there were no school holidays in sight. The forests would be deserted. For close to fifty kilometres, they skirted the forest's edge.

'Perhaps it's the coast,' Fenaux mused. 'Maybe they're taking something off a boat.'

Alarmed, Kate said, 'Crap! Was McElgunn talking about something at sea when he talked about Celtic cousins surfacing?'

Her comment spooked Fenaux. He turned to Dubois.

'How far is the coast?'

'Let me check the nearest ports.'

'Check nuclear power stations in the region also.'

Radio chatter cut in as he looked at Kate.

'Al Qaeda taking lessons from the IRA. *C'est crapuleux!*'

McManus interpreted the radio message.

'They've parked up.'

Fenaux sighed.

'*Mais alors!* At last.'

He pored over the maps and confirmed the location as a forest car park close to Hanvec. McManus googled it on his iPad and found that fewer than two thousand souls lived there. Fenaux pointed it out on the map. It lay on the northwest tip of the nature reserve. The time was 9:55 a.m.

Thirty minutes later Angie's text informed Kate that a grey Ford Transit van had arrived. Minutes later she identified its occupant – '*Nutser's here*', she messaged.

Fenaux greeted the identification with a mixture of delight and trepidation.

'The code analysis was good.'

'Greetings and introductions,' was Angie's next text.

Nutser had brought doughnuts and coffee which they consumed outside the vehicles despite the drizzle. The van was a left-hand drive. Clever, Kate thought, blends in perfectly.

'They're moving,' Fenaux announced, five minutes later. The dot on his screen showed Strain's 4 x 4 setting off along an uncharted forest route. He ordered all crews to back off; they would have to rely on technology for now.

The dot slowed and changed direction as Fenaux's phone rang. The Gendarmerie Colonel. He didn't welcome the distraction but put the call on speaker and kept his eyes on the moving dot. The Colonel informed him that the plane they relied on to bounce the signal from the beacon on Strain's jeep could stay airborne for four hours. After that, it would have to refuel. He also informed Fenaux that General de Hautecloque conveyed his best wishes for a successful operation. Fenaux's expression changed to a broad grin.

'Was he at the first Paris conference?' Kate asked.

'Correct. He's been promoted to two-star General, he'll make sure we get what we need.'

The 4 x 4 was driving deeper into the forest but slowing down. They estimated that it was three kilometres from the car park.

'Looks like terrain that will be difficult to cover covertly and fast,' Kate said.

After five minutes the dot on the screen froze. Fenaux issued a 'hold position and standby' command to all crews. As he considered his next move, he absent-mindedly flicked at strands of hair on his forehead. Up close, Kate noticed the grey flecks through it.

'Let's test the General,' Fenaux said as he dialled.

McManus gave Kate a shrug.

'Salut mon Général,' was the only bit Kate understood. Their conversation was brief.

McManus's three scribbled words conveyed the rest, *Requesting a drone.*

'D'accord, j'attend ton appel,' Fenaux ended the call. Kate understood he was waiting for a callback.

'Rolling the dice,' she quipped.

Fenaux looked over his shoulder at McManus who clarified the risk-taking analogy.

'It's a big ask, but the stakes are high.'

He threw the door of the command post wide open. It had been a nerve-wracking few hours but at least the weather was improving. He looked whacked and cracked his knuckles as he stretched.

Kate stamped her feet to get the blood circulating. After hours in the cramped command post, the fresh air was welcome.

'What's your plan?'

'We'll get a fresh crew into the forest,' Fenaux replied. 'Take it carefully but get as close to where they've stopped as quickly as we can.'

'What do you need from us?'

'Can you stay and see where the operation goes from here?'

'Whatever they're up to, it started with us. We have to see it through. Can you get us hiking gear?'

'Gear will not be a problem. I'm grateful you stay. Do you want your crew to rest now?'

'You will be setting up OPs?'

'Absolutely.'

'We would need to get to them by dusk.'

Fenaux agreed.

'Anywhere to bunk down nearby?'

'Use our campervan,' Fenaux said.

'Perfect.'

'The recon crew will identify observation posts that your crew can use. We'll mark a route that will get you there fast.'

'See you in the p.m.,' Kate replied and hopped into a waiting car.

37

IT WAS eleven o'clock when they reached the rendezvous with the six-berth camper, parked on a municipal campsite outside Le Faou. McManus and Digger dropped their shoes outside under the van, grabbed two sleeping bags, and climbed into the bunk over the cab.

Kate remained outside and briefed Mac on their progress. There were only two other paying customers on the site, a caravan and another campervan. Both appeared empty. She told him what had happened in the early hours, where they had ended up, and what their immediate plans were.

'You're getting some sleep. Good! Fenaux is looking after you, so,' he said.

'Yeah, all good so far. Anything at your end?'

'Butler might have something.'

'What?'

'Slurry tanks.'

'Slurry tanks?'

'Yeah, we have intel on four farmers who recently built new

slurry containment tanks on the periphery of their farmyards. It can't be coincidental that all are IRA sympathizers.'

SIU's experience told them that when the Provos dealt with the Libyan dictator Colonel Ghadafi, he gifted them huge consignments of weaponry which they imported clandestinely into Ireland. In advance, the Provos put a coordinated strategy in place to secure them. Many weapons were stored for years in underground bunkers disguised as farmyard slurry tanks.

'That's interesting,' she said. 'Updates later.'

By the time she got inside the van, Digger was snoring. McManus twisted and turned beside him, trying to escape the incessant din. Kate offered him a set of earplugs, which he gratefully accepted. She took out a sleeping bag and lay on the opposite side of the bed where Angie was quietly sleeping. Sleep came fitfully.

In the middle of the afternoon, everyone stirred. Digger checked the stubble on his chin and decided to leave it. Instead, he retrieved his boots from under the camper and went for a walk around the site. Kate asked McManus to go shopping in the village and he sauntered off with a smile on his face. Angie used the tiny bathroom to freshen up before offering Kate the cramped facility.

'What an *épicerie*!' McManus said when he returned. 'And a fabulous *boulangerie* right next door.'

'Just give us the grub,' Digger said. 'I'm starvin'.'

They put together ham and cheese bread rolls from McManus's shopping. They devoured some and wrapped a reserve for later. They gulped down instant coffees before one of Fenaux's crew arrived and drove them back to the command post. Fenaux and Dubois were inside; neither had gotten sleep.

'All refreshed?' Fenaux asked.

'As refreshed as an hour or two in a campervan will get you,' Kate replied, smiling.

Her eyes were already looking past him, drawn to the photographs pinned on the message board inside the command post. Their clarity was amazing.

'Were these taken from a helicopter?' she asked.

'No,' Fenaux replied 'it's a new system that needed testing. I provided a live environment.'

'Your General friend came through.'

'What altitude were they taken from?' Digger asked.

'More than two thousand meters.'

'Seven thousand feet,' he whistled. 'Impressive! You were lucky with the weather.'

'We got forty minutes when the clouds pushed back enough to get in and out.'

Angie studied the picture of three figures standing outside the open door of the forest shed.

'None of them looked skyward.'

Fenaux began the briefing as the crew pulled wet gear. The photos were a huge help. The three suspects were in a forestry service workshop. Their vehicles were parked at the rear. Nutser's van contained a forklift truck that was still on board, the lifting forks were visible in one photo.

During the day Fenaux's crew had set up OPs around the workshop. Two cameras gave live feed, but the angles were poor.

'They have put timber from a crate into Strain's 4x4,' Fenaux continued. 'It looks identical to the one in the photos you showed in Paris.'

'Anything else?' Kate asked.

'From the noises, we hear we think they're working with metal.'

'Okay.'

She picked up a small backpack and headed out of the command post.

'Point us in the right direction and we'll get out of your hair.'

Fenaux sounded surprised.

'You are going in yourself?'

'Yes. McManus will stay with you and interpret as required. I need to be on the ground to command effectively. I want to see whatever comes out of that shed up close; we don't want to make a wrong move and come up empty-handed.'

'Logical, I suppose.'

'Besides, you need to catch forty winks.'

McManus filled in the comprehension gaps.

'You need to air out that Poste to have any chance of staying alert,' Kate said.

Fenaux and Dubois laughed and waved them off.

Dusk settled over the forest and the pungent smell of pine filled their senses. Kate, Digger, and Angie followed Fenaux's crew who had reconnoitred tracks leading to observation posts. A point man advanced fifty meters ahead, pistol drawn. He indicated where Strain had cut the lock off a barrier encountered on a forest track. He had replaced it with an identical one with a suitably worn look. Nothing left to chance.

It was deadly quiet. As they progressed deeper into the forest their advance slowed. They clicked night sights into place as the gloom of the thickening forest sucked out the light. They carried backpacks with rations and a rain sheet. Their gear was basic, dark, and moisture-resistant; they hoped it would keep out most of the threatened rain.

An hour after leaving Fenaux they reached the OPs. The exercise invigorated Kate. She couldn't dig in but her elevated position shaded by the trees gave some advantage. Surveillance would be awkward and difficult. The rain started and huge spluttering drops cascaded from the trees. A long night lay ahead. Before departing, Fenaux's guide double-checked that everyone knew the fall-back protocol.

Kate's advice was to put SIU in a forward position and be patient; not to move too soon and risk getting only half the picture. Fenaux's crew was down a slope to the rear of the shed. Remote cameras covered the two other sides. They hunkered down, watched, listened, and waited.

Kate asked Digger if he could identify the intermittent sound. He closed his eyes and listened intently.

'Weldin',' he said.

'Are you sure?'

The perfect pitch black at the heart of the forest was undisturbed.

'How come there are no flashes?' Kate whispered.

'Blackout blankets on windows, maybe.'

'Certain?'

'That's a weldin' sound. Some steel cuttin' too.'

'Any chance of picking up some audio?' she asked.

'Cover me.'

'Better tell Fenaux first, it's his gig.'

Kate informed McManus to alert the French of the play they were making. Fenaux was wary but gave the go-ahead.

Digger took a wide arc around the shed and approached it from the rear. He chose an entry point for the tiny microphone behind the area where the targets worked. He had tested the gear with Fenaux's techies when he arrived and knew it would be recorded for transcription.

The French legal system differed from the Irish one. In France, a judge, a prosecutor really, was in charge of and already aware of much of the case. Fenaux briefed him on how the investigation was running and *'Monsieur le Juge'* mostly agreed with his strategy. Any audio picked up might be vital in a chain of evidence to put the suspects away for long stretches.

Throughout the twenty minutes it took Digger to get set up, Kate had her Sig Sauer pistol drawn; ready, if she had to move fast. McManus updated her on what he could see on screen.

'We're up,' Digger whispered when he got back.

'Great work. Let me know if you hear anything interesting.'

Excitement over, Kate settled down to wait out the rest of the night. The rain stopped. The three suspects emerged periodically to relieve themselves in the forest. None showed any awareness that they had company.

At 5:30 a.m. things cranked up a gear.

'Strain wants to move out,' Digger announced.

Kate listened as McManus interpreted the message for the other crews. The adrenaline began coursing through her body as she watched Nutser emerge and stretch as dawn began to win the battle with the night. He scratched his groin and rubbed his eyes before disappearing behind the building. He pulled the Transit around and positioned it in front of the workshop. He opened the rear doors and pulled down steel ramps to reverse the forklift off the vehicle. The racket from its engine shattered the pre-dawn peace of the forest.

'The smart bastard,' Digger said. 'He's suppressed the reversin' alarm.'

Digger and Kate moved to agreed positions when the action began. Angie crawled cautiously to join them.

'He's pretty nifty with it,' Kate said.

They watched silently. Nutser swung the machine around and directed it into the shed. Digger's audio picked up Strain shouting directions. When the forklift emerged, Kate looked at the others and gave a thumbs-up. Their suspicions about the Carlingford crate were confirmed.

The contents had been assembled into three mortar tubes

secured in a metal frame. The frame was made up of forty-millimetre box steel, straightforward to work with, and very strong when welded. The Barrack Buster, Kate thought. Experience told her that the projectiles would be propane gas cylinders packed with Semtex and homemade explosives. Nails or metal shards would be added to the mix to inflict maximum casualties.

Strain and Omar walked up the ramps at the rear of the van and guided him. Nutser worked deftly to position the rack inside the van. Strain picked up a heavy drill and quickly cut four holes into the corners of the unit. He then took four large bolts and unscrewed the nuts that came with them. He handed the nuts to Omar, together with four pieces of flat steel plate. Omar disappeared underneath. They began securing the unit to the body of the van.

Digger attached a camera to the telescope he used on every job.

'I got to get this,' he said.

'What?' Kate whispered.

'The writin' on the mortar tubes.'

She checked out the green cursive script. They couldn't decipher it. Kate thought it was Arabic. Nutser slid the van door closed and went back into the shed. The encroaching daylight made it difficult to remain concealed. Digger's audio picked up Strain giving Omar orders in French. Omar sounded none too happy. Nutser removed heavy blankets from the shed windows front and rear and tossed them into the van. Omar completed his cleaning operation. Nutser collected the rubbish in a black bag which he threw into the van on top of the blankets. He drove the forklift onto the Transit and closed the back doors.

38

THE LOAD WEIGHED HEAVILY on the van's rear suspension. Strain locked the shed and jumped into the 4x4 with Omar. The two vehicles set off slowly in convoy, almost walking pace, back along the forest track towards the public car park. Nutser followed the route Strain carefully guided him along, keeping headlights off. As they locked the last barrier on the track Kate spoke urgently to Fenaux. They were hiking back fast to the rendezvous point.

'Let them go,' she suggested. 'Follow them, don't intercept yet.'

'*Pourquoi?*'

'Because there are no explosives, that's why.'

'No explosives?' he repeated.

'They only have the firing tubes for the mortars. They're planning a close-quarter attack but the van is not ready yet.'

'How do you know?'

'The roof is still in place. They need to cut out a section of the roof and replace it with something sprayed the same colour, so it's easy to remove.'

'What they're transporting and their actions are all the proof we need for conspiracy to commit a terrorist crime,' Fenaux said.

'What if they claim they were just making a film prop?'

'Get back here as quickly as possible and we'll talk.'

McManus was in full flow at the command post urgently conveying the weight and context of what Kate was trying to communicate. SIU had been caught out in the past jumping in early. Digger downloaded his shots when they re-joined Fenaux and he sent them to Paris for translation. Minutes later his office came back with the result. The report heightened the tension in the cramped space.

Islam's elemental message had been painted onto weapons that would bring death and destruction. The message on the first tube read *there is only one God*, the next one, *Mohamed is the Prophet of God*, and finally, *Islam is submission to God*. It sent a shiver through Kate to see the crude but deadly weaponry developed back home carrying a message intended for spiritual guidance.

'Given this,' Fenaux asked Kate, pointing to the laptop screen. 'Do you want to reconsider your advice?'

'It might strengthen your conspiracy case but I advise follow rather than intercept right now. And there's something else you need to think about.'

Dubois was on the radio, busy coordinating the chase cars. Fenaux sounded tired and anxious.

'What's that?'

'Given what's written on the mortar tubes, whatever is being planned is not an IRA attack.'

Exhausted, Fenaux only spoke French now.

'I'm confused. Are you changing your mind, saying it's our problem now?'

McManus, at Kate's shoulder, interpreted rapidly.

'No. What I'm saying is that what we've seen is part of something bigger. I think O'Hare still has a role to play.'

'You have seen this method of operation before?' Fenaux asked.

'Mac many times, me once; we should be patient.'

'We will have to see if *Monsieur le Juge* agrees.'

The evidence was enticing for any investigating magistrate; Kate knew as much. Three suspects could be arraigned and there was the international terrorist conspiracy element. He would have sensational photographs of the homemade weaponry to show the media. It would bolster the country's image of winning the fight against terrorism. Kate believed they had only half the story. Fenaux would have to use all his powers of persuasion to convince the judge to delay and allow them to get the rest.

The two-vehicle convoy was moving south along route N165. Kate released Digger and Angie to join the chase crews. The command post went mobile and alongside Dubois and McManus she was strapped in a seat in the back as they brought up the rear. Up front, Fenaux was having an intense conversation with *M. le Juge*. McManus scribbled translation notes. Kate told him to leave it. She trusted Fenaux to tell it as it was. He looked over his right shoulder briefly when he ended the call.

'We keep going.'

Nutser drove to an industrial estate lockup near Lorient, a 110-kilometer journey that ordinarily would take just over an hour. He was ultra-cautious and maintained a steady speed all the way. Ninety minutes after leaving the forest, he parked up. Strain didn't enter the estate but was not far away. He had followed the van to Lorient, keeping five or six cars between him and his associate at all times. Both he and Omar were on high alert.

Digger followed Nutser's progress through the estate with

his scope. He returned on foot, crossed a busy road, and went into a McDonalds. He ordered coffee and doughnuts and sat down at a table on the drive-through side of the building. After five minutes he stood up and drained his coffee. The remaining half of his doughnut in his mouth, he pulled on his denim jacket and headed for a side entrance. He jumped into Strain's beat-up transport, two cars back from the ordering hatch.

On exiting the drive-through, Strain swung right and headed towards the ring road from where he took the D465 heading south.

'Where to now?' Fenaux asked.

Kate expanded the map on the Sat Nav and saw the nearest large town was Nantes.

'Nutser could be heading home.'

Fenaux turned fully around in his seat and faced her.

'Home?'

'Ryanair has regular flights in and out of Nantes to Dublin or Cork. Penny gets a Pound that's where he's headed.'

McManus clarified her gambling analogy.

'Let him go, for now, we still have only half the story,' Kate said. 'But a good half, lots to work with.'

Dubois looked to Fenaux, who nodded.

Dubois sent an advance crew to Nantes Atlantique Airport. By the time Strain pulled into the set-down area, they had travelled two hundred and eighty-two kilometres from the forest. Nutser jumped out carrying what looked like an overnight bag. It would have no trouble passing Ryanair's strict rules on cabin baggage sizes. He did not say goodbye or look back and Strain headed the 4 x 4 straight for the airport exit.

Fenaux's crew split up. Some stayed with Nutser and the rest took up on Strain who headed towards the centre of Nantes. He wolfed down the burger and chips along the way.

'Is he looking for another McDo?' Dubois speculated. 'How could he still be hungry?'

Instead, Strain drove to the city centre, onto boulevard Stalingrad, and dropped Omar at the SNCF train station. Dubois gave the go-ahead to two of his team to purchase tickets and follow him back on the TGV to Paris.

Angie sat with her knees tucked under her chin in the back seat of the Peugeot 508 in Nantes airport's arrivals car park. She would pass for any petulant teenager. Patrick, the crew-cut wise guy from the briefing sat up front in the driver's seat. Forty-five minutes after they took up position, the Ryanair flight from Dublin was confirmed on time. Using a British passport, John 'Nutser' Treacy, checked in.

Passengers streamed from both exits of the Boeing aircraft minutes after it touched down. Crew-cut's team watched as the outgoing queue began to shuffle. They radioed him and requested confirmation of earlier instructions. He double-checked with Dubois and acknowledged the reply. The sigh told Angie there was no change of plan.

Within thirty minutes of arriving, airport workers had re-fuelled the aircraft and the pilot completed his walk-about inspection. As the jet roared down the main runway with its fresh passenger load, Crew-cut punched the Peugeot's steering wheel.

'*Putain,*' he swore at the departing plumes of aviation fuel.

'*Beidh lá eile,*' Angie's uncertain Irish assured him from the back seat.

He regarded her gruffly in the rearview mirror.

'What does this mean?'

'There will be another day.'

He gunned the Peugeot's heavy diesel engine and headed back to Morlaix as ordered by Dubois.

Kate arranged for a team to take up on Nutser in Dublin

when he caught the Belfast bus on arrival at the airport. A hasty agreement with Symons allowed an SIU team to stay on him across the border into Newry where an MI5 crew took over. Nutser slept most of the way; the only contact made was with a girl who slipped into the seat beside him at the airport. He asked her to wake him before she got off at Newry. He left the coach in the centre of Portadown and walked home. It was twenty-four hours before he was seen again.

O'Hare was wary. The constant shadows in his locality were unrelenting. Nevertheless, everything was moving forward. He held a late-night meeting with Nutser and received a glowing report. Nothing unusual had happened during his five-day trip. The mortars were assembled without a glitch. The young French lad, Omar, had impressed him, a good operator, even if a bit peevish about being told what to do. His associates had fired homemade weapons in Afghanistan and understood how to arm and fire the mortars. O'Hare double-checked with Strain that everything had gone as described. They never spoke directly. Both left messages on the troublesome secret phone that Strain checked daily. It was relocated following his wife uncovering it and misinterpreting its purpose.

'Everything went grand,' Strain's message said. 'It was so quiet, you could have heard a mouse fart in that forest.'

There was one final part of the bargain before O'Hare could concentrate on his war. The final key that would unlock the supply of arms he needed to sustain the young volunteers who would gather around him. The unique inside contact the Paris radicals had generated was a once-in-a-lifetime opportunity. By the time O'Hare helped them engineer their audacious attack, his arsenal would be en route to Ireland. He believed that the

British would never leave Ireland of their own accord. The Peace Agreement had not changed his view. The Paris radicals would claim the attack as their own. He might even get Bob McElgunn to orchestrate a mob outside Theipval Barracks in Lisburn to sing 'Britannia Rules the Waves' on the day he proved precisely the opposite.

39

THE PRESSURE on Fenaux when he returned to Paris was immediate and sustained. His operational decision not to make arrests was derided. Senior colleagues, starved of surveillance resources for weeks, openly questioned his decision not to end the operation in the forest.

When a case update reached the Interior Ministry, political pressure on the DGSI head of service grew intense. He summoned Fenaux and warned him to wind up the case without delay. Fenaux called a twenty-four-hour notice case conference to break the news. Before leaving his office to open it, he spoke to the judge in charge of prosecuting the case.

'I know you are under time pressure, Yves, so I will keep it brief.'

'Thank you, Judge.'

'I intend to charge al-Haddad and the two Irish men with preparing a terrorist act and possession of the mortar weapon. I will issue a European Arrest Warrant for Treacy, the suspect who lives in Northern Ireland; I doubt the British will have any issue with extraditing him. By the time your full investigation concludes, I expect we will get more charges.'

'What about the other suspects?'

'We'll round them all up and see what comes from interrogations. We should at least get a conspiracy charge.'

'Give me another week before moving to arrests,' Fenaux asked.

'*Pour l'amour du ciel, pourquoi?*'

'The Paris group has advanced plans for an attack in France. We're very close to finding out the rest of this peculiar plot.'

'If you know they plan to carry out an attack, then surely the only thing to do is stop them.'

'With respect, Judge, if we don't find out their target, we may never again be in as good a position to uncover it.'

'My God, how do you expect me to hold off the politicians in the meantime?'

'Tell them you decided to charge all known suspects and that the operational timing of the arrests is a matter for the police.'

'You are playing with fire,' the judge warned Fenaux.

'Let me worry about that.'

O'Hare waited until his wife went shopping before packing a bag and preparing to leave. She was used to him being away for days on end and no longer asked questions. He stared out the bedroom window of his home and spotted the tail that would inevitably follow him when he left the house. When he went downstairs, he gave his bag to the teenage son of a neighbour already waiting in his kitchen. He instructed him to wait forty-five minutes before taking the bag to another address in the town where it would be collected from him.

He put on a dark green fleece and walked to the bookies where he placed bets on the first two races. He took a seat facing the window from where he observed the television screens dotted around the betting shop. Twenty minutes later, he tore up his betting slips and went to the toilet. He had clocked two different faces walking past the window and looking in. He removed the fleece jacket and dumped it in a rubbish bin before exiting the rear of the building.

A motorcycle, engine running awaited him. He quickly swapped places with the pillion passenger and pulled on the black leather jacket offered. As he tightened the strap on his helmet, he tapped the rider on the shoulder.

'Go, go, go!

By the time Symons's crew checked the toilet, the high-powered bike had made it to the M1 motorway, propelling O'Hare southwards.

<hr>

Kate and Mac flew into the Paris case conference with crosswinds buffeting their approach for landing. The autumnal city looked very different from earlier in the year. The search-light on the Eiffel Tower struggled to pierce the puffy rain clouds that hung over the city. From what Fenaux told them, his crews were watching the Lorient lockup and all was quiet. She had not expected to be back in France within days.

Two nights in Dublin with Charlie had been the sum of their time together since she returned from Brittany. She was impressed with Charlie's housekeeping skills. He had even changed the bed linen. As she left for Paris, he headed to rejoin his cruise ship at George Town in the Cayman Islands, via a London flight. They planned a skiing break in Austria when he returned.

Fenaux held the conference at his offices in Levallois-Perret. The morning meeting was set for ten-thirty. He seated Mac next to him with Dubois on his other side. He gave no outward appearance of the pressure he was under. The aerial shots from the forest were displayed behind them.

Apart from the French army general, everyone from their first conference was there. Symons, cheerless as ever, was accompanied by Daphne Clarke. Jeffers, the FBI European liaison, and Whatney from the CIA sat alongside four of Fenaux's analysts who completed the group. Fenaux began by recapping the Brittany-based segment of Operation Cassandra. Simultaneous interpretation kicked in on Kate's headphones as Fenaux rapidly outlined events, both in the forest and subsequently.

He passed on the judge's decision to arrest all suspects. He told the meeting the arrests would happen within a week. Turning to Symons he said, 'Treacy resides in Northern Ireland, so the judge will request his extradition through the proper authorities in the UK.

'Finally, action,' Symons replied. 'Our surveillance on O'Hare's gang is draining in every conceivable manner.'

Fenaux asked Mac for an update.

'Arms procurement is the other side of O'Hare's deal,' Mac began. 'Our intelligence indicates that somewhere in Rotterdam port there are containers of weapons awaiting pick up.'

'The Dutch are aware of this?' Jeffers asked.

'The AIVD is on board,' Mac replied.

Mac's boss, Assistant Commissioner Dominic Fox, was personally dealing with the General Intelligence and Security Service (AIVD) in Holland.

'Are the Dutch searching for the weapons?' Jeffers asked.

'We believe O'Hare's containers are warehoused in or near the port area. We don't have an exact location, so no searches yet.'

'What's holding them up being shipped to O'Hare?' Jeffers asked.

'It looks like O'Hare has a final part of a bargain to fulfil before his weapons are released,' Kate replied.

When the meeting concluded Symons and Clarke departed for the London train. Paris-based, Whatney and Jeffers hung back. Mac had elected to stay an extra night when Fenaux offered to show them where the three Paris suspects lived. Kate wondered what was to be gained by doing it but did not object to an extra night in Paris.

Fenaux suggested adjourning to a small bar across the street from his bland new office. He preferred the battered old building they had vacated in Paris before the move to the suburbs. Whatney and Jeffers tagged along. Fenaux had a special relationship with the Americans. Too often, French national pride and American cultural blindness kept the two countries poles apart. He was a practical cop, conscious of the sway America held around the globe. He believed that intel on how European Al-Qaeda cells functioned was most useful when shared.

'Tell the patron what you want,' he said, as they entered the café bar.

The men ordered beers, *grande pressions* all around. Kate took a Perrier. Mac and Fenaux stayed at the counter as the tray of clinking glasses was delivered to their table. Kate took the cue that he wanted a quiet word with Fenaux and chatted with the two Americans.

Mac had warned her not to mention intelligence Detective Sergeant John Casey from Rosslare had passed on as they boarded the Paris flight. Casey had picked up ripples from Customs sources that cigarette smugglers had purchased an old fishing boat. Cigarette smuggling was a lucrative business. It cost the Irish exchequer nearly €1 billion annually in lost excise.

O'Hare's slice of the action was providing a steady income for his nascent secret army.

The boat at the centre of Casey's intel was the *MV Raven*. The fleet register listed it as fifteen years old with a vessel identifier of RTB 11. It was 25.3 meters in length and had a maximum speed of twelve knots. The previous owner had been identified but was not yet interviewed. The vessel had departed early morning from Dunmore East on the south coast, forty-eight hours before Casey was told about it. Neither of the two-man crew that sailed her out of the harbour was known to local fishermen. The boat had not been seen along that stretch since. Kate had expected to spend the next few hours chasing up inquiries on it but perhaps Mac had changed his mind about sharing the intel.

As Fenaux and Mac re-joined the group, Whatney asked 'Could we tag along with you guys tonight?'

Fenaux frowned.

'A unique opportunity for us to see the suspects on their home turf.'

Fenaux raised his glass.

'*Santé*! I will arrange it.'

Back at the hotel, Mac told Kate he would follow up with Casey on the trawler report. He told her that he had shared the intel with Fenaux and seemed relieved that someone else in the Operation Cassandra circle was aware of it.

'Risky,' she said. 'It could turn out to be nothing.'

'We gotta take risks,' he replied, mimicking advice Whatney had proffered earlier.

'Pathetic,' she teased his attempt at an American accent.

Later that evening Fenaux sent a car to their hotel to pick them up. Whatney and Jeffers were already on board. The beat-up vehicle looked like it would blend in best at their destination rather than their midtown hotel district.

They wound their way along the périphérique and soon Seine-Saint-Denis signs began cropping up. Mac asked the driver about the mood in the *banlieues*. Riots were an annual event and often provoked political claims that their regularity was indicative of the fabric of French society tearing apart. As the blocks of La Courneuve loomed into view, the driver assured Mac the area was stable at the moment.

They pulled into an underground supermarket car park that was empty apart from police vehicles.

'Outer cordon rendezvous,' the driver announced.

Fenaux was there, accompanied by two vans with CRS written on the side. The CRS, *Compagnies Républicaines de Sécurité*, the riot police. Their reputation was fearsome. When the order to charge was given, no one in front of them was spared. Their blunt tactics earned them few friends in the media. Tonight, Kate was happy to have them watching her back.

Fenaux pointed to the CRS and smiled mischievously.

'In case things go to shit, our colleagues will extract us. In this location, we take no chances.'

Mac and Kate jumped into Fenaux's car and departed. Fenaux sat up front with his elbow propped on the back of the seat as he continued his briefing. It was a pose with which Kate had become familiar.

'So we get a new point of observation for tonight. It is better this way. No distraction to our colleagues in the main OP. Walk at a normal pace when you exit the vehicle, don't run. Kate, you will carry these shopping bags.'

'Sexist pig,' she joked.

Fenaux looked taken aback until Mac laughed.

'Don't worry — I get the picture you're trying to paint,' she assured him.

'We will stay two, maybe three hours if it is quiet. If for any reason I say we go, we go immediately. *D'accord?*'

A chorus of *d'ac's* assured him that everyone in the car got the message. In this neighbourhood, if you thought you had been burned, hanging about could get you killed.

Fenaux resumed watching everything around them.

'Dubois will give the Americans the same lecture.'

They pulled up near a block whose ground floor was peppered with graffiti. It was the only place in France Kate had seen *Fuck the Police* writ loud and proud. Most floors had lights on but there also seemed to be vacant apartments. She could only imagine the scale of the policing challenge. Staggering!

She surmised that the Nissan that pulled out ahead of them was one of Fenaux's crew guarding a parking slot close to the base. They bailed and walked slowly across the road into the block. The smell of urine and disinfectant hit them straight away. The driver diverted into the stairwell. He put one half of a threadbare blanket down, slumped to the ground, and pulled the other half around him. He placed a half-empty bottle of wine beside him and would stay there for the duration, guarding their vehicle until they needed to leave.

Fenaux's planning was impeccable. They entered an empty apartment on the tenth floor and switched on some lights. Kate dumped the bags and he signalled them across the corridor to another apartment that would function as the OP.

A nice distraction tactic, Kate thought.

There were no lights in the OP, all the bulbs had been removed. The gear enabling them to view the territory and the targets was already in place. Minutes later, as their eyes grew accustomed to the gloom, Whatney and Jeffers joined them.

'Saud's apartment is over there to the right,' Fenaux whispered, pointing across a wide concrete square. 'Fourth floor, count five windows in from the right edge of the building.'

There was plenty of public lighting but less than ten percent of it worked. It wasn't a place to walk about at night.

'Saud's the bomb maker, isn't that right?' Mac said softly.

'We believe he was trained in Afghanistan but cannot be certain,' Fenaux replied. 'He is the quietest. They've only been together as a group twice, each time outside the mosque after prayers.'

Kate asked quietly: 'Do you rate him as out of the picture?'

'Not at all, he's just the one we know least about.'

They took turns surveying the landscape over the next hour and a half.

'The light's just gone out over there,' Whatney said suddenly, as he looked through a scope. His American accent too loud for comfort.

Fenaux confirmed it and as he tuned into the reaction of his team on the ground, his phone rang. The CRS commander.

'There has been an incident at La Cité commissariat,' he told Fenaux. 'We have to deploy there immediately.'

'What's happening?'

'It's sketchy at the moment. I'm told there was an explosion when a colleague started his car.'

'*Merde!*' Fenaux replied. 'Okay, we'll leave now.'

Fenaux's team was tailing Saud and he headed towards the RER. The other two suspects were also on the move. Fenaux radioed the driver to get ready to leave. He didn't bring his blanket with him and for that *everyone* was grateful.

As they drove out of the estate, they saw fire engines racing towards La Cité, followed by two ambulances. Fenaux dialled his friend's number to find out what was happening at his old station. Christophe Reynaud did not pick up.

40

THE NEXT MORNING Mac and Kate rode the bus to the airport. Seeing La Courneuve in daylight as they flashed by on the motorway did nothing to improve their impression of the place. Mac's phone buzzed and, given the crowded bus, he answered cautiously. The colour drained from his face as he hung up.

'That was Fenaux. A friend of his was murdered at La Cité last night.'

'Oh my God! Was it Reynaud?'

'Yes.'

'Fenaux asked him to contact Omar, remember.'

'This is bad.'

'I should stay and see what I can find out.'

Mac agreed and Kate rang Bruno on her way back into Paris in a cab. He re-booked a room for her at her old hotel and arranged a meeting in the afternoon at DGSI headquarters in Levallois-Perret. When she linked up with Fenaux, his ragged appearance shocked her. A bottle of Scotch sat on his desk and he poured a large measure.

'You'll join me.'

More command than an invitation, Kate did not fancy its taste but thanked him. She swirled the peaty blend in her glass as Fenaux twisted his chair so he could gaze out the window. He had not slept, that much was evident.

'Everyone is shaken,' she said.

'What have I done, Kate?'

'Don't jump to conclusions, Yves. Now is the time to support one another.'

'I should never have asked Christophe to go near Omar.'

'You said he spoke to Omar's mother at the market each week, anyway.'

'Yes, that's true.'

'It's too early to say if the two things are connected.'

'You should see what it's like at La Cité,' he replied, his morose mood returning. 'I don't know how long we can hold back the younger agents at the commissariat. They want to pull in suspects and take revenge.'

He downed the whisky. Kate saw tears in his eyes.

'Let's go eat,' she suggested.

He waved a hand and replenished his glass. 'Later.'

'That won't make the pain go away.'

'I don't want to feel, I need to...' Fenaux trailed off. 'How will I face Yvette?'

'Reynaud's wife?'

Fenaux nodded.

'We've known each other since they were dating.'

'Get cleaned up and go comfort her. Bring Jeanne with you, they must know each other.'

'They do but I don't want to intrude on the family.'

'Surely, you would be welcome.'

'Kate, in France we deal with death differently to Ireland.'

'However you deal with it, getting drunk won't help.'

Fenaux stood up and walked to the window. On the street below, a young patron wearing a white apron cleared the pavement tables after the lunchtime rush. Fenaux liked the couple that had taken the café over recently. It was another normal day for them. For him, nothing would ever be the same.

Dubois's knock on his office door jolted him from the dark mood enveloping him.

'You need to hear this.'

Fenaux regarded his deputy cautiously as he accepted the phone.

'Oui,' he began.

Kate watched as the call developed, Dubois standing close to his boss all the while. Fenaux asked rapid questions and scribbled notes.

'A breakthrough?' she asked.

'Come, I'll tell you in the car,' Fenaux replied.

'I'm driving,' Dubois said, firmly.

As they drove to La Cité, Fenaux told her that a young Sergeant who Reynaud had been training in received a tip-off. The explosive device that killed their colleague was planted by a local drug gang. The tip-off had come from a clothes vendor that Reynaud had spoken to recently in a local market.

Fenaux didn't need to ask the name, he knew it was little Omar's mother. Madame al-Haddad told the young sergeant that she found a strange device in a cupboard at her apartment on the night of the attack. She wanted to call Reynaud but her son forbade it. He was behaving more and more erratically; away for days and returning late at night.

What turned out to be a pipe bomb was collected by a local drug dealer an hour before the attack. The dealer had been located and arrested and was on his way to the station. An alert was flashed around the Préfecture de Paris and surrounding divisions to arrest Omar al-Haddad on sight with a warning that he was highly dangerous and possibly armed.

By the time Kate left La Cité commissariat late that evening, she knew that the pipe bomb that killed Christophe Reynaud had most likely been put together by Ibn Saud. The main suspect admitted paying €200 for the device. The homemade explosive used was confirmed as potassium chlorate, the chemical mixture that makes matches ignite. It replaced calcium ammonium nitrate in Afghanistan as the choice for homemade explosives after the US stemmed the flow of fertilizer to regions in Pakistan, close to the Afghan border.

Madame al-Haddad's information confirmed where it had been stored until collection. Fenaux doubted either Saud or Omar had any idea of its purpose. Christophe Reynaud's success rate in putting away petty thieves had been cleaving chunks off the local drug gang's income and this was their response. Fenaux ordered that all the planned arrests in Operation Cassandra be made immediately.

As she waited to board the last Dublin flight at CdG airport, Kate figured that the operation would be as good as over by the time she reached home. Digger rang, a welcome relief from the boredom of hanging around waiting for her flight to be called.

'How did your meetin' go today?'

'You know what it's like when you lose one of your own. Everyone's pretty raw.'

'Any news on who did it?'

'They've got a suspect in custody. There's an indirect connection to Cassandra but I'll tell all when I'm home, I'm at the airport now.'

'Fair enough.'

The long pause that followed spelled trouble. Someone in the unit had done something stupid and Digger wanted Kate to find out before the news reached Mac's ears.

'What's up? Get it off your chest.'

'It's awkward.'

'Someone get caught offside?'

Boredom on ops sometimes led to people making decisions they later regretted.

'No, everyone's behavin',' Digger said. 'There's no problem with the unit, well not really.'

'For God's sake Digger, spit it out. What's wrong?'

'I met Vince Hyland today and he gave me a photo of two suspects he wants us to try and identify.'

'How is the smooth talker?'

Hyland was a legendary interrogator, adept at getting the most hardened hoods to fess up. He told anyone who cared to listen to how he did it, that the secret lay in minute preparation.

'He's fine, he's with CAB now; workin' the McElgunn case.'

'Great! Vince is the most meticulous guy I ever worked with.'

'Well, thanks a lot,' Digger replied.

'You know what I mean. He's a stickler for detail.'

'Yeah, he does my head in sometimes.'

'What's the story with the photo?' Kate asked.

'It's a handover; one suspect handin' a package to another.'

'Does anyone know either of them?'

'I haven't put it up on the squad room notice board yet but Quinlan has IDed one as an O'Hare new blood. You need to see the photo before I show it around. I think I recognize the other one.'

'Why do you want me to see it first?'

'I think the other guy is your boyfriend.'

'Oh my God!' Kate exclaimed.

Her mind went blank. Digger had seen Charlie's photo on her phone.

'Boss, you still there?'

'Yes.'

'I'll hold it 'til you get back. Don't jump to conclusions.'

'I have to tell Mac.'

'My advice is, don't,' Digger said. 'We'll scratch the surface and get deeper. Will I set up a meeting with Vince?'

'Put Vince off for a while. We'll give it twenty-four hours when I come home to find out where the connection is; then I'll break the news.'

'You want me to start diggin'?'

'Look at his phone records, I'll text you his number. Do it for the last six months. Let me know what jumps out at you.'

Kate felt queasy at the thought.

'There's another number I want you to check out,' she said.

She fished out a scrap of paper from the depths of her bag and called it out to Digger. It had been weeks since she uncovered the naked selfie on Charlie's phone. Something about his explanation did not ring true.

'See who owns that phone and check if there are any links back to O'Hare.'

'If we're goin' to keep it covert...' Digger began.

'I know, I know, I'll have to keep things the same between myself and Charlie.'

'Can you handle that?'

'Do I have a choice?'

41

KATE ARRANGED to meet Mac at the SIU base the next morning for a Fenaux update and to assess the future status of Operation Cassandra. They set the meeting for ten o'clock. At 8 a.m. Mac rang her.

'Office, one hour.'

'It's Saturday morning, what's so urgent?'

'Casey rang last night; he's coming here this morning.'

'Okay, I'm on my way.'

Kate had not slept well as she tried to process Digger's bombshell disclosure about Charlie. She hoped to mull over possible ways of breaking the news to Mac as she ate breakfast. First, she needed to check that Digger's identification was correct. She clung to a weak hope that he was mistaken.

Meantime she would put on a brave face and listen carefully to what John Casey believed they urgently needed to hear. He was a veteran investigator, not prone to exaggeration.

The weekend traffic was light. Kate picked up a coffee en route and made it to the base in less than half an hour. Casey was already sitting in the tiny space they dared call a conference room when she checked in.

'Give me two minutes, while I'll dump this cup.'

'Take as long as you like; you're paying my overtime.'

She headed to Mac's office where he was finishing a call.

'Murt Butler's downstairs; the boss is about five minutes out.'

'This must be good.'

'Best hear it from the horse's mouth.'

They arranged themselves around the conference table leaving the top seat free for the boss. Mac sat beside Casey and Kate settled in next to Butler on the opposite side. Butler had brought a forest of intel reports from the analysis section with him.

'You're happy with your source, John?' Mac asked.

'I've no reason not to be. I don't think he would deliberately mislead me.'

'Remind me why he came to you in the first place.'

'He approached me for help last year; his son was done for possession of heroin. I knew the young lad from the hurling and got the case tried in the District Court rather than sending it forward for trial.'

'What was the outcome?'

'The kid got probation, no conviction recorded against him. He's doing okay in rehab.'

The door opened, the boss strode in, and out of deference to his rank, everyone stood up.

'Sit down, sit down. It's Saturday morning for God's sake,' Dominic Fox told them.

He looked around, taking in the four of them.

'So what brings us here?'

Mac turned to Casey, 'John if you lay out your information I'll pick it up from there.'

Casey began without ceremony.

'Information I received last night tells me that the IRA, or whatever they're calling themselves these days, have secured a trawler. Last weekend they fitted steel plating to its hold in a small Arklow dockyard. They began late on Saturday evening and worked through the night to get it done. Two guys with Northern accents gave instructions on the detail of the work. Last night, my man identified one of those as Sean O'Hare.'

'Did you get a description of the other one?' Kate asked.

'Young, early 20's, the same height as O'Hare – around six foot, skinhead. My man didn't care much for him, an arrogant young prick.'

Fox looked in Kate's direction.

'Any ideas?'

'Sounds like Nutser Treacy.' She looked across the table at Casey. 'John, we know him, he's from Portadown. I'll get Digger to show you a photo to confirm.'

'Is your source solid, John?' Fox asked.

'He was forced to do the work. He's petrified that someone will find out he's spoken to me.'

'We need to register him as an intelligence source.'

'Commissioner, there's no point. He's a one-off. I don't think he has any more information to give.'

'Give me a profile on him anyway. I'll review it later. Where does this leave us, Mac?' he asked.

'John's informant said the boat went back in the water early on Sunday morning,' Mac replied. 'It hadn't much fuel. The Arklow fit-out is a prequel to something bigger.'

'Arklow is only eighty kilometres south of Dublin. Any thoughts on what that something bigger might be?'

'There has to be a link to France, Commissioner.'

'What's going on in France?' Casey asked.

'I'll bring you up to speed later,' Kate told him.

'Why weren't we aware that O'Hare knew so much about boats?' Fox asked. 'I thought he had a haulage business and smuggled cigarettes.'

Murt Butler pulled a report from the pile in front of him.

'There's the rub, Commissioner. Only this week, Symons told us that they found out O'Hare worked on trawlers out of Kilkeel for four years.'

'They only learned that recently?'

'He worked on trawlers off and on when he was released early from prison under the Good Friday agreement. The new Police Service of Northern Ireland was part of that deal but with all the resignations and new blood, it took them a while to build up local knowledge.'

'Remind me where Kilkeel is,' Fox asked.

'County Down, it's the largest east coast port in the North,' Mac said.

'On the Irish Sea.'

'Yes,' Mac replied. 'So, O'Hare is familiar with sailing conditions all down the east coast.'

'Another thing,' Casey continued. 'They put dampers under the steel plate.'

'What the hell are dampers?' Fox asked.

'Round industrial-sized pieces of dense rubber designed to cushion the hull from a sudden downward motion. It would keep the steel plating from piercing the sides of the trawler.'

The boss looked toward Mac.

'I'm stumped here on specifics but I'm damned sure we'll find a connection to France.'

'We know they have mortars hidden in France. Could the trawler be some elaborate sort of launch pad?'

'I don't know. I'm getting the D-I in Ballistics to brief me on possibilities later,' Mac replied.

'Are they contemplating a seaborne attack?'

'It would be a first, but I'd rule nothing out. The murder of the policeman in Paris has forced Fenaux to order the arrest of all the Cassandra suspects.'

'Any news on that?'

'I'm ringing him straight after this meeting to find out.'

A staff officer brought in coffee. In the lull, Kate gave Casey a rundown on the French connection. Before he departed, she tasked him with setting up a meeting between his source and a Ballistics expert. She wanted a blow-by-blow account of the work carried out on the boat. Casey wasn't optimistic but promised to push hard to make it happen.

'Fenaux knows we have a lead on a boat; I told him in Paris,' Mac said. 'I'll bring him up to speed.'

'Do it now and keep me posted. We had better brief the Secretary-General of the Department of Justice. Get a report prepared.'

With tasks delegated, Fox departed for his Saturday morning round of golf.

'Do you need me to stay on to help with the Justice report?' Butler asked.

'I'll put it together over the weekend,' Mac said. 'Come in early Monday morning and you can get it typed up.'

'The bastards are always one step ahead of us,' Butler said, gathering up his report pile.

'The Devil's children have the Devil's luck,' Mac replied, morosely.

Kate said. 'Let's hear what Fenaux's got.'

Fenaux sounded despondent when they called.

'*Ils sont disparus.*'

Mac picked up on the anxiety in his friend's voice and stuck with French.

'Disappeared? Who has disappeared?' he asked.

'All three Seine-Saint-Denis suspects disappeared after the explosion at La Cité.'

'*Merde!*' Mac said as he scribbled a note for Kate, *3 Islamic suspects missing*.

'You know how it is,' Fenaux said. 'You lose a target for a few minutes but pick them up quickly. My crews figured after losing sight of them for a short while they would find them again but they simply vanished.'

'Jesus! That can't be too comfortable for you.'

'These past two days have been a nightmare, Mac. The suspects have dropped anything traceable – all the mobiles, the scooter they were using for transport – all dumped.'

'They've moved on to the next phase. Has to be.'

'I should have ended it in the forest. We only have Strain in custody. One, just one prisoner. Symons tells us that they cannot locate Treacy.'

'Would ending it in the forest have saved your friend's life?'

'Who knows?'

'Don't beat yourself up over that, Yves. From what Kate tells me there was a different motivation behind the murder. Is Strain giving up any information?'

'For the past twelve hours, he's refused to answer any questions. Your embassy people are with him at the moment.'

Mac briefed him on the intel about the *MV Raven* – the fact that it was unaccounted for and the modifications carried out. With three key players in Operation Cassandra in the wind, it cast the intel in a sinister light.

'I'll put out a coastal alert immediately,' Fenaux said.

'Where will you focus it?'

'Mainly the ports along the north and west coast, we won't worry about the south for the moment.'

She scribbled a note and passed it to Mac. McElgunn's

cryptic prison remark about Celtic cousins surfacing still bugged her and she wanted to remind Fenaux that Breton sympathizers had to figure somewhere in the plot.

'We're still watching the lock-up at Lorient, but I'll refocus resources to the north-west coast – Saint-Malo to La Rochelle. I will brief the navy, maybe they will assist.'

'And remember, we still don't fully understand what McElgunn meant by the *Celtic cousins surfacing* remark,' Mac reminded him.

'I'll bear it in mind,' Fenaux said. 'Thank Kate for her advice, will you? Tell her it helped.'

'Okay.'

As Mac hung up, her private phone buzzed in her bag. She fished it out and checked the text message. It was Charlie, wanting to chat. She told him she was working and they could talk later. She needed to rapidly resolve the depth of his deception.

'Fenaux says to thank you for the advice,' Mac told her. 'What's that about?'

'Facing up to reality.'

She moved toward the door.

'I've got to go talk to Digger.'

She met him in the Cave, the name everyone gave the office where he worked on the gadgets and gizmos. He showed Kate the six-month printout of Charlie's mobile phone records.

'Something's not adding up,' he said.

'What?'

'From what you told me, Charlie is out of the country a lot of the time.'

'He is. He works on a cruise liner.'

'Well for the last two months, his phone is pingin' in Ireland.'

'What? That doesn't make sense. I mean I speak to him on Skype.'

'I'm only tellin' you what the phone records show.'

'I'll go through them at home.'

'There's something else.'

'What?'

'That other number belongs to Jacinta Fitzpatrick. Her husband is Sean, one of O'Hare's gang.'

'Is he the guy that McElgunn spoke to in Portlaoise prison?'

'The same. He's on remand for murder.'

Kate slumped in the chair.

'What's the connection?' Digger asked.

'Charlie knows her.'

'Oh!'

'What am I going to do?'

'Dump the asshole. Fast!'

'I have to tell Mac.'

'Don't, at least not yet. There's no reason to believe O'Hare's gang knows who you are. If you tell Mac now, he'll have to cut you out of the investigation.'

'Do you think?'

'Talk to Quinlan. He'll find out if there's talk around Dundalk about Fitzpatrick's wife.'

Kate sat staring straight ahead, trying to decide the best course of action.

Digger prodded. 'Better informed is better prepared. You know that's the way we always work. It gets results.'

'I can't talk to Quinlan about this. Would you?'

'Come on! You back down from nothin'. Face it full-on, it's the only way to beat it.'

Shielded in Digger's lair, nervous and fidgety, her fingers tapped her chin.

'Time to face reality, I guess. I'll call from here.'

As usual, Quinlan had his finger on the pulse of her hometown. He told Kate that the drums had been beating around Dundalk and he had picked up the vibes. The prisoner's wife was caught playing offside. The bloke with Jacinta Fitzpatrick had been spared a beating, or worse, by agreeing to help out O'Hare's gang. Quinlan hadn't been able to identify the philanderer but knew that he was from Dublin. He agreed to keep knowledge of her inquiry between them.

42

EARLY THE NEXT day Mac and Assistant Commissioner Fox sat side by side in the Justice Department's opulent conference room. As they began the Operation Cassandra briefing with the Secretary-General, Minister Patrick O'Hagan strode in and perched on the corner of the table.

'Commissioner Fox, you head up the State's Intelligence Service, is that correct?'

No formalities; Fox sensed an ambush.

'Good morning, Minister!' he began. 'Yes, I command one arm of it. As you are aware, the Army takes responsibility for the external threat.'

'Indulge me, if you will. What exactly is it you do?'

'Well, we analyse any internal threat to the nation's security. I am sure you read the intelligence threat assessments we provide periodically.'

'Indeed. Intelligence; what exactly does that word mean to you?'

'Commissioner, if you wish, I'll take that question,' Mac interrupted. 'There are technical explanations for intelligence, but the best way of understanding it is to see it as an intellectual process, regardless of how it is collected, the ultimate product is the result of smart people pondering what is known, what is unknown, and trying to determine what it all means.'

The Secretary-General surrendered his top-of-the-table chair to his Minister and he settled into it.

'So am I right in thinking that you analyse the information you receive and take appropriate countermeasures when a threat is perceived?'

'Precisely,' Fox replied.

'If that's the case, will you enlighten me as to why one of your officers advised our French colleagues that it was a good idea to allow persons, patently guilty of terrorist crimes, to go unhindered?'

'Minister, you will be aware that an international terrorist investigation is a complex beast.'

'Commissioner, I spoke to my French counterpart in Brussels last Friday afternoon. The Interior Minister is not a happy man. A French policeman has been murdered and one of the suspects is at large because the Garda's advice was not to make an early arrest.'

'Minister, we are doing our level best to resolve this case. My people are working flat out; putting in long hours. Hours, I can't pay them for because of budgetary constraints, yet the work goes on.'

O'Hagan blustered. 'What's the current status, then?'

Fox told him of the ongoing search for the *MV Raven*.

'Are you using all the resources at your disposal?'

'Naturally,' Fox answered.

Fox went through the modalities of the searches SIU was carrying out. He patiently listened to suggestions from the Minister before batting them away.

'Minister, trust us to finish the job.'

'Of course, the sooner we cross the finishing line on this one, the better for everyone. Good hunting!'

The Secretary-General cast his eyes skyward without comment as the Minister swept out of the room.

The second day of searches on the Irish Sea yielded nothing. The *MV Raven* was a phantom boat, there one minute, gone the next. Late on Monday night, D-Sergeant Casey called Mac.

'That boat took on fuel at Kilmore Quay yesterday evening,' he said.

'Kate has had crews trying to locate it for more than two days; is your source certain of the identity?' he asked.

'I trust him, one hundred per cent.'

'So your first report put the boat at Dunmore East on the south coast, then Arklow on the east coast where work was carried out and now the south coast again at Kilmore Quay taking on enough fuel to last a few days.'

'That's it in a nutshell.'

'You're a star, John,' Mac said.

When Mac called Kate with the news, something else was playing on her mind, but she did not bring it up. It had hit her on the drive home from work. Her team watching Nasri's every move had reported nothing out of the ordinary lately. He was going to and returning from work as usual. The SIU agent seemed to be working in the warehouse less and less. Kate scrutinized the daily surveillance log from Nasri's warehouse. The crews recognized the agent as the suspect who had been seen passing McElgunn a message, weeks earlier. They logged him leaving the industrial estate in Nasri's car on a few occasions but Kate's strict orders were to follow only Nasri.

After she passed the news on the *MV Raven* to Digger, she

rang Detective Grealy to set up an urgent meeting. His agent hadn't passed on any intel in over three weeks. That made no sense. She opened her laptop and switched on her printer. With time running out, she had to find out what was going on with him.

Kate met Grealy early the next morning in a pub car park near the airport that had barely enough parked cars for them to blend in. She quizzed him on his agent's demeanour at recent meetings.

'He seems okay, Nasri has him running around a good bit.'

'Do you think he's holding back again?'

'Hard to read sometimes but he seems genuine enough.'

'It just doesn't add up, we're getting near endgame and the phones are deadly silent. Your man's running around on business. Did you ask him what kind of errands he's running?'

'This and that is all he told me.'

'This and that, well fuck him.'

'What can *I* do?'

Kate shoved a sheet of official-headed paper into Grealy's hands.

'Show him this. Then, we'll see how keen he is on keeping schtum.'

'A deportation warrant? What the fuck, how come this is the first I'm hearing of it?'

'Look at the signature.'

Grealy recognized her scrawl. He smiled. The warrant was bullshit but worth the play.

'Tell him you've pulled the warrant. Convince him that if he can't deliver; you can't hold off the hounds.'

'I can't wait to see his face.' Grealy grinned.

When Kate returned to base she had a meeting with Mac and Butler. Butler briefed them on a recently identified new blood from O'Hare's gang. She was distracted but tried to focus as Butler explained how an image retrieved from a training camp site indicated that the new volunteers were being trained on using an M72 disposable rocket launcher.

'Depending on the rocket used, it can do serious damage, penetrates armour plating up to two hundred millimetres thick,' Butler explained.

'Do you identify the guy demonstrating it?' she asked.

'We've IDed him as an ex-British soldier from Belfast. Symons's people say he has an exemplary record; did his four years minimum service and got out.'

Mac intervened.

'If they're training volunteers on these, they must be expecting a shipment of them soon.'

'Part of the Rotterdam load?' Kate speculated.

'Probably, can't you imagine Symons's reaction?'

'Wouldn't he be right to be alarmed?'

'No question; it's a game-changer.'

'Has Fenaux turned up anything yet?'

'Nothing so far.'

Kate's phone rang. She checked the screen. It was Grealy.

'I need to take this.'

'We're done anyway,' Mac said gruffly.

Grealy was animated.

'That man nearly shat himself when I showed him the warrant.'

'What's the story?' Kate asked.

'*Money Man* Nasri has been working him to the bone for the last two weeks.'

'Doing what?'

'Hiring four different hauliers to pick up loads in Holland.'

'Fuck a doodle-do!'

'Is that significant?' he asked.

Operation Cassandra intel was strictly need-to-know and Grealy wasn't in the loop on the Dutch end.

'Well it's unusual, wouldn't you say?' she said, regaining composure. 'I reckon it could be.'

'The agent told me he can't meet me until late tonight.'

'We need those four names. Why can't he do it sooner?'

'Look, this guy is shitting a brick. I'm cutting him some slack as regards the time of the meeting. It gives him longer to think about the consequences of any lack of cooperation.'

'You know best.'

'Remember I'm responsible for this guy's safety, I've never seen him so nervous.'

'Okay. We're available if you need cover at the meet.'

'I'll bear that in mind.'

Kate went back to Mac's office. They had worked together long enough to know that the job sometimes gets under your skin.

She tapped on the door frame.

'Safe to approach?' she asked, smiling.

'I hope there's something worthwhile behind that look. What's the news?'

She brought him up to speed on what Grealy had told her.

'This means whatever is planned in France is going ahead,' Mac said. 'I better brief Fenaux.'

43

FENAUX HAD HOPED to get home for a few hours in the afternoon. He was weary. So much pressure comes from within; it seemed forever thus in the French police. It had been a struggle to hold on to his resources. The events following Reynaud's murder isolated him further. He had managed only a few hours of sleep in the past forty-eight.

All three suspects had simultaneously dropped his surveillance teams in central Paris. Two days later, they were no closer to finding them. The search was becoming frantic. He was about to head home to get some sleep when the phone on his desk rang.

He put his briefcase down and took the call. Fifteen minutes later he was still listening and scribbling notes as the Police Judiciaire Commandant from Morlaix recounted his tale.

'Des pêcheurs Irlandais sont ici.'

The Commandant picked up the remark 'some Irish fishermen are here,' while he dined in a Roscoff restaurant. The patron liked to know what was happening in his town. The chief of detectives ate there regularly as the owner also enjoyed a chat.

The Commandant asked the patron what he meant by the remark. He explained that the ferry operator between Roscoff and Île de Batz had recently encountered Irish fishermen. They had sheltered in the island's port two nights earlier; the night of the storm.

A little over five hundred people lived on Île de Batz which lay off the Brittany coast. It took fifteen minutes to make the ferry trip from Roscoff. The island ran three and a half kilometres in length.

When the patron concluded his tale, the Commandant took out his phone and punched the speed dial for his office. He passed concise orders and then savoured the sea bream in a delicious sauce that the patron served for lunch. He had never figured out the sauce's secret ingredient. He skipped dessert and was finishing his coffee when his phone rang. The young detective told him he was at the port. The Commandant ordered him to hold the ferry for his arrival. He demurred on the offer of a digestif from the patron, threw back what remained of his espresso, and left the restaurant walking briskly towards the port.

'The Captain', as he liked to be called, suggested to the detectives that they could talk as he went about his business. He would not expect either of them to pay the usual ten euros charge to make the return trip. Both smiled at his generous offer. They would have preferred to take him to Morlaix and increase the pressure, but time was against them. They allowed him to clear the jetty before the younger one began throwing questions at him.

The smell of oil and diesel fumes filled the wheelhouse and made the young detective nauseous. He fired questions staccato style; easy ones at first. The captain tossed back fast and straight-forward answers.

He had been in the business for over ten years; the season was average; he would halt the service and tie up for the winter probably after the first week in November.

'Did you see an Irish boat recently?'

The captain grew restive.

'Yes.'

'When?'

'About a day and a half ago.'

'Be precise,' the detective said. 'Date and time.'

'The twenty-ninth, at fifteen hundred hours.'

'You spoke to the skipper?'

'Yes.'

'Who were these Irish men?'

'Fishermen, as far as I know.'

'Did you see fish in their boat?'

'I didn't see into the hold.'

'How many did you see on board?'

'Four.'

The Commandant was growing to like the young detective, he was sharp.

'Anything else you can tell us?'

The captain did not answer immediately as the island jetty approached.

'I need to concentrate on docking.'

The detective had found his sea legs and was hitting his stride.

'This can't wait. Is there anything else you can tell us?'

The captain's head jerked back and forth as he made a big deal of the boat's docking manoeuvres.

'They were fellow seafarers. They needed assistance I was only helping them out.'

'What are you talking about?' the detective pressed.

He pointed toward the mainland.

'Fuel; I brought them fuel. It saved them having to put into port.'

'Surely it would have been quicker and safer to pump it at Roscoff?'

'Of course, but they told me they had other repairs to carry out; a fisherman's life isn't easy.'

'How much fuel did you get them?'

'Nine hundred litres.'

'How the fuck did you manage that?'

'I made three crossings, I pumped three hundred litres each time.'

'Did they pay you well?'

'Just the price of the fuel.'

'So you didn't charge anything for *your* fuel?'

'They paid me for the fuel I pumped and a little for my expenses,' the captain outlined.

'So they did pay you,' the detective pressed.

'Just my expenses.'

'How did you work out how much to charge them?'

'We agreed on a fee for each trip.'

'How much?'

'Fifty euros per trip.'

'So, in fact, they paid you a hundred and fifty euros on top of the price of the fuel? Is that right?'

'I made three trips that would be right.'

'Didn't you think that was a bit unusual for poor fishermen?'

'At sea, many things that happen might seem unusual to landlubbers. I was only trying to help out.'

They continued to question the captain while he waited to make the return trip. He confirmed that he had been paid in cash for his services. He sighed in relief when the ferry tied up back at Roscoff for the final time that evening. Another big wind was brewing and customers were in short supply. The departing detectives advised him to guard his money as he might need to hire a lawyer as their investigation progressed.

Fenaux thanked the Commandant for his diligence. 'One final question, did the captain confirm the name on the boat?'

'The ferryman told us the name was *Raven*; there were numbers after the name but he couldn't recall any of those.'

As the Commandant's call began, Fenaux had thrown his coat onto one of the chairs facing his desk. He now returned it to the stand inside the door. He knew he wouldn't be heading home any time soon. He called Jeanne to tell her that he would miss another dinner with her. She asked him to be quiet coming in as she would probably be asleep. His next call was to the Duty Officer. Fenaux ordered him to recall the crew from the early shift.

He called Dubois and asked him to pick up something to eat. Nothing exotic. He settled for pizza. He had a shower and put on the last clean shirt from his locker. As he closed the card-board lid on his dinner, Mac called. Kate was with him in his office.

Mac's call was to tell him about identifying the hauliers. Fenaux's news trumped that. He explained that the *MV Raven* was somewhere off the French coast. The news shocked them both.

'We know there are four on the boat,' Fenaux said.

'We know that O'Hare and Treacy were together on the boat at Arklow,' Kate replied. 'Do you know if all four on board are Irish or could some of them be your lot?'

'You know, Kate, we lose the three suspects from Seine-Saint-Denis for two days,' Fenaux replied. 'It's possible some of the suspects are ours.'

'At this stage, it doesn't matter who they are,' she replied. 'Finding them and stopping them is all that matters.'

'Mac, I need to locate this gang rapidly and take them alive if possible. Is it possible you can support us with a team?'

'Why do you want us over again?'

'Kate's crew knows the Irish suspects. This gives us a greater chance; do you agree?'

Mac looked across his desk in Kate's direction, deflecting the question her way.

She nodded.

'If Kate travels with her team, I'm also sending a SWAT.'

'We can protect them.'

Mac cut in.

'This is life or death, Yves, you know that. I'm not risking things going bad because of mixed signals.'

'What about sending the man who came last time?'

'McManus?'

'Yes, Tom; why not send him to us?'

'Too risky, he's an interpreter, he's not operational.'

A veteran of several firefights, Mac knew the risks.

'The SWAT team, ERU we call them, work with Kate's crew all the time.'

'Okay; I will try to get an agreement,' Fenaux said.

'I'll do likewise.'

Ireland's neutral status in international conflicts meant a high-level decision was required to allow Kate to travel with armed support. The Cabinet security committee held a hastily arranged telephone conference. The Justice minister cautiously explained what lay behind the French request to allow an SIU team to assist in the operation to locate the lethal gang. The operation would be dangerous but they could only speculate on how high the risk was.

Along with O'Hagan, the Taoiseach or Prime Minister, and his deputy fired questions at Mac and the boss. The vagueness of the intel on possible targets was dissuasive, but the knowledge that an Irish group was involved forced their hand. They gave a hesitant thumbs-up to the operational assistance the French requested. As on-scene commander, Kate would have operational command.

Operation Cassandra had careered forward in twenty-four hours. From the intel Grealy's agent supplied, SIU had details of the four hauliers Nasri had hired. They were playing catch-up. With registration details of each truck, John Casey at Rosslare confirmed that the vehicles had travelled through the port on ferries bound for the UK. The vehicle details were flashed to MI5 but when checked out, each truck had entered and exited Britain for Europe.

Each haulage company was contracted to pick up a forty-foot container in Rotterdam and deliver it at yards close to Rosslare Harbour. The AIVD, Holland's General Intelligence, and Security Service agreed to identify and follow the trucks when they entered their jurisdiction.

PIERRE-JEAN SILLEC LIKED the commune where he lived. Guilers lay fourteen kilometres north of Brest. About seven thousand people lived there, workers mainly, like the Sillecs trying to keep their heads just above the water. They had a routine lifestyle. At eight o'clock Stéphanie was trying to restore order at the breakfast table. Their two children were arguing over who got to pour their cereal first. The doorbell rang and Pierre-Jean went to answer.

'*Oui?*' was all he managed before he was roughhoused inside. He heard a voice speaking to his wife in the kitchen. Omar al-Haddad pushed him through the hallway and joined them.

'*Pas d'école aujourd'hui,*' Omar announced to the children. '*On va rester à la maison.*'

The two children smiled nervously and looked at their parents, seeking reassurance. One of the two men who had come in the back door had his hands on their mother's shoulders. The children didn't understand why they should feel unhappy about staying home from school.

'*Il faut parler avec Papa au salon*,' Omar said as he pushed Pierre-Jean towards the front room. Omar's clipped instructions explained what he had to do to keep his family alive.

With a thumbs-up from the suits, Kate's team scrambled. Six hours after talking to Fenaux she was on a Casa CS235 that the Air Corps had laid on for them. They were cruising at 25,000 feet and she sat facing down the cabin. The pilot announced that an approaching low-pressure system from the Bay of Biscay was likely to cause turbulence. A crewman passed around sick bags. Kate knew her fear of flying was rooted in the wrong conclusions she drew from things that happened during a flight. If a flight attendant looked serious, Kate took it that something was wrong and they were keeping quiet about it. Part of her brain told her that she had to be wrong because her conclusions always turned out to be incorrect. She tried to focus on what lay ahead but when the aircraft dipped suddenly in a violent wind gust, she threw up into the bag provided.

'I hate flying,' she said as she stowed the bag at her feet and prayed for the storm to abate.

It was a no-brainer as to who she selected for the mission. Digger, Angie, and Zoom sat across from her, trying to keep down the meal they ate before getting on board. Tom McManus sat beside her, reading over pages of vocabulary, blissfully unaware of the rocky nature of the flight. Mac had relented and allowed him to travel on Kate's insistence. Bill Twomey's ERU team was six strong. Their gear sat on the seat beside them.

Lieutenant-Colonel Shaw from G2 Army Intelligence completed the party, although his cockpit seat separated him from the plebs. The Casa was configured for parachute troops.

The Air Corps had carried out exercises with the Army's Ranger Wing the previous day and there was no time to strip it out and change the layout. In this configuration, the plane could carry thirty-six fully-equipped troops. It was less than half full.

Before leaving the Air Corps base, a nagging voice in Kate's head had reminded her to call home. She felt an irrational need to hear her mother's voice.

'Hi, Mum, what are you up to?'

'Oh, the same old ding dong. How about you?'

'I'm fine, working long hours at the minute.'

'Where are you, it's very noisy?'

'Yeah, just out near the airport. How is everyone?'

'Everyone is fine. Mary D'Arcy is here having a cup of tea with me.'

'The shrink; she's not trying to psychoanalyze you, is she?'

'Don't be silly, we're just chatting. What about you? Are you keeping warm when you're out working?'

'Yes Mum, we're mostly in cars these days.'

'Okay, smarty pants!'

'I know that tone, what's on your mind.'

'Kate, you're my daughter; I worry about you. Just take care.'

'I will Mum,' Kate assured her. 'Look I have to go, we'll chat in a few days.'

'God bless.'

Kate smiled and hung up; the familiar sign-off was a salve to her rising anxiety.

The agreed plan was to land at Villacoublay base, outside Paris. There, the SIU and ERU teams would link up with Fenaux's crew. After a joint briefing, they intended to redeploy as a group towards Brittany in helicopters. They expected O'Hare to move the mortars from the lock-up in Lorient for pickup on the coast. They planned on being close behind. However, with surveillance little usually went according to plan and as the plane cleared the pockets of turbulence, Kate was unaware of how much was about to change.

Days earlier, beneath the Atlantic Ocean, a Warrant Officer on board the *USS Thalassa* had fretted about Petty Officer William Lacey. Detailed to keep an eye on the radioman, the Warrant Officer had tracked him down to one of the communications panels. He was hunkered down behind it. All the systems on board, from the sensitive sonar equipment to the atmosphere regeneration system, were classified as Top Secret. The communications system, vital to the submarine's primary function of preventing nuclear missile attacks on the United States, had the highest classification.

'Lacey,' he shouted. 'Why aren't you at midrats?'

Lacey replied without getting up.

'I'm changing the emergency batteries for the main radio.'

'Go and eat. I'll get relief to you.'

'Sir, thank you, sir I'm not hungry,' Lacey replied.

It was rare for men to miss out on the midnight meal.

'No, thank you. That's not an option, sailor. Standing orders are to eat when the opportunity presents.'

'Sir, yes sir,' Lacey replied, his head still buried behind the panel.

Lacey was one of the twenty-five crew members 'on watch'. Routine preventive maintenance, such as changing the emergency batteries for the radio gear was carried out when the radiomen were off watch.

With a capacity crew on board, some of the crew had to

bunk down in the torpedo room and Lacey had drawn the short straw. When he finished behind the comms panel he returned there rather than going to eat. The Warrant Officer came up fast behind him and stuck a pistol at the base of his skull.

'Remove what's in your right pocket,' he shouted. 'Do it slowly.'

The startled sailor fished out a smartphone and held it up.

'Hand it to me,' the Warrant Officer ordered. Lacey complied.

'Unlock code,' he shouted.

Lacey stuttered out the four-digit code and the Warrant Officer quickly accessed the images surreptitiously gathered. All were gross violations. The Warrant Officer radioed the Captain who placed the errant seaman in lockdown. He was taken aback at having a traitor on board and ordered a twenty-four-hour watch on the prisoner. Lacey was a textbook sailor who had increased his skills incrementally to become a valuable crew member. He had married his high school sweetheart during shore leave a year earlier.

Fearing sabotage, Captain Anderson ordered an immediate audit of all equipment on board. It was carried out in record time and his XO reported that all systems were functioning normally. The *Thalassa* was not due to make port for another three months. Keeping a prisoner on board for that length of time was unconscionable. It would impact morale and affect their mission.

Captain Anderson decided on a bold course. He would have Washington innovate. Anderson spoke to his Quartermaster of the Watch and determined their position in the ocean. If the *Thalassa* was to become the first American fleet ballistic missile submarine to make port outside the United States, France offered the best option. They could make a west coast port with the least delay.

The tiny tracking beacon Lacey had secreted beneath a tangle of wiring in the comms panel matched the green cable colour around it and went undetected. The periodic ping it emitted was the only testament to its presence. It enabled its trackers to chart the progress of the *Thalassa* and plan for its arrival.

PART 4

45

THE AMERICAN EMBASSY in Paris sits on avenue Gabriel. Next door is the British embassy and to the rear, Palais d'Élysée, the French President's official residence. A stroll through a picture-perfect park leads to avenue des Champs-Élysées.

By eight o'clock in the evening, the human traffic on avenue Gabriel thins out. Many of its restaurants only do a lunchtime trade. Usually, if he were still in the office at this time, Robin Jeffers liked to sit back and listen. The extensive embassy block was full of mature trees, manicured lawns, and well-tended floral borders. Evening birdsong occasionally cut through the ceaseless drone of traffic on the Champs-Élysées.

Jeffers loved the unique opportunity he had to savour the ambience. The history of the place fascinated him. His late evening office sojourns were precious moments of calm before returning to his apartment replete with the noise his pre-teen daughters generated.

This evening his moment of perfect Zen disintegrated when his call ended. He could not shake off the gnawing feeling that started when he heard the gossip from home. He continued to stare at the phone after Carrie Grey hung up.

Grey had graduated with him from Quantico. They remained close throughout their service even though their careers had taken them in different directions. He liked the operational, field work. Management was her talent. Her sharp survival instincts meant she kept her ears open in the circles that mattered. Washington was six hours behind Paris and she had returned from lunch when she filled him in on a case in his neck of the woods. NCIS; the Navy's Investigation Service was handling it. Service personnel had been dispatched to France the previous day to pick up a sailor from the submarine fleet, sometime in the next twenty-four hours.

'It'll be a 'touch and go' operation,' Grey had told him.

'What does that mean?'

'They won't hang about because of the kind of vessel. Coming into a foreign port at all is highly unusual.'

'Carrie, courtesy calls with allies are a dime a dozen. I've seen US submarines in ports here on previous occasions.'

'For the attack subs maybe, not the Boomers.'

'Boomers?'

'Fleet ballistic missile submarines, SSBNs, they're the ones with nuclear warheads. Everyone in the Service calls them Boomers,' she educated him. 'They stay at sea for months on end and only make port in the good ol' US of A.'

'Why are they making an exception in this case? What did this guy do?'

'He took photos in the Comms Room on a cell phone,' Grey said. 'All that shit is Top Secret.'

Carrie Grey enjoyed working as much information as possible from her sources. She had told him that's how Washington worked; friends helped friends.

'Who discovered the photos?' Jeffers asked.

'A Warrant Officer seized his cell at his bunk in the torpedo room.'

'Does that sound odd to you?'

'Nope! When they have a full complement on board some of the crew sleep on makeshift bunks in the torpedo room.'

'That can't be much fun.'

'Guess not. The Warrant Officer was watching out for this guy's flaky behaviour.'

'Good job! Do they need me to tag along?'

'I don't think so, they haven't requested any assistance.'

'Okay, thanks for the heads-up. By the way, do you know where they're putting into for the handover?'

'Brest,' Grey said. 'If I hear anything else, I'll let you know.'

It was a wonderful evening in Paris. The morning's heavy rain had given way to bright, late autumnal sunshine through the afternoon. Rain dripped from trees with leaves changing irrevocably from glorious gold to dull brown. One gale would rip them from their branches. The birds were in full evensong. The beautiful noise did not register with Jeffers.

He pulled up everything he had on Operation Cassandra and re-read it. Kate had given him a copy of the prison transcript with McElgunn's cryptic reference to Celtic cousins surfacing. He paced back and forth working through the evidence for what he was about to propose. Irish terrorists helping Al Qaeda prepare an attack on a U.S. submarine. It was crazy. He'd come across as a nut job.

Perhaps the Navy's choice of Brest was just a coincidence; it was an important base for the French submarine fleet. There would be established links between the two Navies, for sure. It was likely one friendly service helping another deal with its dirty linen discreetly. It had to be a coincidence.

He didn't believe in coincidences.

He called Grey back and re-checked the facts. Then he rang Mac.

Mac told him: 'Full briefing for all colleagues 8:00 a.m. tomorrow. The past hours have been manic here.'

'I saw the note on the briefing,' Jeffers replied. 'Can we discuss it now?'

'Switch to secure mode.'

Jeffers waited. Static crackled. The line cleared and he heard Mac's voice again.

'We have confirmed intel that O'Hare is on a trawler, with other unidentified suspects, off the west coast of France. The last sighting was at Roscoff thirty-six hours ago. The three Paris suspects are unaccounted for during the same period and we suspect a link-up. We think an attack is imminent. Kate and her crew are en route to France to assist in the search.'

'Great God Almighty!'

'What?'

'I think I know the target.'

He outlined his suspicions and consented to Mac sharing them with Fenaux.

Jeffers rang Carrie Grey next, the third time in thirty minutes. She instantly patched him through to the Director of the FBI's Office of International Operations.

The Air Corps pilot had barely alerted his passengers that the white cliffs of Dover were on the right when Kate's phone vibrated. She glanced out the window as a string of twinkling lights along the coast faded into the sombre darkness of the English Channel.

'Diversion to Brest,' Mac told her. 'Full briefing when you get there.'

'Does the pilot know?' Kate joked.

'Of course, G2 arranged it, they are here with me.' His voice sounded strained.

'Can you tell me anything else?'

'Jeffers has changed the game; we'll talk when you're on the ground.'

Kate decided not to push him. She shouted the news to her crew. It was greeted with a shrug, even from McManus. Permission for him to travel was granted on the proviso that he stayed well clear of any action. Moments later, Shaw emerged from his comfortable cockpit seat.

'Have you heard?'

She told him that she knew of the new destination.

'Mr. Fenaux is on his way to Brest in a Fennec.'

'What's a Fennec?'

'A fast military helicopter, the French use them for air cover over Paris. If a civilian aircraft starts acting erratically over the capital, they send a Fennec first to intercept and ascertain if the pilot will comply with directions.'

'Pretty quick then.'

Shaw nodded.

'How many passengers can it carry?'

'Depends on the version; certainly four at least.'

The military angle struck Kate as odd. Why use the military? The French police were well provisioned with choppers. The capacity of the Fennec meant Fenaux would probably have Dubois and Patrick Leclerc with him. What had Jeffers found out that merited such an accelerated deployment?

She systematically reviewed the intel as the aircraft banked due west.

'Penny for your thoughts?' Digger said.

'Not worth a penny,' she smiled.

She could not work out the reason for the sudden change and chose not to speculate. When they landed at Brest they taxied towards a hangar at the edge of the airfield. Through the thick fog, Kate noticed three military green helicopters sitting alongside. Even inside the hangar, the air had a chill.

Fenaux welcomed them. He looked tired. He smiled and greeted Kate and Angie as usual, a peck on each cheek. Everyone else from the flight spilled onto the hangar floor, yawning, stretching, and checking kit. Twomey and his ERU team exchanged embraces and back slaps with their French counterparts. The bonhomie was genuine; back in Dublin, six months earlier they had carried out joint training exercises. Underlying the novelty of the occasion was a reality everyone understood. This situation would likely be resolved only with lethal force and they would be the ones deploying it.

Fenaux directed them towards a door at the end of the Gendarmerie hangar. It led along a narrow corridor not designed for crowds. Twomey and his men pushed through carrying their gear in front of them. Some bumped off walls as they moved along at pace humping awkward loads. Weapons were slung over shoulders, Heckler and Koch HK33 assault rifles mainly. Twomey hung his H&K MP7 sub-machine gun to the front. One of his team guarded the Steyr SSG69 sniper rifle he carried, as carefully as a newborn. Pre-op adrenaline kicked in and any weariness they had been feeling quickly dissolved. There was no time to call Mac. Kate would have to improvise.

In a briefing room, set out theatre style to accommodate the mixed assembly, Fenaux shepherded Kate to a top table facing the room. She acknowledged Daphne Clarke, Peter Symons's number two at MI5. Jeffers and Whatney were also in situ. The place was top-heavy with Brass; Police and military of a hue that Kate didn't recognize. She motioned McManus to join her and he slotted into the last available seat up front.

Fenaux began. He spoke in French and then in English to welcome everyone. He informed them that time was a luxury they did not enjoy. He would proceed in French with an interpreter from the Navy putting English on his words. He invited Robin Jeffers to deliver his briefing.

'In the past few hours, the FBI has received information that leads us to believe that Al-Qaeda is planning to attack an American nuclear-powered, ballistic missile submarine.'

Kate unscrewed the top of her water bottle and sipped.

Quite the opening line!

Jeffers paused as if for effect; the translation evoking audible gasps as it swept through the room.

He continued, 'We believe the attack will take place in Brest. The *USS Thalassa* is due to dock here in the next twenty-four hours. The purpose of the visit is Top Secret. I have been authorized to share it with you.'

Palpable silence prevailed as he raised a glass of water to his lips.

'The US Navy's Investigation Service, NCIS is to take one William Lacey into military detention sometime tomorrow. Lacey is a sailor, who has been with the submarine service for ten years and was due to be promoted to Chief Petty Officer. Now he is under guard, on suspicion of attempting to steal military secrets. When the vessel docks NCIS will take him into military custody. The FBI suspects him of being part of an Al-Qaeda plot.'

Jeffers turned slightly to his left and nodded in the direction of a middle-aged guy sitting two seats away.

'We have this man to thank for getting us here. Commander Harper, sir can you fill us in on Lacey's background?'

Harper struggled to make much above five foot six. His silver-grey hair was immaculately coiffed. He did not rush; rather he gave everyone sufficient time to take in the array of service ribbons on his Navy dress uniform. He was in France as part of a tour of European capitals promoting his candidacy for a senior post in NATO. He jumped at the opportunity to command the naval side of the operation, immediately offering to use his Navy jet to ferry Jeffers and Whatney from Paris to Brest.

'Commander Avril Harper,' he announced.

Kate did a double-take. Isn't Avril a girl's name?

He got straight to business.

'As Agent Jeffers outlined, Lacey has been with our submarine service for ten years. He did two years on a cruiser before volunteering for the subs. Up to this, he was an exemplary sailor.'

The Commander brought them through the story. Lacey had been working in the sub's Operations Department. That meant he had spent most of his career working for the navigator and in communications.

'Based on what the FBI has told us, we think Lacey engineered the timing of the discovery of his cell phone. Cells don't work on subs and even having one with him is a code violation.'

He paused to make sure he had everyone's attention.

'The cell contained photos of *top-secret* communications equipment, the discovery of which Lacey knew would trigger his detention. Given the seriousness of the offence, we believe he knew he would have to be removed swiftly from the vessel. We believe he planned on the basis that there was only one possible port where we would disembark him – Brest.'

Jeffers was about to stand up believing the Commander was done.

'In fact,' he carried on, 'Boomers do not put into foreign

ports, but this SOB figured, correctly as it turned out, that we would want to get him off ASAP.'

'Has the captain been warned?' a question came from the room. Kate could not see who asked it.

'The vessel's running silent,' the Commander replied. 'When the Pentagon decided to break the age-old protocol of only home porting the Boomers, they also decided to turn it into a challenge.'

Fenaux bristled at the Commander's brash style and his takeover of proceedings. He shifted in his seat and shot Jeffers a glance which left him in no doubt that he needed to take back control of his briefing.

'Can you *briefly* explain what that means, Commander?' Jeffers interrupted.

Unaccustomed to having his rank taken lightly, Harper glared as if kicked in the rear.

'Gladly, Agent Jeffers. The captain will communicate with nobody until he surfaces his vessel in the harbour. To arrive at Brest harbour under zero communication conditions is now his challenge. I would lay odds on Captain Anderson achieving that goal.'

He resumed his seat.

'Is it possible to block the harbour entrance?' Fenaux enquired of no one in particular.

'Possible, but undesirable,' came the reply from a French naval bigwig.

Kate guessed the bigwig bit from the rainbow of ribbons on his chest.

'Creating conditions that could lead to a subaqueous collision involving a nuclear-powered submarine is not desirable,' he told Fenaux, disdainfully.

'Surely they have warning systems that will help them avoid such an outcome?' Fenaux pressed.

'Passive sonar, of course, which will also help them evade any blockade,' the bigwig replied.

'Not if you devise a large enough blockade.'

'Monsieur Fenaux, my service believes a blockade is too high risk.'

'As opposed to...' Fenaux stopped, having second thoughts about escalating this difference of opinion in public.

'Would you like to finish your briefing, Robin?' he invited Jeffers.

'Our inquiries, with the cooperation and support of NCIS, lead us to believe that Lacey has been radicalized. He converted to Islam, a year before he married. His wife's family are immigrants from Georgia, the country, not the State. We have confirmed in the past few hours that he spent two weeks of his shore leave there last year.'

Fenaux listened intently, although Kate presumed he was already aware of this information. Jeffers continued.

'Our inquiries into Lacey have been rushed. However, a local Georgian intelligence asset believes he met a group of returned jihadists from Afghanistan during the same shore leave.'

Jeffers swiped up grainy black and white photographs of the alleged meeting onto the screen from an app on his phone. It was impossible to pick out Lacey as an obvious Westerner in the group. Jeffers pointed him out and followed up with a Navy photo. There was nothing remarkable about his appearance.

'Do you have specific intelligence on the target?' Fenaux asked.

'The FBI's conclusions are drawn from the intelligence in Operation Cassandra and our recent discovery of Lacey's radicalization.'

He looked to his right towards Dan Whatney, the Paris CIA liaison who sat beside him.

'Dan, maybe you would like to add something?'

Whatney nodded. He stood up and introduced himself.

'Thanks, Robin. At my Service, we have been re-evaluatin' all our Al-Qaeda intel in the past twelve hours. It is an ongoin' process,' he began.

Kate could tell the naval interpreter was struggling with Whatney's Texan drawl.

'We're focussin' in particular on obscure reports comin' outta Pakistan 'bout cutting the head off the monster. Now we get this from time to time - 'kill the crusader, slay the westerner' type-a-lingo. We'll continue doin' our thing, collatin' intel and analysin' it. If anythin' jumps out at us we'll share it right off the bat. Nobody's holdin' back on this one.'

So nothing really from the CIA, Kate thought. He could have said it in a word. Nothing.

'Thank you, Dan,' the ever-polite Jeffers said, closing out his contribution.

Fenaux stood up and cued Dubois on the lights. He displayed the photo SIU had supplied of the *MV Raven*. Fenaux was concise. He stated his belief that this would most likely be the attack vessel, which he believed was likely nearby. He summarised DGSI's role, since Operation Cassandra began, in tracking the activities of O'Hare's IRA splinter group in France. He outlined the analysis of their motivation for involvement in exchanging their skills for a substantial arms shipment. He asked Kate to fill in the blanks.

She stood up and glanced around the room, exhaling quietly before taking a deep breath.

'Our suspect, Sean O'Hare, is the one most callous terrorists we've ever encountered. He's fearless, ruthless, and remorseless. Bear in mind that he has killed more people than we'll ever know for sure. The clique around him is his army.'

She was conscious of the silence in the room. She had everyone's attention and established an even pace with the interpreter.

'O'Hare was the main man in the Provisional IRA weapons department before the ceasefire. Let me remind you of some of the attacks they carried out over the years.'

Kate highlighted a small number of incidents; the failed attempt to kill the British cabinet in Downing Street in 1991 in a homemade mortar attack. The two massive truck bombs in the City of London, Bishopsgate in 1993 and Canary Wharf in 1996. Those two bombs killed three people and injured many. Damage caused ran to hundreds of millions of pounds.

'O'Hare is highly competent and driven. Apart from his bombing prowess, he trained up and deployed a sniper team in Northern Ireland. Daphne will testify to their kill rate.'

Clarke nodded in consensus.

'O'Hare is a meticulous planner,' Kate continued.

'Why attack an American submarine?' the interpreted question of a French naval officer interrupted.

'I don't know,' Kate replied.

The naval officer continued, 'All submarines are painted black to help them hide,' the naval officer explained. 'An ordinary citizen cannot tell one from another, perhaps the terrorist doesn't know.'

She replied: 'O'Hare may believe he's attacking a British vessel and for him, that would rate as a bonus. This is a trade-off deal; his skills for Al Qaeda weapons.'

She answered questions as they came, explaining that O'Hare's group was well-funded and not averse to taking extreme risks as the Greenwich attack proved. The group's known activities in France confirmed as much.

Fenaux outlined that the mission was to intercept the *MV Raven* and confirm its status. He reiterated his intel on the sighting of the vessel off Roscoff.

'Trawlers travel slowly and use a lot of fuel,' the naval officer explained. 'Seven to eleven knots per hour is the average speed. One knot means one nautical mile.'

'The Irish fleet register records the *MV Raven* with a top speed of twelve knots,' Kate told him.

'The sighting by the ferryman at Roscoff was forty-eight hours ago,' Fenaux said.

'The trawler took on nine hundred litres of fuel, is that correct?'

Fenaux nodded in confirmation.

'Well, only sixty-seven nautical miles separate Roscoff and Brest; which means...'

'If the target is at Brest, they're already here,' Fenaux concluded.

46

WITH THE BRIEFING COMPLETE, the brass, bigwigs, and liaison people departed, leaving the teams who would have to find and intercept the gang. Kate remembered most of the faces in the semi-circle, it was the names she struggled with.

'The future is not written,' she told the stripped-down meeting, 'it's ours to shape.' McManus interpreted and there were nods of agreement all around.

'We've all seen our targets in action. That advantage gives us a head start.'

The French surveillance officers understood what Kate meant. Knowing the way their targets walked, talked, or moved their heads meant you picked them out quicker. There were mutterings of agreement throughout the group. Previous knowledge of the targets was a small advantage but Kate had planted a positive seed.

'Okay,' Fenaux clapped his hands to get everyone's attention. He spoke in French and McManus interpreted. 'Locating this damn boat is our priority.'

'Doing it undetected is critical,' Kate added.

Fenaux continued. 'A Navy dive team is on standby. If the boat is moored; I will pass them the location. At that stage, we all pull back a safe distance and they will mine it with Limpets.'

'Then what?' Kate asked.

'We give the *MV Raven's* crew one chance to surrender. If the *Thalassa* surfaces meantime, the Navy will blow the trawler regardless.'

Nobody commented.

'It's a poorly maintained boat - a gas cylinder could explode at any time. At least that's what any inquiry will say – an industrial accident.'

Kate said. 'We know O'Hare and Treacy better than anyone else in this room. Use that advantage.'

'How?' Fenaux asked.

'Allow us to carry out a covert search around the harbour. Give us an hour before you send in your team.'

Fenaux looked to Dubois as he processed McManus's translation. He shrugged.

'Two teams?' Fenaux asked.

'Yes,' Kate replied.

'I will put one of mine with each team,' Fenaux said looking around. He fixed on his number three. 'Patrick you're up.'

Crew-cut smirked and gave Kate a thumbs-up.

Fenaux put a harbour layout map on the screen.

'Arsenal de Brest is the main French naval base on the Atlantic. It extends along the banks of the Penfeld River which, as you can see, is lined with docks. The Navy's ballistic missile fleet is based here. Searching this area can be left to the military.'

He continued: 'Lots of well-guarded no-go areas. The Navy says that they have doubled the guard until this situation is resolved. The berth for visiting subs is in a public access area.'

'What's this?' Kate asked, pointing at what looked like a castle.

'Château de Brest. One of five national naval museums in France.'

'The ramparts of the castle seem to look directly towards the berth designated for the *Thalassa*.'

'Do you think they might use it to spot the submarine?'

'The height would give them a good tactical advantage if they used it as a point of attack,' Twomey chipped in.

'How close to the target do you think they will risk taking the trawler?' Fenaux asked.

'It depends,' Digger said.

'On what?'

'Whether they intend launching mortars from the boat as the intelligence suggests they might or otherwise.'

'And if they use mortars?'

'Distance is its Achilles heel. Homemade mortars like those we photographed in the forest have a limited range. They had to get within a few hundred meters of the Police and Army barracks they bombed in Northern Ireland.'

'How accurate are they?'

'Depends on the team that does the setup; O'Hare's considered the best in the business.'

'The Château's a good starting point,' Kate suggested.

Fenaux nodded his consent.

'Two teams, one on either side of the river,' Kate said. 'Best on foot, I think, vehicles might attract attention. Twomey will need an inflatable to support us from the river if things get hairy.'

'We can get you a RIB no problem,' Crew-cut said, 'but searching on foot will take too long, we'll use a scooter.'

She didn't fancy the idea but they were running out of choices.

'Okay, a scooter.'

'You will sit behind me as my girlfriend,' Crew-cut told her in his best English.

Sniggers echoed around the room.

'I'll need a coat and some kind of headgear,' Kate said.

'No problem,' Crew-cut told her. 'We can borrow.'

One of Fenaux's crew handed out copies of a port map which they pored over, getting bearings straight in their heads, picturing where each team would be searching. Protocols were agreed upon in the event of a confrontation. If the SIU teams encountered the target they would adopt a defensive stance and wait for Fenaux's intervention teams. Twomey and his men would be embedded with them. The Navy had a Special Forces team on standby.

The juice of anticipated action kicked in. Kate took a few minutes with her crew. Fiery blood-and-bandage speeches were not her style. This op was unique. They were away from home; a new challenge and they did not want to mess up. She talked about the processes they needed to go through to achieve their objectives and stay safe.

Surveillance ran a fine line between pushing hard enough to see what you needed to see and doing something rash that gave the game away.

'Go with your gut and react fast,' Kate said.

Fenaux reiterated that if the boat was located, no approach was to be made. The Navy got first dibs on getting some pre-emptive insurance in place on the hull. Limpet mines would surely scupper any attempted attack.

Twomey and his crew gathered their gear and departed. Kate picked up her shoulder bag and followed, with Digger, Zoom, and Angie mixing in with Fenaux's crew.

They drove to the service car park of a Super U supermarket not far from the town centre. At 1:00 a.m. the Brest streets were eerily quiet. If anything, the fog had gotten thicker since their arrival. The autumn chill had taken on a colder wintery feel and Élodie, from Fenaux's crew, loaned Kate a parka jacket and beanie. Crew-cut arrived with the sad-looking scooter he'd secured for the job. Kate did not fancy it much but hopped on board.

She saw Digger, Angie, and Zoom climbing into the cab of a small Renault truck that would drop them at *Quai de la Douane* where customs boats were berthed. This would give them precious moments of orientation before they made their way to the marina. More than twenty jetties lay ahead of them. They would have to check all the vessels moored there.

Kate headed towards the river. Crew-cut was good. He rode the little bike nonchalantly; for all she knew he owned one of the bloody things. He rolled along at a steady pace until they got to the Château car park where they stopped. He told her to stay seated while they scoped the area and he smoked a cigarette. The car park was deserted apart from a solitary service van. He tossed the butt, and as they took off again she clamped her arms around his waist. They needed to cross the river and headed towards the higher streets to get to *Pont de Recouvrance,* an old bridge spanning the Penfeld. They reached the other side without encountering a single vehicle or skidding on the tramlines.

What she could see of Brest was atypical of her image of France. Just block after block of utilitarian granite and concrete. Aware that the town was blanket-bombed by the Allies during the Second World War, she guessed reconstruction had been done fast and cheap.

They watched everything that moved. The thickening fog blotted out the far side of the river. The ramparts of the castle disappeared beneath its clinging, freezing cloak. It was the best and worst of worlds from a surveillance viewpoint. While it restricted the view, it also diminished the chances of detection.

Kate picked up the negative reports on the regular radio feedback to Fenaux from the other team.

They reached the pier end; any further and they would be in the Atlantic. Crew-cut turned the scooter off. Total darkness prevailed out to sea. The water was relatively calm. An outer harbour wall accounted for this. Small waves lapped below them. Back towards the town, they could see the arc lights of the freight yards burning through the fog. It was quiet, almost peaceful.

Suddenly, Crew-cut grabbed her in a tight embrace. He was strong, and not likely to let go without a fight. He kissed her on the lips, his nicotine tang repulsive. She was confused and angry, betrayed by the violation. Had Bruno been bragging? Her head blazed with indignation. She twisted and prepared to knee him, hard in the groin. She heard it at the last minute, the gentle beat of water against the bow of a boat and the faint sound of an engine. It was barely visible; a small vessel moving slowly, almost silently, with no lights.

Crew-cut stopped kissing her. She took his hand and walked towards a container that looked like a permanent fixture on the quay. Anyone seeing them from the boat might assume they were lovers, taking their encounter to the next level.

They pressed their backs against the container's corrugated sides.

'*Desolé,*' Crew-cut whispered. 'I could not think to do any other thing.'

'Forgiven! What do you think?'

'Sailing on this night without lights; strange, I would say.'

'Call it in and let's get going.'

47

ANGIE, Digger, and Zoom had Élodie with them and split into couples to search the jetties. The harbour master had been roused. One of Fenaux's men was stationed with him in his office which overlooked the elongated harbour. The view always pleased Monsieur Beressi even though he had looked at it almost every day for the past thirty years. Tonight, only his reflection stared back as he peered through the window. He supplied answers to queries from Digger's group as they searched the marina. Checking the boats was a slow, tedious job and nothing showed up.

With Crew-cut's call on the sighting of the boat, everything changed. He told Fenaux the boat was following a course towards *Le Goulet,* the bottleneck, the final section of the harbour. Beressi pulled out mooring maps and strew them across his desk. The DGSI man put him on the radio. Kate listened intently.

'There,' he stabbed a finger in the direction of a wall that ran parallel to the river. 'Two large berths there. One of them is free.'

Fenaux thanked him.

When she arrived back at the command post, he briefed her.

'The berth Beressi suggested sits below a small harbour wall. It's 300 meters from where the *Thalassa* is due to berth.'

'That has to be it,' she replied.

'Beressi is saying only someone who knows these waters could get a vessel through on a night like this.'

'They've paid someone,' she suggested, 'they could be waiting for him. Is Digger's group aware?'

'Yes, and reinforcements are en route,' Fenaux assured her.

Kate's brain was working overtime, considering the possibilities.

'I don't think O'Hare or any of Omar's gang are on that boat.'

'Why?' Fenaux asked.

'What's to be gained on a night like this?'

'You get the boat into attack position.'

'Spend hours on board risking detection? I don't think so.'

'So what are you telling me?'

'Whoever is sailing the boat knows nothing of its purpose.'

'Do you think O'Hare and the others are watching in the port?'

'I doubt it. I suspect they're well away from the port. Waiting for a call. Don't rule out coercion.'

'How do you mean?'

'Hostages; I can't imagine any sane person putting out to sea in this kind of weather just for money.'

Digger radioed in, saying he had sight of the boat. Élodie was with him. Zoom and Angie had taken up positions on an empty yacht that gave them a line of sight on the direction of travel of anyone leaving the port.

Fenaux conferred with Dubois, Crew-cut, and Kate; McManus at her shoulder.

'Whoever gets off that boat, we follow him,' Dubois suggested. 'If Kate is right he will lead us to the gang.'

'What do you think?' Fenaux asked her.

'In theory, Bertrand could be right. Problem is, following anyone out of the port in this fog will be a nightmare.'

'Do you have a better idea?'

'The IRA used proxies in the past.'

She outlined that when British Army bases in Northern Ireland became too difficult to penetrate with mortar or machine gun assaults, the IRA switched to proxy bombs. This involved identifying a person with an entry permit, kidnapping his family, and getting him to drive a vehicle armed with a bomb into a base or checkpoint. It was one of the IRA's most cruel tactics; the person delivering the bomb inevitably became its first victim.

'*Merde*,' Fenaux swore. 'So you think the bomb is already in the harbour?'

'I don't know. I think the fog has forced them to alter their plans. On a night like this, would you risk losing your main weapon before you even got close to your target?'

'Get the boat in position first,' Dubois said.

'Yes and arm the bomb later,' Kate added.

'What about the guy who skippered the boat in?' Dubois asked.

'In most of the attacks in Northern Ireland, the families were held hostage until the bomb detonated.'

'So getting the boat to the harbour will not get him off the hook?'

'If my theory is correct, not likely.'

McManus tapped her shoulder. The radio crackled another message.

It was Digger.

'Boat is being tied up,' he said.

'Location?' Kate asked.

'Berth nearest to harbour wall. The guy seems to know what he's doing.'

'What now?' Fenaux asked.

'You need to talk to this guy,' Kate replied.

'*Une photo,*' one of Fenaux's techies shouted, '*incroyable.*'

Managing to get any kind of photo was a surprise but the image was blurred.

'Anyone we know?' Kate asked.

'Check it,' Fenaux ordered. She knew they would run facial recognition software against it. It would take time.

'One of Omar's mates?

'Definitely not,' Dubois replied.

'An innocent is my guess,' she added.

Fenaux tapped his temple as he contemplated what to do.

'Take him before he gets to the port exit,' he commanded. 'Put him in a van and meet us at Super U.'

In 2009 all French police intervention units were brought under the control of one authority, *FIPN (Force d'Intervention de la Police Nationale).* The head of RAID was given operational control. Twomey's ERU maintained close links with them. They were one of the best in their deadly business.

Dubois primed the RAID team. As the situation developed they moved closer to the port. They only had minutes to get into position.

Digger relayed commentary and Élodie passed it over the radio.

'Suspect has left the boat.'

'Suspect double-checking the mooring ropes.'

'Suspect appears nervous.'

· · ·

The port was deserted. Nothing moved on the quay. Boats bobbed silently at their moorings. He headed from the gloom towards the brightness of the street lights, fidgeting in a pocket of his working trousers. He had his hand on the phone when they hit him.

Perplexed, he found himself on the ground. Face pushed into the tarmac, a gloved hand covered his mouth, his hand snatched from his pocket. Knees fell heavily onto his back and pinned him to the ground. Both his arms were trussed behind his back. Before he realized what had happened double-flex handcuffs were zipped on his wrists. His head was pulled back, the gloved hand replaced by duct tape. A hood was roughly pulled over his head and he was aware of four pairs of hands lifting and carrying him.

He grunted in pain as he landed on the van floor. The door slid shut and it drove off at normal speed; no fuss, no panic. He didn't bother struggling. Compliance was foremost on his mind.

They pulled him up onto a bench seat and stripped off the hood. He gasped when they ripped the tape from his mouth. The figure seated in front of him wore a ski mask. He held a finger to his lips indicating to the prisoner that he should remain silent; then he used his phone to photograph him.

The drive lasted five minutes. The van stopped and reversed. The driver kept the engine on. A blast of cold air entered as the door opened. His four captors got out. Three men and a woman replaced them. The guy who appeared in charge took out a pocket knife and cut the plastic ties on his wrists.

'No need for these anymore,' Fenaux said.

The pick-up had been fast and efficient; the suspect was disorientated. Fenaux regarded him cautiously and spoke rapidly.

'My name is Yves Fenaux of DGSI; this is Dubois, also DGSI. Kate and Tom are from the Irish Police.'

The suspect rubbed each wrist in turn. The ties had left no imprint on skin well used to outdoor work. He shifted his gaze in Kate's direction.

'Irish police?'

Fenaux's eyes had not left the suspect's face, trying to read what it had to offer.

'Listen carefully, we need you to tell us why you sailed a boat into the harbour tonight in total darkness. Leave nothing out.'

The suspect looked at each of them in turn.

'Who are you again?'

Fenaux pushed his badge impatiently in front of him.

'DGSI, *Police Nationale*. 'You're wasting time we don't have; talk.'

Tears welled in the suspect's eyes.

'You have to help me. They're holding my family hostage.'

'Who's holding your family?' Fenaux asked. 'Start at the beginning.'

Dubois poured a coffee from a flask and handed it to the prisoner, who sipped it tentatively and began.

'Stéphanie was preparing breakfast for our children this morning when they came to the house.'

Fenaux cut in.

'Start with your name. What's your name and where do you live?'

McManus offered Kate a whispered interpretation as the suspect resumed his story. He was Pierre-Jean Sillec and lived in a small commune called Guilers fifteen kilometres north of Brest. He worked as a pilot in the port. Dubois ordered the photo sent to the Harbour Master immediately. Beressi confirmed his identity.

Sillec and his family had been having breakfast when a knock came on the front door. As he answered it, two young men walked into the kitchen from the rear of the house. The guy out front had pushed Pierre-Jean back inside. All the hostage-takers spoke French. They were unmasked and acted calmly. They told the children that they would have a day off from school. One of them then took Pierre-Jean to the front room.

This was the one who spoke the most. He told him they needed his expertise. If he performed the service they required his family would be released unharmed. If he did anything stupid, like informing the police, they would be killed. He would have to live with the consequences.

Crew-cut climbed into the front of the van and handed a sheet with eight mugshots on it to Dubois.

'Do you recognize any of these men?' he asked Pierre-Jean.

He took the sheet and perused each image carefully.

'This one, he's the leader,' he said pointing out Omar. 'He drove me from my house to Anse de Sainte-Anne. This is where I boarded the trawler.'

McManus explained that this was a cove close to Brest harbour.

In turn, he pointed to Omar's Paris associates, Said al-Khayyan and Ibn Saud.

'What are your instructions?' Fenaux asked.

'Get the boat in and tie it up at berth 202. Call home to confirm it's done and then come back to the house.'

'Pierre-Jean, trust us. We'll get you and your family out of this situation if you follow *our* instructions. You must be patient and remain as calm as possible. We're in control now.'

He was overstating it a bit but Pierre-Jean nodded, his face weary from the day's events. The night-time sea journey would not have helped.

'Have they people watching the harbour?' Fenaux asked.

'I don't know. They called a number from my house phone a couple of times today. The leader spoke to whoever answered in another language, English I think.'

Dubois looked towards Crew-cut who nodded. He had already ordered a printout of calls from Pierre-Jean's number in the past twenty-four hours. It was being processed as an absolute priority; a telephone intercept was being set up with equal haste.

'Can you tell us anything else?' Fenaux asked.

'They have a laptop and were reading a map on it.'

'Did you get a look at it?'

'I caught a quick glimpse,' Pierre-Jean replied. 'I know it.'

'A map of where?'

'I'm certain it was a nautical map of the western approaches to Brest harbour. There was a blinking dot on the screen.'

'Thank you. You've been very helpful. Dubois will brief you on how we will protect you and your family. *Bon courage, eh!*'

Dubois took him outside.

'Looks like they have a tracker in place,' Kate said.

'Confirms the sailor as part of the plot,' Fenaux agreed.

Acting solely as an observer of the unfolding action felt strange to Kate. There was more to come; she would be patient. For now, Fenaux had delicate matters to weigh before deciding his next move. She did not envy his task.

48

BACK IN DUBLIN MAC was trying to make sense of the bombshell that had just dropped.

'Can you repeat that, please?' he asked the Justice Department's Secretary-General.

'The Minister has ordered that SIU stands down from operational cooperation with French forces.'

'The decision on full cooperation was made hours ago,' Mac said. 'What's changed?'

'The Assistant Attorney-General has suggested to the Minister that while intelligence sharing is perfectly acceptable in this context, active participation in operations on foreign soil might infringe our constitutional neutrality.'

'Where did he dream up that notion?' Mac asked in exasperation.

'As you know the Assistant A-G is an imminent legal scholar and the Minister values his opinion.'

'Has the Attorney-General changed his mind too?'

'I'd rather not comment on that, Chief Superintendent.'

'The Minister's instructions are received and understood. I

place the safety of my team above any other consideration. Remember that.'

'Is that the message I give the Minister?'

Mac left the question unanswered.

Before Fenaux's men dropped him back to the harbour, Pierre-Jean rang home. He explained that the voyage had taken longer because of the fog.

When he answered, Omar al-Haddad was curt.

'Just get back here if you want to see your family alive.'

The RAID team drove Pierre-Jean to an alley off the quay. He unlocked the gate to a compound where a scooter was housed. The harbour pilots used it to get around the port. Pierre-Jean kicked it into spluttering life and rode out of the compound. He locked up and headed slowly towards the ring road that brought him in the direction of home.

Digger and the three others had remained in their OPs. They were uncertain whether O'Hare had the harbour under surveillance.

'If he has, they're well concealed,' Digger said. 'It would be pointless to be anywhere other than deep in the harbour; the fog's gotten worse and we haven't seen a soul.'

Fenaux ordered everyone to steer clear of the berth where the *MV Raven* was securely lashed. Kate reviewed Digger, Angie, and Zoom's proximity to the vessel and as far as she could tell, they were safe.

The command centre moved closer to the harbour as Fenaux spoke to his Navy contact. McManus scribbled notes and turned the notepad towards Kate as the call ended. Identifying the hull of their intended target was a challenge, the navy said. Fenaux told them they were the experts and to go figure it out.

His people were thin on the ground now. He had another scene to manage, a delicate one. Four innocent lives depended on them staying undetected until intervention was possible. His second team was still in transit from Paris. He needed SIU more than ever.

'What will O'Hare's next move be?' he asked Kate.

'It's hard to predict.'

'Try.'

'Working on the assumption that O'Hare has the weapons in place on the boat, someone has to come and arm them. Almost certainly, it will be O'Hare himself.'

'What will this involve?'

'He will have to wire the firing mechanism. I am assuming there's no new technology in place. A timer wouldn't work in this scenario as they're unlikely to know the precise time of the sub's arrival. O'Hare will have to have a firing point from where he'll detonate it.'

McManus interpreted.

'Tell me what O'Hare has to do to make the explosion happen.'

'Usually, he encodes a specific signal into a receiver linked to the bomb. This means it won't trigger if it receives *any* radio signal, just the one O'Hare sends when he pushes the button.'

'Can he do that from anywhere?' Fenaux asked.

'In the past, just like the electronic lock on your car, you needed proximity or even a line of sight to make it go boom.'

'He will need to get close then?'

'A couple of hundred meters used to do the job. I can't be sure of the range he needs nowadays. There is another possibility.'

'What's that?'

'Recently, IRA dissidents tried to shoot down a British

Army helicopter north of the border using a mortar detonated by an infrared laser.'

'What advantage would that give them?'

'Distance, they could afford to be further away.'

Fenaux's face was grim; he didn't have to wait for McManus's translation.

'Aside from the method of detonation, he will have this attack planned meticulously,' Kate continued. 'We need to consider what elements there could be other than the boat.'

'What do you mean?'

'The people who have agreed to supply weapons to O'Hare in return for his expertise will drive a hard bargain. They will want the world to know that one of America's most potent weapons has been damaged.'

'Or at least made to look weak, I suppose.'

'Precisely! They'll want to prove once again to America that it is vulnerable to attack anywhere in the world.'

'So what are we looking at – another team? Doing what?'

'Supporting fire, we need to think about where that could come from, who'd provide it, and what they'd use.'

'There's the military doctrine,' Dubois began. 'Height gives you a greater spread of fire. Keeps your enemy pinned down.'

There were nods of agreement.

'Here,' he said pointing at the screen. 'The Château, the ramparts, in particular, offer possibilities to set up supporting fire to the main attack.'

At 4:30 a.m., three and half hours since their initial deployment, he dispatched an intervention team there. It was still pitch black, none of the fog had lifted. The backup team arrived from Paris. Fenaux commandeered private cars from the local Police Judiciaire and deployed them around the harbour.

He was planning the next move when a call from the Navy interrupted him.

'The Limpets are in place,' he said when the call ended.

Kate pored over her copy of the harbour map, rechecking distances between Digger, Angie, and Zoom and the doomed trawler. She reminded them to maintain cover.

Thirty minutes passed. They watched, listened, and waited. Fighting off fatigue is toughest early in the morning. The air in the command post didn't help.

Radio traffic jolted McManus into action. He grabbed his pen and began scribbling furiously. Fenaux and Dubois were already animated. He pushed his pad in front of Kate. *Van at pilot's house – Nutser sighted.* Kate's brain kicked up a gear and she secure texted the news to the teams in the harbour.

The van picked up Saud and left immediately. At 5:25 a.m. it was turning off the port access road, rolling slowly up the quay, as daylight crept into the sky. It was too early for any activity at the port. Fenaux could not send in any more resources without being detected.

Zoom and Angie tracked the van as it entered the harbour. It quickly drove out of sight. Halfway down the quay, it turned right, into an alley. Seconds later the lights disappeared. Fenaux spoke rapidly to Dubois. He was agitated.

McManus whispered to Kate. 'He wants to get a visual in that alley.'

Dubois radioed a RAID Commander and ordered him to get an optic fiberscope in place.

'They're going to gain access from neighbouring roofs,' McManus whispered.

Risky, Kate thought.

A Google Earth image of the alley taken on a sunny day showed a mix of old buildings cheek to jowl with newer ones.

The more recent buildings had flat roofs that could be crossed silently.

Tension escalated in the cramped command post. A radio message confirmed that a fire escape ladder had been located. A RAID member would continue the high-wire act. They estimated Nutser's van could only have been halfway up the alley when it disappeared. The only buildings that offered storage large enough for a van were on the right-hand side, so he had to negotiate a treacherous slated roof.

Minutes ticked by. Their hearts collectively skipped a beat when the door of the van slid open without warning. A RAID member handed a monitor to Crew-cut and departed as quickly as he had arrived.

A grainy picture fuzzed onto the screen. The camera struggled with the light. The doors of the shed were slightly ajar. The RAID commander told Dubois they would keep the camera in place for as long as possible. Kate didn't envy the guy trying to hang on undetected on the slippery roof.

Their eyes didn't leave the monitor. The light was growing brighter; the image improved in tandem. At 6:20 a.m. Saud poked his head out and checked the alley in both directions.

Everyone was on maximum alert. At the harbour pilot's house, street lighting made Nutser's identification possible. They expected both him and Saud, who was picked up there, at the port. The identity of the third passenger was a mystery. The passenger shifted inward when Saud got into the van. Kate believed it had to be O'Hare.

Saud tentatively pulled open one door and then the other. The van slowly reversed out. The RAID cameraman stayed in place. Saud closed the shed door and jumped into the front passenger side of the van. As the van moved off, the camera feed faded.

Angie moved swiftly to another jetty while the van was

housed. The alley was a dead-end and her new position gave her a view of the only exit.

'Only Treacy and Saud in the van now,'

'Repeat,' Fenaux asked.

'Confirm! Two suspects visible in front of the vehicle.'

'What about O'Hare?'

'Not visible in vehicle. Just two heads,' Angie confirmed.

Fenaux, Dubois, and Kate reassessed what had transpired in the past hour. Nutser did the driving when it entered the shed and the crews had counted three people in it. Angie confirmed Nutser as the driver when the van exited.

The alley was the only blind spot where he might have slipped out. Why he would do it like that baffled them.

'Search and find him,' Fenaux ordered Dubois.

He spoke rapidly to the RAID commander who sent a team to check nearby roofs. Meanwhile, Digger had taken up the commentary on the progress of the van. Élodie transmitted his observations. When it came to the end of the alley it turned right, in the direction of the MV Raven.

'Two passengers in front – confirm.'

Nobody in the command post spoke.

'Saud and Treacy – confirm.'

The intervention point was set. Fenaux and Dubois had agreed with RAID as to how close they would allow the van to get to the boat. The choices were limited. It was a challenging environment to operate in for anything but a Navy unit. Fenaux wanted to keep it Police.

Élodie's radio reports filled the command post. Kate heard Digger's calm tones in the background.

Just under a hundred meters from the corner of the quay, he began the countdown.

'Seventy-five.

'Sixty.

'Forty-five.
'Thirty.
'Fifteen.
'Approaching corner NOW.'

The site was well chosen. RAID had commandeered a fish wholesaler's premises. If there was any tactical advantage at all it was minimal. It would only work if they moved at the right moment. The distance between their hideout and the target at that point was three to five meters. Chances were the driver and passenger wouldn't see them before they heard the booms. Then it would be too late. The van turned towards the boat.

The monitor flickered into life again. The command post went mobile as a chaos of noise erupted from the live feed on RAID helmets. Kate couldn't make out what was happening. Their driver careered along the quay towards the action.

'Two prisoners. Standby. One down. Standby. One dead.'

Fenaux was on his radio immediately.

'*Allez, allez, allez,*' he shouted. McManus scribbled. He didn't need to; Kate got the picture. He was sending in the teams at the harbour pilot's house. Plugged into the juice, she wished she was closer to the action.

Pierre-Jean had explained to Dubois that his family was being held in a utility room beside the kitchen. Their captors had allowed them to get sleeping bags. Stéphanie was lying with her two children on either side when he left.

The RAID commander had given precise instructions. 'Stay with your family; lie down. Cover your ears when the windows break. Don't move. Don't run.'

When Pierre-Jean got back to the house he had asked permission to stay with his family. The one in charge let him reunite with them on condition he kept them quiet. The wait had seemed like an eternity. When the first sound of breaking glass erupted around the house; he sprang into action. He had decided it would be too frightening for his family to hear the police instructions. As glass crashed and door frames splintered, he threw himself on top of his wakening family.

'*Ne bougez pas!*' he cried to his hysterical children and screaming wife. '*Ne bougez pas!*'

His pleas were unnecessary; they were paralyzed with fear. The noise around them was apocalyptic. First explosions; then doors and windows being broken down; calls of 'Surrender or die.' Rapid gunfire, '*Allahu Akbar*' shouted. Pierre-Jean didn't move in the deadly silence that followed. He was afraid to look until a hand touched his shoulder.

The RAID commander smiled through his ski mask and gave him a thumbs-up. '*Bravo!*'

49

WISPS OF SMOKE from the stun grenades and weapons mingled with the early morning fog. The smell of cordite hung in the air as Fenaux and Kate got to the shot-up van. RAID members took up defensive positions around their prisoner.

'Hold positions,' Kate ordered her crew. She didn't know the status of the limpets and felt uncomfortably close to the *MV Raven*.

'You can allow them to come out soon,' Dubois told her. 'They won't blow it now.'

Fenaux was still anxiously holding the radio in his left hand and pacing.

The message finally came. 'Family safe and secure.'

The group around Fenaux cheered on hearing the message.

'Status?' he asked the RAID commander.

'Two in custody with gunshot wounds. They'll survive.'

'Good work! Have we taken any hits?'

'One of ours is down.'

'How bad?'

'Medics with him. Neck wound. We're rushing him to the hospital. Status unknown for now.'

'What about the suspects?'

'Ambulance is en route.'

'Keep me posted,' Fenaux said.

The van was peppered with RAID rounds. Nutser Treacy was trussed on the ground; his wrists bound with flex handcuffs pulled tight.

'*Chef – s'il vous plait.*'

One of Fenaux's crew called him to the rear of the van. The doors were wide open.

'*C'est vide.*'

Kate's eyes took in the reality. There was nothing in the back of the van. No person, no tools. A Leatherman in a black web pouch, found in Nutser's trouser pocket, was the closest thing to any kind of tools needed to wire a bomb. One of the RAID team examined it, opening it up and checking out its various accoutrements.

Kate looked to where Nutser lay on the quay. A RAID boot kept his head pressed sideways to the ground. He wasn't struggling, there was no anger. His expression worried her. He was smirking and deadly calm.

An eerie feeling washed over Kate. O'Hare had succeeded in drawing everyone to the trawler. His plan had to still be in play.

'We're not done,' she said to Fenaux.

He tilted his head, not understanding.

'It's not over.'

'But we're in control now.'

She took him aside, out of Nutser's hearing.

'My advice is to get your people back from that boat fast.'

'But the Navy will not blow it now.'

'We don't know what devices are on board,' Kate warned Fenaux. 'Nobody's safe until we find O'Hare.'

'Okay,' Fenaux nodded. 'What's your call on what to do?'

'I'll redeploy my team to the Château and join them there.'

She called Twomey. He was in a RHIB in the harbour. She told him to go slowly upriver past the Château and be prepared to move fast if they needed him.

Crew-cut pulled up alongside the command post in a car that had seen better days. McManus jumped out of the van and moved toward it. Kate didn't want him in harm's way.

'Stay on the radio,' she shouted. 'Keep me updated.'

'My orders are not to let you out of my eyes,' Crew-cut told her.

'Out of your sight, perhaps. Whatever, we need to pick Digger up.'

Angie's voice cut in on the radio.

'There's a van in the Château car park. I don't like the look of it or where it's parked.'

'That was there last night,' Kate reminded Crew-cut. He was already revving the engine of the dated motor as Digger exited his OP and jumped on board.

Kate shouted to Fenaux.

'The boat's not the main weapon.'

'*Putain*! Get going. I'll tell the Navy to blow it.'

As the command post started to reverse Fenaux and Dubois jumped in and slammed the doors. The RAID teams frog-marched Nutser towards an armour-plated car. The last image Kate saw in the wing mirror was the lumbering command post van straightening up and beginning its trip up the quay. The thing was built for neither comfort nor speed.

She checked with Twomey, he was returning downriver. A

Navy RIB had intercepted them and warned all police units to stay clear. They were controlling the entry points to their bases and wanted no complications if they had to defend them.

She ordered him to get as close as possible to the Château and find somewhere from where he could deploy fast.

They swung into the Château car park. Kate jumped from the car as it slowed and crawled towards a public toilet building. Her phone rang as she got to the wall of the block. It was Mac.

'Kate, Minister O'Hagan has ordered we restrict our involvement in this operation to intelligence sharing only,' he said, urgently.

'Jesus, Mary, and Joseph, you have to be joking.'

'I'm not. That's his order.'

'Bullshit! He can't just switch us on and off like that. I'm in a highly volatile situation right now.'

'Kate...' Mac shouted. 'What if Charlie has compromised you? Let Digger command the rest of the operation.'

'How...?'

'Vince Hyland talked to me a few hours ago. He knows about Charlie's female associate, Kate.'

'Sub's coming up,' Twomey reported into Kate's radio earpiece.

Kate's head throbbed with information overload. 'I'm killing this phone. An operational imperative.'

Angie's alarmed voice cut in on the radio.

'The rear doors of the van have opened,' she reported.

'What's your ETA?' Kate radioed Twomey.

'Thirty seconds.'

Her peripheral vision caught a glimpse of the sub.

Twomey's RIB was bumping across its wake. The *Thalassa* seemed to grow as it moved along at a steady pace; a sleek black monster rising serenely from the deep.

For an instant, the scene was utterly calm.

Then the ear-splitting sound of heavy weapon gunfire erupted from the van. Spent rounds spilled from it into the car park.

'Jesus Christ,' Kate shouted. 'That's a big fucking gun.'

Almost simultaneously, Kate saw the fireball, milliseconds before she heard the explosion. The days of the *MV Raven* as a working boat were done. Another burst of firing came from the van.

Kate was hunkered behind the toilet block.

Twomey came on the radio, shouting. 'Kate, we've taken shrapnel to the RIB. Don't count on us.'

'Can you get ashore?'

'Affirmative.'

Another burst of fire came from the van. The attacker's tactics were simple. Lay down a field of fire and wait for the target to move inexorably into it.

'Can RAID take out the van?' Kate shouted into the radio.

'Their shots on the van aren't impacting,' McManus replied. 'They think there's some kind of steel plating inside the roof and sides.'

'Tell them to hold their fire. We'll take it,' she shouted.

Digger was behind her, she told him what she wanted from him. She worried about Angie and Zoom until Angie confirmed they were inside the toilet block, spotting for the crews outside. She motioned to Crew-cut that on her signal she wanted him to shoot out the van's windscreen. A momentary distraction to stall the shooter. He gave a thumbs-up.

Water spewed around the sub as the weapon in the van fired again. Kate took off, running hard, staying low. The action around her seemed to play out in slow motion, her focus solely on her objective. She heard glass shatter; Crew-cut had done his job. Digger immediately shot the tires out and the van sagged. No stopping now.

Hunched over, Kate edged closer. Up close the weapon was a brutal cannon, the noise from it, horrendous. A fearsome tongue of flame shot out each time it fired. No stopping now.

Kate's side-arm was nothing special. A Sig Sauer pistol; the kind most detectives carried. The one concession the procurement officer made to SIU was to get them fifteen-round magazines rather than the standard ten.

Kate rolled in front of the open doors and came up low, both hands grasping the Sig in a fist grip. She didn't aim, didn't look but let loose a guttural scream as she emptied the full clip into the rear of the van, and rolled away.

The noise stopped.

A voice in her head told her to run. She got to a grassy embankment, jumped over, and kept rolling. Her mind in turmoil, she struggled to grasp anything that would halt her momentum. Had she holstered her gun? It was still in her hand. She ditched it as she tipped over a ledge. She clung on for dear life and scrambled for a foothold. She was suspended over some kind of drop but did not know how steep, and did not dare to look down to check it out. Her strength ebbed and she began to feel nauseous.

'We've got you, Kate,' she heard a voice above her say.

Fenaux's classic Gallic good looks came through her blurred vision as Digger grabbed her other shoulder. Together they hauled her up and she glanced down towards the moat. Her head began to spin as she pulled back. A strip of green grass had replaced the water of medieval times. She was glad to have been spared the ten-meter drop.

'Nobody touches the van until RAID checks it,' Fenaux shouted.

He wanted to ensure nobody got caught out by secondary devices.

Twomey appeared. He had led his men from the river to safety.

'You okay?' he asked her.

'I'll live,' Kate said 'What about the guy in the van?'

'His fighting days are over.'

'O'Hare?' she asked.

'Definitely not,' Twomey replied.

50

KATE'S HEAD cleared as Fenaux discussed their next move.

'He'll go to ground for...' she began.

The static of Fenaux's radio cut in as a message came through. He looked at Kate.

'The Château crew is reporting a naval museum fire door has been forced open.'

'O'Hare. It has to be.'

'I'll task RAID with the arrest.'

'You have to find him first.'

'This is what they train for.'

'Let us lead you to him, we know him better than anyone.'

'Kate, you're shaken up. You and your crew have done enough today.'

'Nothing's done 'til I see O'Hare's face and he knows it's over.'

'Let's go inside and discuss it.'

Inside, a map of the Château hung on a wall of the small security office. It was a huge site; advertised as a veritable open-air museum. A series of towers constructed over centuries connected by ramparts offered a perfect view of the harbour entrance. It was a well-chosen site from a defensive viewpoint and boasted of never having been taken by force. They focused on the naval museum. The map showed fire exits, ground-floor windows, public entrances, and exits. All were possible escape routes.

'He'll try to go to ground. He has done this many times in the past after border attacks,' Kate explained.

'Any particular place he might choose?' Dubois asked.

'We know he has used extremely tight concealment areas in the past.'

'We saw the photos of the truck cab.'

'We believe he has holed up in rural bunkers for up to a week. He's cunning.'

They examined each floor plan minutely. The RAID Commander wanted to drive O'Hare upwards using two search teams. One would take the basement and ground floor and the other, the first floor upwards to the ramparts.

Angie and Zoom began in the basement. Kate brought Digger with her and headed towards the first floor. A four-man RAID team came with both.

The first hour of the search was tense. They checked every crevice and found nothing. The exhibit rooms portrayed Brest's connection to the rich French maritime history. The search teams did not allow it to distract them. They were more inter-ested in the small service rooms off them. They found nothing. Angie reported that they had cleared the basement and were en route to the ground floor.

The stone steps between the floors were well worn by centuries of use. Kate's group ascended cautiously towards an exit onto the ramparts. Fenaux had locked down all exits from the Château. As they reached the landing she radioed him to release the door that would allow them to access the ramparts.

As they waited, a shadow crept across her vision. She glanced behind to the offside of a turret, but it was too late. An arm came round her neck and pulled her back towards the door. Cold metal pressed hard against her temple as the door clicked open.

Digger trained his pistol on O'Hare.

'Let her go,' he roared.

'Try anything and she goes first.'

Kate struggled. O'Hare's breath smelled foul, his eyes were frenzied, and his face contorted in a feral snarl.

'Take me,' Digger said, 'release her.'

O'Hare kicked open the emergency exit and growled, 'This bitch will do. Back the fuck off.'

Digger's weapon followed O'Hare's every twist and turn. He had counted his shots from earlier in the car park; six. He still had more than half a clip.

'Where she goes, I go.'

O'Hare stabbed his gun at the RAID team that had assault rifles trained on him.

'Tell them not to come out in the open or I'll do her.'

Digger shouted into the radio for McManus to pass the word. He frantically gestured at RAID to stay put.

O'Hare pressed to Kate's head.

'Close that fuckin' door.'

The RAID commander pulled it inward.

'It's closed,' Digger told him.

He did not lock the door, however. Instead, he delicately pushed a tiny camera through the open crack. Twomey and Fenaux followed events on the tiny, temporary command post screen and held their breath.

O'Hare dragged Kate backwards towards the edge of the ramparts. She began to see the panorama of the harbour unveiling as the fog cleared. He hauled her towards the edge. The sight of the dry moat below made her head spin; she was going to puke. She couldn't stop and began to spasm. O'Hare tightened his grip. Her knees sagged as she vomited copiously onto his hand.

'Oh, ya dirty...' O'Hare exclaimed, his sentence unfinished. Kate felt propelled backwards until she hit the ground. Digger pulled her free from beneath O'Hare's writhing body as the RAID team spilled out onto the ramparts and disarmed him. Blood flooded O'Hare's throat and frothy bubbles spewed from his mouth. A RAID medic emerged from the castle and asked Kate if she was okay. She nodded and he went to attend to the dying terrorist.

Twomey had told Fenaux about Kate's fear of heights. Fenaux worked it to their advantage. He ordered RAID to take the shot on O'Hare if a clear opportunity arose. When Kate slipped, the closest sniper didn't hesitate.

Fenaux charged through the emergency exit; his face a mixture of anxiety and elation.

Surveying the mess of puke and blood on Kate's parka, he smiled.

'This is going to be a big cleaning bill.'

'Oh crap! Someone better break the news to Élodie. This is her coat.'

The Thalassa berthed as they hunted O'Hare. Pilot boats guided it into position, nudging it against the quay wall where mooring ropes secured it.

Lacey was brought up and handed over to NCIS personnel who transferred him to a car and drove off. Jeffers briefed Captain Anderson, the master of deception, on the FBI's investigation into the planned attack on his vessel. Until the shots rang out, the captain had achieved his goal of a silent arrival into Brest.

While the Captain was brought up to speed, a human chain formed from a delivery van. Conscious of the daily needs of their brothers in arms, a French navy catering crew was delivering fresh vegetables, freshly baked bread, and finally croissants and pain au chocolat. Kate guessed the Thalassa crew would enjoy a rare culinary treat that day somewhere under the Atlantic Ocean.

Traffic was picking up on the roads around the quays as Brest came to life. A submarine in port was not exactly an event for the locals. The only onlookers were early-morning joggers. Whether the shooting had been captured on camera was anyone's guess. The noise would certainly have attracted attention.

Captain Anderson didn't raise the Stars and Stripes and didn't hang about. Fenaux and Kate's crews watched from the ramparts of Château de Brest as pilot boats steered the Thalassa from its berth. Within minutes of leaving the quay, it was already fading into the depths heading out of the harbour, back to its natural habitat of the open ocean.

At 8:00 a.m. a RAID bomb disposal team gave the all-clear on the van. A team approached it, retrieved the body, and laid it out on the tarmac. The crews approached in silence.

Fenaux squatted to view the body. He turned the head sideways.

'Any ideas?' Kate asked him.

'Not immediately,' he replied.

'Let us have a photo when he's cleaned up,' she said, maintaining an outward calm. Inside, she was a mess. She ached all over from the morning's action and was looking into the face of the first person she had to kill. Digger stayed by her side. He knew the feeling. Killing another human being, whatever the circumstances, was a life-defining moment.

They looked into the back of the van. The metal-on-metal clang they'd heard from the van was the machine-gun belts holding the 12.7 mm rounds for the DShK anti-aircraft weapon. Spent shells spattered with blood lay on the floor of the van.

Kate moved away and sat in the back of a RAID van. She had removed Élodie's damaged parka and began to shiver. Digger took off his jacket and put it around her shoulders.

'Mac knows about Charlie,' she told him.

'Fucking Vince Hyland couldn't help himself. He had to keep snooping.'

'It doesn't matter. He was going to find out anyway.'

Meanwhile, Fenaux called Mac and told him how the final parts of the drama had unfolded. He sang Kate's praises, and of her crew, assuring him that everyone was well.

Crew-cut leaned into the van.

'The Press is here,' he told Fenaux.

Mac overheard the news.

'My crew must leave now,' he said, urgently. 'Don't tell the Press that there were Irish police near the scene. Okay? Just tell them we helped you out with intelligence sharing.'

'Leave it to me,' Fenaux said.

While he broke the news to Kate, she looked at his hands rather than directly at him. He had pockmarks on his skin from which blood had been cleaned. She had missed it in the hurried briefing before the searches for O'Hare began.

'What happened?' she asked.

'The command post caught some of the blast from the boat. The windows shattered.'

'What about McManus?' she asked.

Fenaux pointed across the car park where a medic was bandaging his head. He looked like a rugby player after a France-Ireland game.

'Shit,' she laughed. 'The interpreter's the one going home with stitches.'

51

O'HARE HAD TRIED to choreograph both sides of the deal. When the harbour pilot's house was taken over, the green light was given to move the containers. While the frantic action played out in France, the other pieces of Operation Cassandra were being relentlessly fitted together.

The first truck made its pickup. Belgian traffic cops then sighted another en route to Holland and called it in. Dutch Intelligence took over at the border. Within hours, they identified the Rotterdam warehouse, the destination of the Irish hauliers. AIVD had surveillance teams in place by the time the second truck arrived.

In most European countries investigating judges direct how criminal investigations proceed. In Ireland and the UK, police make these calls. Assistant Commissioner Fox brokered an agreement that accommodated all sides.

By the time the AIVD operation cranked up, the first truck had left Holland. Daphne Clarke, acting MI5 liaison link for Ireland, confirmed that it had entered the UK at Dover. Its whereabouts was unknown for a few frantic hours.

Fishguard in Wales was the most likely port of exit and inquiries there confirmed it was booked onto a late evening sailing to Rosslare. Clarke agreed to let it proceed to Ireland unhindered.

Fox ordered Mac to concede seizing the remainder of the trucks to the Dutch. They had played their part and had to be rewarded.

Around the same time, Kate's crew learned of the scale of the task ahead of them in Brest, Detective Sergeant John Casey was giving another SIU team a 'heads-up' at Rosslare port. Nasri's truck had rolled off the ferry. They watched it wind its way up the narrow roadway from the port. They tailed it to a freight yard twenty kilometres north where the trailer was dropped. The driver was allowed to leave; he would be picked up later.

The team set up around the yard and waited. At 2:00 a.m. Bob McElgunn arrived, unlocked the gate, and drove in. He made a phone call and nervously checked his watch. Twenty minutes later another truck arrived.

The watching team was patient and it paid off. McElgunn checked the numbers on the trailers and directed the driver towards the one he wanted. They hitched it to the cab and drove out. McElgunn locked the gate behind them. Mac ordered the ERU Commander to hold back. He wanted to get as far as he could with the deadly load and discover its destination.

Everyone got twitchy when the driver turned onto secondary roads near Arklow. Kate's crew had scoped the area out a few weeks earlier and Mac directed units to where he believed the weapons were headed. McElgunn led the truck to a farmyard and opened the gates. The team allowed them to unload the first crate into the underground bunker before hitting it. In the telling, Mac recalled with relish how the ERU had dropped stun grenades into the bunker to encourage compliance. Seconds later, McElgunn and his accomplice crawled out screaming.

Telephone intercepts picked up Nasri's frantic calls to the other three hauliers as he tried to cancel their jobs. He was too late for two of them; they were already in custody in Holland. They would be hostages to fortune for as long as it took the investigating judge to conclude that they were duplicitously drawn into the affair. The fourth driver was at the Belgian border when Nasri got through to him and cancelled. The fifty per cent fee he received would barely cover his expenses. He would never connect the dots and thank his lucky stars.

<hr>

Mac was waiting when Kate and her crew landed at the Air Corps base outside Dublin.

'Alright kid?' he asked all fatherly, as she stepped onto the tarmac.

'I'll live; I've got a splitter of a headache. The flight didn't help.'

'Let's go get you checked out.'

'What about the debrief? Don't you want to know how it went down?'

'Fenaux's filled me in. The debrief can wait.'

'Will the Commissioner or Minister for Justice not want to make a statement to the Press?'

'For now, that will be along the lines that we're cooperating in every possible way.'

'So, what we've been through never happened?'

'Kate, you need to look after yourself. Get yourself checked out.'

'I'll do it after I change my clothes back at base.'

'Better if you do it straight away.'

'But my clothes are in shit,' she said, annoyed at the muted welcome home.

'The hospital will give you sweats.'

'What hospital?'

Kate was pissed off. She could see most of the team piling onto a minibus that had drawn up alongside the plane.

'The Blackrock Clinic. I know one of the consultants there, we spoke this morning, and you'll get priority treatment.'

The Blackrock Clinic was a private hospital with a coterie of rich clients.

'If you're taking me there, I need to change.'

'Don't worry. We've arranged to get you in quietly. We're even picking up the bill.'

'What about everyone else?'

'The CMO will look after them.'

'That'll be fine for me too. I want to stay with my team.'

The minibus driver seemed to be waiting for a signal. Mac gave it and the door closed. The bus drove off. Mac walked with Kate towards the car which had brought him to meet the plane.

'If you go back now, people will want to grill you straight away. Do you think you're up to that?'

'What people? We brought the case to a successful conclusion, didn't we?'

'Kate, you disobeyed direct orders.'

'We were under fire when the order came to stand down.'

'Listen to yourself. Do you think that kind of answer will keep you out of trouble?'

Kate shook her head.

'Believe me, before we're done with Cassandra, things will get dirty. Politicians always cover their arses before worrying about ours.'

Kate didn't answer.

'I've arranged sick leave for you for at least a week. The dust might have settled by then.'

'I'm not running away from anything. I did nothing wrong.'

'Take my advice, Kate, just this once.'

She nodded and slumped into the back of his car. He sat up front with the ERU driver.

'Blackrock Clinic,' he ordered.

'Your weapon, please,' Mac said as the car pulled off. Kate knew it was routine after an officer-involved shooting. She slid the mag out, pulled back the slide, and cleared the Sig before handing it over to him without query.

He overheard Kate tap a message on her phone.

'Who are you texting?'

'My mother.'

'Okay.'

The text she sent to Digger read: *Deep shit – all actions on my orders – get me all info possible.*

She entered the exclusive clinic round the back, walked through the kitchens, and took a service lift. Mac accompanied her all the way. Any insulin burst her body gave her as a shield against trauma had long since drained away. She was stiff and sore. At the diagnostic suite, she showered and changed clothes. The hospital supplied disposable underwear and sweats. She stashed her stained gear in a plastic bag and brought it with her. They poked and prodded; blood tested and X-rayed her before advising that she needed a week's rest to recover. While Mac waited, they filled a prescription for painkillers and sleeping pills.

He dropped her outside her apartment block, a kilometre away.

As she exited the car he said, 'I'll let everyone know you'll be back in a week or so to give them grief.'

The painkillers were kicking in and she was too weary to reply.

Familiar afternoon smells greeted Kate in the entrance hall. Cleaning solvents mainly, but it was home. She called the lift and ascended. As she stepped onto the landing, her warning antennae switched back to full alert.

Light shone from under her apartment door and she could hear music playing. Instinctively she went for her weapon but came up empty-handed, Mac had commandeered it.

She fumbled for her keys, opened the front door quietly, and stepped inside. No stopping now. The music thumped loudly and she could hear the shower going. The hallway was empty. Kate moved cautiously to the bedroom. It was clear. Charlie's suitcase lay open on the floor; she had a bad feeling. He had been gone less than a week. Her head began to throb.

Silently, she made her way back towards the lounge where Adele was belting out 'Set Fire to the Rain'. Her heart pounded. Should she duck out and call back up? She decided against it. She needed to verify how many people were using her apartment.

Kate swept into the lounge but there was no one there. When she killed the music she heard movement from the bathroom behind her. Charlie appeared with a towel draped around his waist.

'What are *you* doing here?' she demanded.

He fidgeted nervously with the towel.

'Kate, what's happened to your face?'

A dark blue-grey bruise had welled up on her left cheek.

'Answer my question?'

'I got cancelled by the company; had to head home.'

Kate looked at him coldly.

'Charlie, I know.'

She hadn't taken in that the shower was still running.

'I loved you, but you ruined everything.'

A voice from behind startled her.

'You might be overstatin' it a bit there, darlin'.'

Instinctively, Kate lashed two swift defensive kicks in its direction and Jacinta Fitzpatrick crumpled to the floor. Her towel slipped revealing opulent breasts still slick from her shared shower with Kate's boyfriend.

She screamed in agony. 'You fuckin' bitch, you broke my leg!'

Kate stood with arms raised defensively between the cheating couple, a residue of adrenaline sustaining her.

'Jesus, Kate, there was no need for that,' Charlie shouted.

'Her leg's not broken. She'll get feeling back in about twenty minutes. Get your clothes and get out.'

'At least let us get dressed first.'

'Scoop up your clothes and get out. You can dress on the landing. Otherwise, I'm calling the Guards.'

Charlie walked over and picked up his concubine. She hobbled through the hallway, picked up a bundle of clothes, and pulled on pants. She slumped to the floor to stuff the remainder into a weekend bag and Charlie offered his hand to help her up. As the pair shuffled through the apartment door, Kate noticed something they had forgotten. She grabbed Charlie's iPod from the stereo dock and threw it after him.

'Take Adele with you!'

It clattered off his head onto the landing floor. She slammed the door and chained it securely.

52

THE NEXT MORNING Kate woke up stiff and sore. She had slept on the couch and took a warm shower to ease the aches and pains. She rang her mother.

'Mind if I come down for a few days?'

'Of course, I'm delighted to hear you're taking a rest. I'll cook something nice.'

'No need to fuss, Mum, I just need to get out of Dublin for a while.'

'Well, I'll be delighted with the company.'

The drive to Dundalk took under an hour. Kate's happiest memories were of growing up near the centre of town. Her Mum greeted her at the front door of their red brick, two-up two-down, terraced house. Kate had helped her mother purchase the property when the local council decided to sell off its housing stock.

'You look pale,' she said.

'Can we at least get in off the street?'

'Let me get some of your stuff.'

Before Kate could protest her mother had grabbed her

weekend case and headed indoors. The kitchen was warm and spotlessly clean. The kettle was boiled. Her mother made tea and filled her in on all the local gossip. When they finished she lay out on the couch in the front room. Familiar sounds from the street helped her drift off. When she woke up, she was covered by a warm blanket, and orange light from the street lights was filtering through the window blinds.

'How long have I been out?'

'Six hours,' her Mum told her.

'Oh crap, I won't sleep tonight.'

'Girlie, by the look of you, sleep won't be a problem.'

'What do you mean?'

'Kate, I have eyes in my head, I can see you've been knocked about. All the make-up in the world won't cover it up.'

Her mother was used to seeing Kate with bruises from Ju-Jitsu. This looked different.

'All part of the job, I'm afraid.'

'Tell me what happened.'

'You know I can't, Mum.'

They ate dinner together in the kitchen, one of her mother's famous Irish stews. It was delicious. The phone rang as they tidied plates off the table.

'A rape victim,' her mother said as she hung up. 'I have to go to the hospital. One of our new advocates is nervous the first time around. Will you be okay on your own?'

'I'll be fine. I can catch up on some telly.'

'Norrie will bring the kids around tomorrow evening after work.'

'Fine, Mum. Get going.'

When her mother left, Kate called Digger at home.

'How are you feeling?'

'Shite, if you must know,' he replied.

'Yeah! I've got a few aches and pains myself. I guess we got lucky overall, do you think?'

'Maybe! Maybe not.'

'What do you mean?'

'I don't like what's goin' on,' Digger said.

'What do you mean?'

'We fronted up for the debrief today and the first thing we saw is that you weren't there.'

'The hospital put me on the sick for a week. I thought Mac wouldn't hold the debrief without me.'

'Mac told us you were certified unfit for work but I'd have preferred to hear it from you.'

'Jesus Christ Digger, I had other shit to deal with.'

'What other shit?'

'Charlie!'

He paused.

'Sorry, I forgot about that. I thought he was away.'

'So did I. It doesn't matter now, he's gone for good. What are you worried about?'

'You know the way our debriefs usually roll?'

'Yeah, sit down, coffee, tell the story.'

'This time's different. We're bein' interviewed individually.'

'What? By who?'

'The Commissioner has set up a board of inquiry into SIU actions in France. The head of CID is chairin' it and Detective Chief Superintendent O'Driscoll from Special Branch is advisin' him. You know what he's like.'

'Holy crap! And no one thought to tell me?'

'Check your phone. I've tried a few times.'

Kate dug her phone out of her bag. It was dead. She found a charger and plugged it into a socket in the kitchen.

'So everyone from the mission is bein' interviewed separately,' Digger said.

'Were you first?'

'No, kind of weird; they started with the most junior of Twomey's crew. They grilled him for an hour.'

'It's a bloody setup,' Kate exclaimed.

'No, I think we're cool. Like you said in the text, we were actin' on your orders. You were actin' on orders from on high.'

Kate didn't respond immediately.

'That's the case, isn't it?'

'What I'm going to tell you now stays between us.'

'You don't have to say that, you know I won't tell anyone else.'

'They tried to call us off at the last minute.'

'How do you mean?'

'Just as we got to the van, Mac rang to say that the Minister ordered us to steer clear of confrontation. I ignored him.'

'Oh fuck me!'

'Digger, it was too late at that stage.'

'Yeah, but...'

'I know, someone high up the chain wants cover in case there's kickback.'

Digger ended the call with a warning.

'Think carefully about what you say to the inquiry board.'

Kate checked her phone as it came to life. She had a 'call me' text from Mac but it was too late now. There were four missed calls from Digger. Her mind was swirling; the turmoil of the past twenty-four hours tipped her brain towards overload. She scribbled a note for her mother about having an early night and went to bed. Her eyes closed the minute her head hit the pillow.

Kate could only see the sky. Her feet weren't touching the ground. Foul-smelling breath invaded her senses. She was being pushed closer and closer to the edge of a cliff. She was panicked, screaming...

As she sat bolt upright, her mother threw her arms around her.

'You're okay, Kate. It's just a bad dream.'

It took Kate a few seconds to realize that she was sitting in her own bed. She took in short, fast breaths. After moments in her mother's embrace, her breathing stabilized. She was drenched in sweat.

'I'll get fresh bed linen,' her mother said.

'Sorry, Mum.'

'Go change and put the kettle on. We need to talk.'

Kate showered and changed into pyjamas she found in the airing cupboard. It was 1.00 a.m.

'How long have you been in my room?'

'An hour or so, I came home around half eleven. You were crying out in your sleep. I wanted to be there when you woke up.'

'Oh Mum, I'm sorry for keeping you up.'

'Kate, stop right there. Was this the dream about Grandad again?'

'No, something else.'

She held both Kate's hands and looked into her eyes.

'*Tell* me what happened.'

Worn down by exhaustion, she told her mother most of the details of the previous two days. How she had pushed on when others wanted to pull back. How it appeared likely she could be seeking a new job when the whole thing got threshed out. She explained that her enforced rest was an immediate outcome.

'Right,' her mother said, 'you speak to nobody until Mary sees you in the morning.'

Kate said she would talk to her mother's psychologist friend and take it from there. At three o'clock she kissed her mum goodnight and hugged her tighter than she had in a while.

***

Shrinks hold much fear for police, one adverse report could stall a career. Mary D'Arcy was Kate's mother's best friend and confidante, who helped with cases at the Rape Crisis Centre. The next day when Kate met her, the Doc began by explaining that she knew what it was like to work in a male-dominated world. Margaret Bowen had filled her in on how Kate came by the bruise on her face. Kate told the Doc that having a 'meltdown' report on her personnel file would sink her career.

'That's not a problem,' Doc D'Arcy replied, 'because you didn't have one.'

'What have the past few hours been about then?'

'Let's go over what brought all this on.'

Kate reiterated the near-death experiences and threw in her acrimonious bust-up with Charlie.

'You've been through multiple traumatic events. Now your future seems under threat. It's all too much for your brain to cope with. It just needs a rest.'

'As simple as that? What about post-traumatic stress?'

'Too soon to say for sure, Kate; nothing is straightforward when understanding how our brain works. Just be aware that a life-endangering trauma, as you've experienced, leaves a profound mark on the emotional brain. Here's what we're going to do.'

She certified that Kate needed a further week off. Simple fatigue was the diagnosis; rest was the only cure. No exceptions.

'We'll ward off the vultures, and work identifying any triggers that might set off a PTSD episode.'

Kate nodded.

'We can't control every aspect of our lives. You've always rolled with the punches. Keep it like that!'

'I can go back to work?'

'What happens with this whole inquiry business?'

'I have an order to appear before a board of inquiry, next week. I tell my side of the story. They decide whether I did anything wrong.'

'Focus on getting a precise sequence of events straight in your head. Remember your primary duty is always to protect life.'

'What are you saying? I was wrong to shoot the attacker?'

'No, no, quite the opposite; your action protected the lives of your team and those you were working with.'

'Glad we cleared that up.'

'Don't go back to work until the inquiry is done. When you go before the board keep emotion out of the equation. Wait and see, mercy will season justice.'

'Shakespeare! Really, Doc.'

'Isn't justice what drew you to the police? Your mother worries about you, you know. She thinks what happened in the past might have affected you. Do you want to talk about it?'

'Another time.'

***

At the end of the following week, Kate felt rejuvenated as she collected a visitor's badge at the Garda headquarters main gate. Her mother's pampering had revived her. Her sleep pattern was still all over the place and she napped most afternoons to catch up. She spent hours playing with her niece and nephew, revelling in their innocence. Norrie showed her how best to apply the Touche Éclat she had bought her the previous Christmas. It had lain unopened in Kate's bag. Now it would cover up what remained of the bruising on her face.

She walked confidently to the Officers' Club where the inquiry board was conducting its business. She wore her full dress uniform as required and bounded to the top of the wide stairs two steps at a time. Outside the conference room, a Special Branch D-I stood guard. Kate recognized him. He had been passed over the year she was promoted to Superintendent.

He smirked as she slowed down near the top.

'Judgment Day! They'll call you when they need you.'

'That makes you surplus to requirements.'

He squared up but she did not flinch. The inquiry board chairman opened the conference room door and glared at the pair.

'Dismiss!' he ordered the narky D-I.

Before taking her seat, Kate saluted the triumvirate that comprised the head of CID, the Special Branch head O'Driscoll and a Minister's appointee. They fired questions and Kate batted concise answers in reply. For two hours it went back and forth; the operation was dissected from beginning to end. The chairman then informed her that the taking of evidence stage of the inquiry was now complete. He had maintained a neutral expression throughout and told her that he would draft a report for the Commissioner, who would be the final arbiter.

Kate stood up and saluted her two senior officers again before departing. The Commissioner would not have total independence; the pompous Justice Minister was lurking in the wings and he would have his say.

53

SKY NEWS HAD LOOPED footage of the attack scene in Brest as the lead item on their bulletins for two days following the incident. American networks were similarly intrigued. They had to content themselves with images of the wreckage of the *MV Raven* floating in the harbour. A crime scene tent completely covered the van near Château de Brest. The ramparts where O'Hare met his demise were out of bounds to the media.

Various anti-terrorist experts were wheeled out to give their views on the involvement of the captured Irishman. O'Hare's pedigree was outlined and mulled over. The true scale of his ambition never became public.

During his first court appearance, Nutser Treacy pulled a stunt, shouting random Islamic phrases; all carefully coached it seemed. He told the judge that his actions were motivated by his devotion to Islam. He claimed that he had been converted through meeting Muslim brothers at truck stops around Europe. It was preposterous and did not help his case.

Kate returned to work the Monday following her appearance before the inquiry board. Relations with Mac cooled. She talked to Mary D'Arcy about her sense of abandonment having narrowly avoided death in the line of duty. Doc D'Arcy counselled reflection on Mac's actions. Who were they designed to safeguard? Kate's immediate response was that it was all about him. The Doc advised her not to rush to judgment.

When she saw the first Sky News report on O'Hare's death, Michelle McKittrick screamed so loudly that neighbours on either side of her Belfast apartment knocked in to check that everything was alright.

She dried the tears streaming down her face, before answering her door.

'Is everything alright?' the pleasant girl from number three asked.

Michelle was unaware that her neighbour was a member of the Police Service of Northern Ireland. A Polish guy lived on the other side. Her mind was in turmoil as she scrambled to explain her distress.

'Oh, I'm sorry if I alarmed you. I thought I saw a rat in my apartment.'

'A rat?' the policewoman said. 'God, that's terrible. Do you want us to get the council out to get rid of it?'

'No, don't worry,' Michelle replied. 'I'll be fine. I think it scuttled out the back way.'

'I will check for you,' the Polish guy said. 'Get me brush to hit the rat.'

'Yes, come into my apartment for a minute. Piotr will get that rat out if it's still around.'

'You're very kind, there's no need.'

The policewoman insisted and placed a protective arm around Michelle's shoulder guiding her next door.

'At the very least, you need a cup of tea. Come on.'

For an hour, Michelle had to endure idle chit-chat while in the background, every fifteen minutes, a television report looped news that caught her completely unawares. The love of her life was a deadly killer.

Two weeks after she threw him out, Charlie sent his brother, Ed, around to Kate's place to collect the rest of his clothes. Ed had played a part in getting them together in the first place. A year earlier, Kate had him trapped in a headlock when Charlie arrived at the Ju-Jitsu dojo to pick him up.

'Sorry about this,' he said, shyly, 'my big brother's a dope.'

'Don't worry. Everything with us and the club stays the same.'

'He's still a dope.'

Operation Cassandra wound down. SIU's main task was preparing case files for court. McElgunn and his accomplice faced multiple charges arising from their arrests. SIU left Nasri untouched.

The identity of the shooter from the van remained a mystery. Fenaux trawled databases in France and beyond to no avail. On a hunch, Kate had the photo shown to the SIU agent. He confirmed that the shooter was the jihadi who had met O'Hare a year earlier. He had no idea what nationality he was and could not identify him further.

Nutser Treacy's appearances before the French courts attracted less and less attention. In a plea bargain that allowed him to serve his twenty-year prison sentence back home, he gave up some details of O'Hare's pact with the radical Islamists.

The mortars made up in the forest were a prototype for the jihadists to use in future attacks. They were competent bomb makers and knew how to build projectiles. O'Hare planned to blow the trawler's fuel tanks as a distraction. The fog had changed their plans to sail the boat into the harbour ready to detonate. Nutser's task on the morning of the attack had been to wire the detonator to blow a small charge over the boat's fuel tanks. The French limpets did the job for him. The attack with the DShK was the key part of the bargain. The best guess on the provenance of the weapon was that it had come from Afghanistan.

Strain received a ten-year sentence on a guilty plea of conspiring to cause explosions. Omar al-Haddad and Said al-Khayyan recovered from their wounds and received twenty years on conspiracy and kidnapping charges. The injured policeman died two weeks after the successful hostage rescue. Only Mac was authorized to attend his memorial service. Fenaux managed the media successfully and SIU's presence in France never surfaced.

His final act was a return trip to Dublin. He brought Dubois and Patrick 'Crew-cut' LeClerc, with him. They tagged along on 'Nutser' Treacy's repatriation flight. Kate greeted them in Dublin. An ERU crew took over the prisoner and escorted him to Portlaoise Prison which would be his digs until his fortieth birthday.

Fenaux was in an ebullient mood. He was bookending a case that stretched everyone to the limit. They had proven a point that good detective work could counter the terrorist menace. The attempt at a spectacular attack against French and American interests had been stopped in its tracks. Plans for a deadly resurgence of a terrorist campaign in Ireland never got off the ground.

They planned to eat together and meet the boss in the afternoon. Kate had donned her glad rags for the occasion. They jumped into cars and headed towards town with Zoom driving. Dubois and Crew-cut were in the following car with McManus. Fenaux informed Kate that his rank obliged him to make a courtesy call on his country's ambassador so they diverted off route.

Dublin's embassy belt is located in Ballsbridge, the most expensive real estate in the country. They crossed the Grand Canal at Leeson Street, diverted onto Ailesbury Road, and drew up outside number thirty-six a short time later. The Gendarme checked them in and told them to park around the back.

'We'll wait in the car for you,' Kate told Fenaux.

Fenaux opened the door on her side.

'Please. You are expected.'

'I'm expected? Why?'

Fenaux just smiled. Further over in the car park, Kate noticed Assistant Commissioner Fox's car. A black Mercedes was parked alongside, the Justice Minister's official vehicle. Her suspicious mind aroused.

'What's going on?'

Fenaux opened a side door and guided her inside.

'Please, just be patient and come.'

The polished smell of decorum hit them as they walked along a corridor. Fenaux directed Kate towards the front of the building and they entered a large room, opulently decorated in a classic French style. A magnificent glass chandelier hung in the centre of the wide corniced ceiling. There was a dark wood, claw-footed table to one side set out with snack food. She had little time to take it all in.

The number one Commissioner, alongside A/C Fox and Mac, was standing in the centre of the room. Alongside the group Justice Minister, Patrick O'Hagan chatted to the French ambassador. The CIA's finest, Dan Whatney shot a 'howdy' as

Fenaux steered Kate into the limelight. Jeffers, the urbane FBI man was chatting to Daphne Clarke, a welcome replacement for Symons, who had returned to MI5's Berlin bureau. When the ambassador saw Fenaux, he broke off his conversation and began to applaud. His staff joined in and soon clapping reverberated around the room as the Irish contingent followed his lead.

Kate was gobsmacked.

'All of it is not for you,' Fenaux whispered. 'Some for us also,' he said as Dubois and Crew-cut trooped in behind him.

Digger and Angie were there already with Twomey and his mob. Zoom was the last to enter the room and he closed the door.

The ambassador indicated that Fenaux and Kate should join him. As she walked towards the centre of the room Kate glared at Mac – *you knew about this?* He shrugged.

While Kate was questioning his motivation, Mac was strategizing about what to do with Charlie. If word of Kate's relationship got to the inquiry board, she would have been dead in the water. Mac convinced Vince Hyland to use Charlie as an informant in the Criminal Assets Bureau case against McElgunn.

It worked like a dream and CAB froze accounts containing €5.5 million that belonged to O'Hare's gang as a result. Charlie had been supplied with a false passport and opened bank accounts at George Town in the Cayman Islands. He had deposited and withdrawn money for the gang for more than a year. When the case concluded, Charlie received a relocation allowance from witness protection and was warned to quit the country permanently.

Without any forewarning, Kate was nominated to accept a Distinguished Service Award from the Fifth French Republic to the Commissioner. Everyone thought it best to spring it on her. They were probably right, if anyone had asked, she would not have volunteered for the job.

French is spoken at all official ceremonies in the embassy. Just before the ambassador began, Fenaux whispered to him.

'Monsieur McManus, s'il vous plait, can you reprise the role you performed so admirably in France?' the ambassador asked.

'*Avec plaisir, Monsieur l'Ambassadeur,*' McManus smiled and stepped forward.

Despite her college debating team experiences, Kate did not care for speeches. Having to listen to them or having to make them. Today was no exception. She tuned out shortly after the ambassador began. A/C Fox glared at her as if reading her lack of attention.

She observed the bigwigs, Minister O'Hagan beaming; in his shadow, the number one Commissioner was equally expansive. Neither seemed bothered by the irony that it was another country that recognized the actions of Kate's crew as meritorious. Either would happily sacrifice her, should the need arise.

When it became apparent that their presence in France had not leaked to the media, the board of inquiry delivered its verdict; no one from the mission had any case to answer. Kate's actions were necessary to protect the lives of the police involved in the operation. She would remain vigilant; O'Hagan was a vain politician who bristled at his authority being undermined.

On behalf of the Commissioner, the man who might have fired her, Kate accepted the medal awarded to An Garda Síochána, the Irish Police. Was it this that stalled Minister O'Hagan's desire to sanction her? It looked impressive; a silver cross with blue tips adorned with a red ribbon – *Ordre Nationale de la Légion d'Honneur.*

Such awards are usually made at the Élysée Place. This one was different; no official announcement would ever be made. It would be noted somewhere in Paris in a record that would gather dust over time. Knowledge of Operation Cassandra would remain strictly between governments and police. The award would be stored at SIU; the unit that earned it and conserving it out of public view would soothe political sensitivities.

She walked slowly to the centre of the room and made a short speech. It expressed her belief that when police worked together in trust, great things could be achieved. Like Fenaux, she believed that security services, absorbed with gadgets and technology, lacked belief in human capacity.

Kate concluded to heartfelt applause and Minister O'Hagan thanked the ambassador for the honour bestowed on behalf of the government. As guests sampled the dainty *amuse-bouche* snacks, he muttered congratulations to Kate and left.

An hour later she departed with her entourage. Everyone relaxed, ate lunch together, and laughed a lot. Fox insisted on a diversion to his office before Fenaux's party returned to Paris. Kate correctly deduced that a bottle of Midleton Very Rare Irish whiskey was the objective. The boss poured and they drank a toast to past and future successes. Kate clinked glasses with Mac.

'Thank you!'

She ducked out of the 'boys club' after one nip, saying her goodbyes en route to Fenaux, Dubois, and Crew-cut. She had other plans.

It was April and the Phoenix Park was coming to life. A green sheen was emerging in the park as trees put out their buds and grass began to spring up again. The black cloud that sucked the colour out of her life months earlier had lifted. Kate had chatted with Doc D'Arcy a few more times, mainly over coffee in her mum's kitchen. Occasionally images from Brest bombarded their way into her dreams - O'Hare's grip around her neck - the ground collapsing beneath her feet. The Doc reassured her that the night terrors would subside and her sleep pattern would return to whatever normal had been before Brest.

Her niece and nephew jumped up and down excitedly beside Norrie's car when they saw Kate.

'Let's do a big hug,' she said, spreading her arms.

Her mum was at the centre.

'Now, what do you want to see first?' Kate asked.

'Elephants,' the children replied in harmony.

The trip to the zoo was her treat; her way of saying thanks for helping haul her back from the brink. The family planned to go to the Tea Rooms nearby when the kids had seen all the animals. Margaret Bowen wanted to taste their Panini and the kids wanted milkshakes. Kate wanted to make the most of the quiet time.

She was reunited with her crew. Their core values of loyalty, courage, and belief held them together. Her world had been shaken but had stood the test. She was exonerated, toughened, and ready for business.

This is what Kate Bowen believed on that warm, carefree, spring afternoon.

ENJOY THIS BOOK?
YOU CAN MAKE A BIG DIFFERENCE.

I hope you enjoyed reading The Devil's Luck.

Reviews, short as you like, are powerful tools. They assist self-published authors like me to attract new readers. Also, more reviews enable us to advertise our work on major advertising platforms so we can reach a larger audience.

Thank you.

ACKNOWLEDGMENTS

I am deeply indebted to everyone who gave their time or used their knowledge to bring this story from manuscript to published novel.

Especially my editor, Lizzie Harwood, for her constant patience and encouragement and for expertly guiding me along an untrodden path.

My wife Eva, patiently read and re-read the manuscript. My daughters, Sarah and Emma, read early drafts and suggested improvements, together with Tim, Kathy, Martin, Robyn, Philip, Maureen, Schira, Peter, and Katherine who did likewise. My thanks to Michelle and Caroline who proofread the manuscript.

Tom Holland's Channel 4 documentary, Islam: The Untold Story, provided useful context on how that Islam emerged and where it stands today. 'Intelligence' has dozens of definitions in a policing or security service context but I used the version offered by Mark M. Lowenthal, author of many books on the subject.

To my fellow officers in An Garda Síochána whose professionalism and courage over many years still inspires. I am very grateful to you all.

ALSO BY T. R. CROKE

THE TRINITY ENIGMA

FREE to download.

This free-to-download novella centres on Trinity College, Dublin. Kate's surveillance crew work to halt a serial killer's murder spree.

The Trinity Enigma regularly charts in the top 10 of Amazon's 90-minute Mystery, Thriller & Suspense short read category.

THE PRIZE PRINCE

Detective Kate Bowen suspects Dublin gang boss, Don Bailey, is up to no good when she sees him greeting Middle Eastern contacts in Limassol, Cyprus.

When she returns as Garda surveillance boss in Dublin she trains her sights on Bailey. She has no idea of the scale of the score he is planning or that unscrambling his lofty ambitions will change her life forever.

Hard-hitting and tense from beginning to end.

STRIKE BACK

This fast-paced, action-packed thriller scorches across Europe and the Atlantic. Detective Kate Bowen is forced to work scant clues to foil an ISIS attack security chiefs reckon is looming. Nobody can tell her what, where, or when.

As Kate works frenetically to unpick the ISIS plot aimed at causing maximum death and destruction, a spectre from her past threatens biblical revenge. The dynamic surveillance detective is hit with a double whammy when her private world descends into crisis.

By the time her thirst for justice is satiated her life is changed utterly.

BITTER JUSTICE

Detective Superintendent Kate Bowen inserts an undercover agent inside a far-right extremist group. This collective of anonymous activists is different; a group of young radicalized police embedded inside the Garda.

Kate has no idea that the phantom figure pulling the group's strings from the depths of the Dark Web is a nemesis she believed was put away for good. As the group's far-right terror intentions are uncovered, the mystery man zeroes in on *his* objective.

To kill Detective Kate Bowen.

TAINTED JUSTICE
COMING IN 2025....

The first daunting journey for a young African girl becomes her last. For weeks, Kate's team has been shadowing the logistics company owner whose trailer shipped the murdered girl amongst other undocumented immigrants via a French port. Kate vows to bring her justice.

Her new role as the Dublin Surveillance Squad's strategic commander pitches her into direct conflict with a Deputy Commissioner she doesn't trust. She uses her FBI contacts to dig deeper and expose the company's links to organised crime. Nonetheless, the DC decides the surveillance operation is a costly trawling exercise he will no longer pay for and orders it to be shut down.

Set in modern-day Ireland, against a background of organised crime's global reach, Can Kate expose the corruption facilitating lethal human trafficking or will she be its next victim?

ABOUT THE AUTHOR

T. R. Croke is the author of the Detective Kate Bowen crime thriller series. He also wrote the British crime fiction novella, One Night at the Perseverance Hotel.

He is married to Eva and lives in County Laois in the Irish midlands. Read more at
https://trcroke.com

info@trcroke.com